I lift my eyes from the boy and there he is, the Silencer, his eyes hooded and dark under his heavy brow. The square jaw locks into a smiling grimace. We stand there frozen for half a moment before he kills the silence with a yell. The rage takes over, wild and hot and out of control. The boy is back on the ground and I am racing toward the Silencer, grabbing his throat, squeezing, squeezing, squeezing to stop the sound.

PRAISE FOR THE WORKS OF E. J. WENSTROM

"Wenstrom's debut is the catalyst for a planned series of fantasy war tales, kicked off with this thoroughly expanded retelling of the Orpheus myth...the clever use of weathered fantasy tropes and occasionally lovely turns of phrase will propel readers into book two."

- Publishers Weekly

"MUD, I loved this book!! So unique so engaging, a Keeper and must read!!"

- Nelsonville Public Library, Heather Bennett

"I really like books about uncommon supernatural creatures, so, when I saw MUD had a golem as the protagonist, I jumped at the chance to read it. A well-written and enjoyable read."

- Metaphors and Moonlight, Kristen Burns

"There's something primal in Mud. It's a reverent, mythical story of supernatural beings who justify desperate measures in their quest to feel complete. They struggle with emotions we all understand, even as they challenge the very rules that govern all of creation."

- Fantasy Author, Robert Wiesehan

CHRONICLES OF THE THIRD REALM WAR

E. J. WENSTROM

CITY OWL
PRESS

MUD
CHRONICLES OF THE THIRD REALM WAR: Book 1

CITY OWL PRESS
www.cityowlpress.com

Cover Design by Heather McCorkle & Tina Moss. All stock photos licensed appropriately. Edited by Heather McCorkle.

For information on subsidiary rights, please contact the publisher at info@cityowlpress.com.

Paperback Edition ISBN: 978-0-9862516-6-5
Hardcover Edition ISBN: 978-1-944728-01-4

Printed in the United States of America

For Christopher,

who keeps me at least partially in the real world,

and makes it all matter.

- E. J.

CHAPTER 1

A STAIR CREAKS.

With the rain pounding down on the temple's rattling roof, the human may not have even heard the sound. But I do. It is too close, just outside the door of my tower. I look up from the Texts and listen.

There it is again.

A cold darkness tosses in my stomach.

Another stair creaks, and I know I'm about to kill again. The boiling thrill for blood rises within me and I know better than to bother suppressing it. It will happen anyway, no matter how much I try to bury the monster I really am.

Over the centuries, I've at least learned how to make it quick. My hand has already dug the box from the breast pocket of my cloak. I stride across my small room, my bare feet collecting dust. My back to the door, I lean on the mantle to lure the Hunter in. Then, I stare at the blank dusty wall and wait. The rustle of his cloak breaks the quiet with each step.

I want this over.

I hold the box high in my hand for him to see, as if I am inspecting it. So small, so delicate. It nestles easily against my palm, comfortable and sure. It knows I must serve it.

Padded steps lift from the wood and onto the worn rug. My spine prickles with anticipation. Dread, heavy and thick like a storm cloud, wells up inside me. Have they learned nothing from their many losses? So many I cannot count them anymore.

I lay the box on the mantle for him to reach. My fingers itch for the fight, but I will not destroy the human of my own will. He must bring it on himself. I step away from it, leave it there for the Hunter to set his fate.

A rustle of rushed steps, a grunt, and a blade slices through my back, cool and slick. They keep trying to hurt me as if I were human, as if I felt the pain as they do. I reach around and remove the blade from my back. The skin knits itself back together.

I turn to him. Rain beats at the window. Wild dilated eyes peer up at me from under a deep red hood. Young. The cloak slips at his neck, too large for his growing body. It is the same deep red cloak all the others wore. Rich, dark, velvety, with the same gold braided trim. My own cloak, worn and ripped, seems even worse next to it.

The boy is trembling inside it. Waiting.

Has he even experienced a true fight before? Why did they send someone so young? Guilt twists through me.

"It's not too late. Leave." My voice is rough with

disuse.

I shift the knife in my hand, holding it away to show him I don't mean him any harm, not if I can help it.

Like their cloaks, the Hunters' blades are fine, an elaborate pattern carved into its handle. It seems out of place in my hand, even after so many times. I run my fingers over its familiar ridges and wait. My ears are hot with anticipation, with dread of what I know comes next.

He gapes up at me, my monstrosity. I fight the urge to drop my gaze to the ground and instead keep my eyes locked on his. I try to will him to turn away, to go back to wherever he came from.

But I already know he won't. They never do.

Instead, he gives himself a quick shake and recovers his warrior's front. "The Sworn will not rest until it is destroyed. Give me the box."

Courage glows in his eyes. Strong. Fresh. What a waste of a life.

The Sworn? What is the Sworn?

"I cannot."

If only I could. It would save both of us.

He reaches for the box on the mantle.

"Don't—"

His fingers wrap around it.

The box's force takes over and my arms reach for him. I wince as my hand slips the Hunter's own blade through his soft middle. In the back of my mind, years and years of all the others who came before him flash through my memory. My hands buzz with mad hunger for the fight.

But it's already over.

He gasps, clasps his hands to his open belly, trying to hold it in. Then he slumps to the floor, spilling his life across the wooden panels. He opens his mouth to gasp, but it comes out as more of a gurgle, blood rising in his throat.

Not much time left. I try to push down the throbbing anger, the monster in me that hungers for the fight. I kneel beside him, gripping his head urgently so he is looking at me.

I hold the box to his face. "What is in it? Why do you come for it? Who are the Sworn?"

A red line dribbles down his chin. He looks up at me, trembling, shakes his head side to side.

"You don't know?"

His words come out in a hoarse whisper. He is shaking all over now in a struggle for his life. He opens his mouth again, tries to push out more. But the dark puddle grows fast below him, and it is over before it begins. Again, I am alone in the heavy dark of the temple tower.

****

The Hunter's eyes are cold and dead and open wide.

Watching, judging, condemning.

And they should. They have seen what I am.

I used to tell myself I would get used to it. I got used to snapping bones, last cries, pools of blood. But the eyes. The eyes freeze in an echo of their final panic and pain. When they realize these are their last breaths. Paled. Filmed. Hollow.

The Hunter's eyes stare up at me and I can't bear it.

I step out onto the balcony to escape them. Try to clear my head, still buzzing and grainy from the kill. Rain squeezes out of the sky like teardrops over the cobblestone streets in the marketplace below, over the thin rotted roofs of the laborers' quarters beyond it, over the wall that traps them within the city's borders. Even over the city center, where Epoh's elite rest, safe and dry. It pounds down on me, drop, by drop, by drop.

So close, yet again.

I set the box next to me on the railing, finger the curves of the delicate patterns painted over it. Such beauty. But it's what's inside that the Hunters come for, die for. That much I know. If only it would open. If only I knew what my body betrayed me for, why my hands are covered in blood yet again.

They will send another. They always do. I will be waiting. It goes without end, back further than I can remember. Centuries. Years trudge by, bodies pile up, the weight grows heavier.

I cling to my new clue. *The Sworn.* The phrase is meaningless to me, but it's a little more than I had before. Next time, maybe I can learn even more, if they keep sending their young and untested.

Already the dark sky is lightening toward a troubled gray. Another weary day is here in the city of Epoh.

Which means I'll be stuck with the Hunter's cold stare all day. There's no time to move the body now. Soon Epoh's Silencers will be out, the city's guards who keep the order with fear and clubs. Ever since they burned down the Holy District and all the Texts so many years ago, anything related to the Three Gods makes them jump. Any sign of movement from a temple like this would trigger a full search of the grounds. Then where would I go? There's nothing else left beyond Epoh's walls. Nowhere else to go.

It wasn't always like this. The realm was happy once. There were tons of other cities like Epoh, and they were thriving. But something shifted in the Second Realm War.

Some say the Three saw the destruction and anger and hate that spread throughout the realm of Terath in the Second Realm War and abandoned it. Others say the Three themselves were on the battlefield, and They came with Their soldiers to beat at Epoh's wall, begging to be let in and shown a little of kindness — care for wounds, a drink of water — but the people would not let them in for fear of the rebels, and They gave up on us. Others say the Gods simply saw how few men dared fight for Them and turned away.

Whatever it was, the Gods are gone, and the people won't dare invoke Them for anything, afraid of Their wrath. The realm is in ruins. Only the Gods know what lies beyond Epoh's high walls. If They care enough to look.

That's why I hide here, in the temple. I keep to where the humans don't dare wander. The Gods don't worry me. They forgot this realm long ago.

I force myself back inside and quickly step toward the body. I drag my fingers over the grayed lids, closing them. I untie his cloak and pull it from under him to mop up the congealing blood from the floor.

With his eyes off of me, my entire body finally begins to relax again.

It must be such great relief, knowing you can end. I envy them that, the humans. But not like this. Not before your time. Not alone, with no chance.

When I'm done with the floor, I lay the cloak over the body. His legs jut out at the end, the hand still pushing against the sliced organs. A grotesque empty shell.

The eyes still haunt me through the cloth. But there's no time to do anything more.

I pick up the Texts from the mantle and move quickly past the body to the window, trying to push the Hunter out of my thoughts. Below my feet the ornate rug, once rich and brilliant, is worn so deep I can feel the wood's grain under my toes. Decades of standing in the same place day after day after day. Here, I am in the shadows. A human peering in from the streets would not see me. But I can see out.

I watch them. Completely alone, silent, still, there is nothing else to do.

My temple tower rears up against what's left of the holy district, tall and tired, leering over the market. I watch each day play out on its wide streets and small carts. Behind it, the expired grandeur of the aged towers rises, a rotted reminder of a lost past.

There was a time when Epoh was Terath's shining jewel. Its streets bustled with life at all hours. But the Second Realm War changed everything. The First Creatures tore through the realm like it was paper, their battles destroying men's cities, homes, the land itself. And the men, they took part. Some stood up and fought for their Gods. But others turned away from them in anger. Others' loyalty was easily bought with magic, jewels, or promises of safety after it all ended. Still others ran, cowered, and just waited for it to end.

I'd never, in all my years, seen such destruction.

This is when Zevach arrived at Epoh, with his flock trailing behind him, desperate to believe his promises of protection and hope. Then Zevach told his followers if they wanted the city, they must take it for themselves. Desperate and scared, they fought their way in and destroyed most of its people.

They should have known then what he would become, that this is the city's fate. I should have.

The sky turns from pitch black to a troubled gray. The rays of light touch over the battered city. Silencers' boots tap against the pavement. Another weary day in Epoh is here.

CHAPTER 2

EVERY DAY IS the same. There is no rest.

The Silencers are the first to take the streets. Zevach's trained men, guards he collected to protect the people he brought here in the Second Realm War. In the beginning, he handpicked men for this great honor. They watched the city's borders, made sure nothing got in. But when the war was over, they turned their eyes and their weapons inward. Their ranks are filled with laborers eager to escape life on the bottom, and the children of prisoners taken from their homes. They leave their people proud and hungry. When they come back in their fine black cloaks and shining silver armor, it is as if they don't even remember. Zevach told the people the Silencers are here to keep the peace. But all they sow is fear.

Each morning the Silencers circulate through the roads and alleys, clinking in their armor, their heavy black boots tap-tap-tapping through the fog before curfew lifts. Steam pours from their mouths like dragons in the damp morning freeze.

As the sun pulls itself up, the rain tapers down to nothing. Shopkeepers drag their wooden carts to their usual places along the sides of the street and arrange their displays, pulling their cloaks around them tight. Their jobs carry less risk than the laborers, but their hours are earlier and later, working around the laborers' strict shifts and the elite's late night amusements. The market is the one place in Epoh all the classes share. The air here is always tense.

Soon the laborers come. The ones who grow the food, sew the clothing, create the luxury items for the city's elite. They flood the streets in a rush to get the day's meals before shift. Tired, beaten. Their trampled voices throw off tower walls and bounce up to me amid the morning quiet.

Inside the teeming mass, a young boy with bright red hair stands very still. He stares up at my tower. He can't possibly see me, not from all the way down there. But still his stare prickles behind my ears like pins. Ever since he and a few others slipped into my temple through a shattered window, he does this.

It happens, sometimes. Just restless laborers' children curious about the things no one talks about, mostly. Sometimes the helpless get desperate and come here hoping the Gods will listen. I keep to my tower, and soon they are gone again.

Except this last time. This time they climbed the tower stairs. They had explored every room. Anxiety spread over my shoulders and down my back as their hushed voices had crept closer and closer up the tower, pausing at each room on the way. I buried the box in my pocket and hovered in the room's darkest shadows.

When finally they reached the top and swung open my door, I tried to be as small as I could, tried to let the shadows swallow me. But there was no hiding. As soon as they saw me, the other boys gasped and fled. But the red-haired boy, he had stayed. He stepped closer. He reached his hand toward me, fingers stretched and palm out as if feeling for something. He frowned as he looked me over. "What are you?" he asked.

The other boys seem to have forgotten. They never look to the temple. They don't dare go near it, or anywhere on the Holy District's border. It's only this one, this boy with the red hair. He looks up at my window and his face reminds me how quickly I could lose it all.

What are you?

The question grates and scratches along the walls of my mind. All he has to do is tell someone I'm here, and I'm forced out the temple, out of Epoh, into the wastelands beyond the wall.

But now the other boys call to him and pull him back to the street. They greet him with grins and friendly slaps to his shoulder. Before they run off, the boy runs to a woman and pulls on her skirt. She always comes to market with him. She leans down and says something to him, her fiery braid swinging off her shoulder. In a different world, one where life had not wrung so much out of her, she would have been beautiful. She turns away and begins her morning shopping at a nearby cart.

The boy turns and races toward the middle of the street with the others. They split up, their eyes glued to the streets. The boy pushes against the flow of traffic, hardly noticing as the others shove and knock him as they pass. It takes only a few minutes, and with a shout to the others, he dives under the crowd. He emerges victorious, waving a flat smooth stone over his head.

They cheer. The stone is dropped back to the ground and the boys kick it back and forth, weaving through the morning shoppers. While the rest of Epoh drag themselves awake and brace for another day of work and abuse, the boys play. Some of the shoppers frown, even snap at the boys as they rush through. Others crack a rare, weak smile. The boys tease, laugh, and run free through the streets.

Free. In Epoh.

The tension in my shoulders loosens as their laughter floats up. I drink it in while I can. It can't last long. The woman will return and call him back any moment.

The more they play the more they forget themselves. The boys get bolder, run faster, call louder, leave Epoh far behind. Their calls throw off the cement, brick, glass, and race toward the sun's open arms. Escape into the sky.

No one escapes.

A knot tightens between my shoulders. They will pay for this if a Silencer catches on.

One already has. Tall, with a furrowed brow and jutted jaw. His club is already clenched tight in his hand. Hungry for action. He wafts in the tail of their shouts, trailing behind. Waiting for his moment.

They have done nothing wrong.

It will not matter.

But any moment the woman will step out from the

carts, give a shout, and the boy will be back by her side. They will walk away together. The stone will lay still in the streets again, trampled by numb passersby. The play will dissolve.

She should be back any moment.

Where is she?

The streets are swarmed, but I cannot see her in them.

There it is—a glimpse of flashing red. Behind the crowd, in line at a shopkeeper's cart. I strain to peer through the stream of passing workers, my forehead pressing into the glass. She waits, her arms juggling too many things. At the front of the line, a man waves wildly at the store clerk, his face flushed a deep red.

Meanwhile, the boys are still playing. Every call, every laugh winds the tension in me tighter and tighter now, trapping me in a coil, squeezing too tight. The Silencer trails them, wafting in the wake of their cheers. Still the woman could appear and with one call shatter the moment into pieces, pieces too small for the Silencer to pick up. But she is still waiting in the line. The game continues, and the Silencer is closing in.

A hard kick sends the stone flying. It spins overhead, floating, soaring, and bounces off the Silencer's head.

The moment seeps in, steals the grins from the boys' faces, and sinks into the crowd around them. It spreads across the Silencer's face and drips like poison from the thin smile crossing his lips. The Silencer picks up the stone. He rolls it over in his hand, holds it out to the nearest boy to come take.

And suddenly the boy looks so, so small. Small

except his eyes, which are huge, bulging with fear. A fear that traps him to the spot where he stands. The Silencer's sharp jaw tightens and grinds behind his grin as he waits.

The boy slowly steps toward the Silencer, his face tense and blank. Nearby shoppers step away, make room, as if the moment will combust. When the boy is near enough, he reaches out cautiously for the stone. He almost gets it.

At the last moment, the Silencer's smile disappears and he snatches the stone away and grabs the boy's arm.

Through a clenched jaw, he growls with anger: "I'll teach you to get in the way of a Silencer of Epoh."

The crowd watches in fascinated horror. The Silencer lifts his club above his head and whips it down, striking the boy across the face. No one moves. No one speaks. No one stops it. It happens all the time like this.

He lifts it again, his expression loaded with hate.

Suddenly something jostles through the crowd from one side, and before the Silencer can strike again the fiery-haired boy has pushed in front of his friend, is taking his blow.

A flood of words spill from him onto the Silencer. "Stop it! It's not his fault, leave him alone—"

The Silencer snarls, forgets the other child, and grabs the redhead by his shirt. He spits out words sharp as blades inches from the boy's face.

"Stop? Are you telling *me* what to do?" The Silencer shakes the boy. "How dare you use such a tone with a guard chosen by Zevach. Maybe you need a lesson more than your friend."

Then he strikes. Again. Again. Again. Each time staining the stick redder as the blood pools and drips from the child's face. The boy cries out, but he doesn't fight.

The crowd jostles again and the woman is now at its center behind the Silencer. Too late. When she sees, she screams and runs to the boy, pulls him back from the Silencer's wrath.

"How dare you," her words spit out in sharp tones of jagged glass. "He's just a boy! Don't you ever touch my brother again."

In the moment she has while the guard is stunned, she frantically checks the boy's dripping face, brushes back the fire-red hair, runs her hands over his face and head. She crumples to her knees and wraps her arms around the boy, presses her face against his shoulder. And then she forgets herself in her relief, she must forget herself, or she would know better than to do what she does next.

She says, "Thank the Gods."

It's quiet. Most of the humans don't hear it. Only a few of those closest look up. But as soon as the words escape her lips, as soon as the first accusing eyes flit to her, her cheeks burn red. The whispers travel like lightning and soon the whole square is buzzing, followed by deadly silence and stares. Her flush spreads, covering her face and down her back. Burning hot, angry, and defenseless.

No one, no one, no one invokes the Gods. Not in Epoh. It is a death wish.

I clutch the Texts in my fist tight and battered,

afraid of what will happen next, unable to look away. The woman's words still float heavy in the air. An awful blackness builds in my chest, coursing through me and into my head, my fingers, my toes, filling me, emptying me, consuming me. Helpless.

The Silencer's flat eyes ring with sadistic joy. The woman looks back to him. For a heartbeat, they turn the air between them to ice.

Still clasping the child, she whips around and pulls him behind her into the crowd. I follow the trail of jostling bodies as long as I can, clinging to whatever I can of her. It could be the last time I see her.

The Silencer doesn't bother to follow. He stands watching as they run, a calm smile baring his teeth. He knows there's no rush. Even if she escapes now, they will find her later. There's only so much space to search inside Epoh's walls. She will be a warning to the others to keep their minds on their own realm. Her best hope is that they will be carried away early on, and she will die quickly.

They'll take the boy too. Throw him in training to be a Silencer as they've done with so many others. He will forget his home, his family, whatever the woman has been teaching him about the Gods. He will come back blank-faced and cold.

But for now the show is over, and the crowd begins to move again, tending to their business. The rest of the day passes quietly. I watch without seeing as the laborers leave, the elite make their leisurely strolls through the carts in bright fresh tunics and cloaks. The Silencers step down, becoming less harsh when the elite shop.

Finally, the market dies down, the shopkeepers pack up their days work, the sun sets, and the Silencers forfeit the streets to the dark. Night settles in as it always does, over empty streets that have already forgotten what happened this afternoon. But my hands are still clenched in anxious fists, nails digging into my palms. Epoh hasn't forgotten what happened. The Silencer hasn't forgotten. Fear rattles in my chest when I think of what's in store for the fiery-haired boy and his sister.

CHAPTER 3

AT THE OTHER end of the room, the cold stare of the Hunter's corpse watches me through the sheet. I want it out, buried deep, deep, deep, so deep even I could never find it again.

Even so, I let another hour pass before daring to move. I wait for signs that Epoh's underworld is stirring, to be sure none who would care are here to see me haunting the temple's empty halls. The box is still gripped tight in my hand, so hard its pointed corners pierce into my skin. So hard the tension pulls on my knuckles. So hard it should break.

If only it would break.

Once the shadows start lurking in through the alleys, I know I'm safe.

Even through the blanket, those cold, knowing eyes send quivers down my back. I brace myself and step toward it, and quickly sling it over my shoulder, sheet, and all.

It is surprisingly light for such a great burden.

I open the door from my tower and make my way

down the cold stone steps to the temple's sanctuary. The air trapped in its dark pockets is thick with dust and memory. So many bodies I've already carried down these winding stairs.

The sanctuary is an abrupt burst of light at the end of the stairs. Full moon tonight. It pushes through the temple's stained-glass windows, spills fractures of blue, purple, red, and green. The pews awaken beneath its light and the pulpit is restored to its former glory. I quicken my stride as I walk across the back of the room to the wooden door at the other end.

The door creaks as I push it open. The rich smell of sod beckons and repels me. I force through the door's small frame and the dark swallows me back into its comfortable emptiness. The old stairs groan under my weight. I tread slowly so they don't snap under the pressure. Onto the compact earth of the cellar's floor, I step, past the rows of raised mounds in the ground, each marking a life gone. A life I took.

It's dark, but I feel each one below my feet. I remember. Down here they will always be freshly murdered, their blood still warm and sticky on my hands.

This easy deposit is one of the reasons I've stayed here so long. The Hunters would have found me anywhere. They have not always been so easy to hide.

I reach the row's end and release the body to the ground. My fingers sink easily into the dirt. Cool and rich. I crumble handful after handful and push it away, lulled into an easy rhythm in this hidden safety.

Before I drop the body in, I fumble through his cloak pockets. Even in the dark, I can feel the flat eyes on me, but if there is anything to find, I have to know. I stretch my fingers into each pocket. I find nothing but crumbled breaks of stale bread. It's always this way. But it doesn't stop the hope from burning in my chest as it dissolves.

The body drops into the hole with a soft thud. I fold the dirt back over him, smooth it out.

He didn't deserve this. To be hidden away, forgotten.

On top of the mound, I push in a small dot with my thumb to mark where he lies. The symbol of the temple's Goddess Theia — a seed. It is the least I can do; leave him with some kind of blessing. Maybe it makes no difference, if the Three have really abandoned Terath. But maybe not.

Going back, I move quicker. My eyes have adjusted to the dark and I don't have to rely on memory.

Past the long line of the dead.

Up the whining stairs.

Through the door — and I freeze.

Something is wrong. Through the half-opened door, a flickering light bounces off the atrium wall. Not the diluted colors of the temple's colored panes. Pure, clear, white. Flickering…like a candle.

There's humans in here.

****

Humans, here in my temple. To be wandering the night in Epoh, they must be reckless. To be here, in this place of the Gods, they must be completely desperate.

I don't dare move. The stairs are too loud for retreat — it's a miracle they did not already hear me. I cautiously pull the door back in best I can, and watch their flickering shadows on the wall, distorted and strange, through the crack.

Their whispers magnify off the walls. A man and a woman. Her voice quivers, matches the faded sanctity of this place. His is gruff and hurried as he pushes himself in through the broken sanctuary window.

"We shouldn't be here," he growls. "We should go."

"By the Gods, you will stay."

"I can do this ritual just as well in my tent—"

"No." Her voice sparks like flint. "You will do it here. In Theia's house. Where the conduit to Them is strongest."

The voice is familiar. It hovers in my ear, waiting to be known.

The man's shadow moves away from her another step. She closes the gap. When she speaks, again it is so soft it is almost nothing. "Please. In Theia's name, I beg you. My brother—"

"Yes, you told me already. I know." The man's shadow shifts and fidgets. He sighs. "We need to get started. I told you, we cannot be here long."

Her shadow nods eagerly.

They move to the front of the sanctuary, their shadows stretching across the back wall. He grows as the stairs to the pulpit creak under him. She kneels to the ground.

They pause: a true silence.

Then the man stretches out his arms, tilts back his head, and becomes a great stretching shadow-tree against the back wall.

"Most holy Mother, Theia the Creator —" The prayer transform his voice, strengthens, deepens it. "Have mercy on your beloved child, who lives in your Order..."

A draft pushes past me, forces the door wide enough to walk through with a loud whine. Anxiety rises in goosebumps over my skin. They heard it, they had to have heard it, and now they will come to see what caused it. They will find me, and all will be lost.

But the man's voice continues to echo through the building without pause: "...we beg you, protect this child from the forces working against your Order..."

I exhale my panic and let it break away into the air.

The woman speaks now, a rhythmic response in the prayer, her voice — that voice I somehow know — rustling down the aisle and tickling my ears, stirring up a restless ache inside me, an ache that unsettles and surprises me.

The door is already open. They are at the other end of the large sanctuary. Her voice tugs at me, and curiosity wins out.

I place my hand on the floor to lean out into the atrium. My arm quivers with caution. Their ritual could end any moment. If I'm going to do it, I need to do it fast.

I push myself forward onto my arm.

I catch just a glimpse before I pull back again. But a glimpse is all I need.

A thick braid twists down the woman's back, a fire-red rope. It's the woman from the market, the one who always comes with the boy. The one who whispered her own death sentence today. My stomach flutters with excitement, confusion, curiosity. Who is this woman, so willing to do these reckless things no one else in Epoh would dare?

I pull back behind the door and lean against the wall. I hope they are done before sunrise so I am not stuck in the cellar with the dead all day. But for now I can only wait. I settle into my spot, close my eyes, and drift into the rhythm of their chanting prayer. It's soothing, somehow. Not just the voices, but also the presence of someone familiar. If only she didn't have to leave. But she does, for both of our sakes.

No wonder she is desperate. Breaking into the temple in the dead of night is nothing to what she already did in the glaring midday. I wonder where the boy is now, how badly the Silencer hurt him. And what horror lies ahead for the woman when they find her. Because there's nowhere they could hide that the Silencers won't soon find

Something twitches near my arm and pulls me out of my thoughts. As if the air itself pinched. It grows larger, tightening, pulling, and snapping into a tense current. I open my eyes and stand alert, looking for the cause around me in the cellar's darkness.

And then, a blinding light comes from the cellar and washes out everything else.

CHAPTER 4

I AM FROZEN, caught, blind in the glaring light. Adrenaline charges through me, pulsing in my wrists and pounding my ears.

The light wanes to a low glow, beckoning across the dark cellar, and takes shape.

A figure like a man, but larger. Too perfect, a chiseled marble statue under an airy white robe. Silvery blonde locks curl around a brooding forehead. Skin glows pale and soft as the moon. But a darkness hovers around him—two inky black wings burst from his back.

His eyes glow hot as embers, burn through me with a steady gaze. My fingers wrap around my blade in its hilt, but he reaches out an arm toward me: *All is well.* My body's chaos quiets.

"I am Kythiel, angel of Theia." His voice is pearly smooth.

Theia. The Goddess they used to pray to here.

I blink. An angel, one of the First Creatures. Right here in front of me. They were rare enough before the war, but since then they've been assumed dead, or at least that the gods locked them out of the realm.

His eyes bore through me, hot with intensity.

"They're upstairs," I say. It comes out weak. My face stings.

The perfect face clouds into confusion. "What?"

"Theia's followers. They're upstairs." I whisper the words, afraid they will hear us.

"*Theia's* followers?" he scoffs. "I am here for myself. I am not Her mindless slave like some of the others. Those worshippers' prayers merely opened the way for me. I came here for you, golem."

It's too much, too fast. It doesn't make sense, and my mind won't wrap around it.

"But—"

"Stop it. Be still."

He circles me slowly, those burning eyes passing over my every inch.

"And you needn't whisper, by the way," he chuckles. "I've taken care of it. Simple charm, really. For an angel, at least. But they will not hear us. Not from upstairs, not from anywhere. So stop. It's irritating me."

Charms? Angels? It's more than my mind can take in.

"But *why are you here*?" The question escapes in spite of me.

He purses his full lips into a line. "I have been watching you, golem. I require your help."

What could I possibly have to offer such a creature? And that word again. *Golem.* It unsettles old things I pushed aside long ago. Reminds me of everything I wish to forget.

"Adem." I say it as loud as I dare.

"What?"

"My name. It's Adem."

The angel observes me with sharp eyes, catches every twitch of my face. Every muscle in me tenses. I try to stop the twitches, not to let my edginess show.

"A golem with a name. How original," he says. "But then, I knew you were exceptionally well crafted or I would not be here. And it's even clearer close up. You radiate like a furnace, such great magic compounding inside you for so many years. I can feel it from across the cellar."

He stretches his hand out to me like he is warming his fingers.

"Which, of course, is why I am here."

"I am nothing."

He stares at me blankly. "Nothing? Do you know what a golem *is*?"

I know. More from the Texts than my own experience, but I know what I am. "Mud."

He shrugs, light and shadow dance over his shoulders. "Mud. Dirt. Dust. Whatever debris men can find. But it's more than the materials. Men create golems to do the work they can't, or won't. For their strength and durability. For their mindless obedience. But men were not meant to create in the first place — that is for the gods alone. Man's magic is stolen from angels, and they do not wield it well. Very few men have succeeded in creating a golem, and even then, the process is precarious and unpredictable. Most golems who succeed are grotesque, miserable, broken things."

His words pile up, confirming what I've always felt. "Like me."

He frowns. "Not like you. That's what I'm saying. You are a masterpiece compared to most. You may be hardly more than a live puppet, but most golems are much less."

If I'm among the better ones, the others truly are doomed.

"But enough of this," Kythiel presses. "There is much to say and little time. The reason I have broken through the Host to find you in this temple is this: Golem, there is a way for you to be free."

The words seep deep into my chest.

Free.

The world around me fades and I drop into a haze of disbelief.

"Do you understand me, golem? I can free you." Kythiel's voice is laced with impatience. It's too much, too good to be true.

"How?"

"I can give it to you. But first you must help me."

"Help you?" What could I possibly have for so perfect a creature?

But...to be free.

"How?"

His lip quivers at the corner.

"For you to understand, I must start at the Beginning. Listen. As it reads in the Texts, in the Beginning—Terath's true Beginning, when man was new—angels had open passage between the Host and Terath. There was no need for a divide between the realms back then. The First Creatures walked side by side with man."

"I know about the Beginning," I say. I've read the tired Text pages over and over and over. Everyone knew them, once. The humans looked after the realm; the angels were Theia's messengers to them, teaching Her Order. The Beginning was beautiful, perfect. Until the men and First Creatures broke the Three's will.

Kythiel scoffs. "From what? The Texts? The Three did not share everything with men. To know all, you had to be there."

But what more could there be? The Texts are everything. "What do you mean?"

Kythiel leans toward me. "The Texts only tell what the Gods wanted to share with men. But for the First Creatures, it was different. When the Three created men, we did not understand. They already had us. The humans did not have our beauty, nor our understanding. But, their great heart and individuality soon won us over."

He pauses, his gaze drops to the ground for a moment.

"One of the first women was Rona. She was different from the others — truly different, not in the trivial ways the others were. Theia singled her out with a special gift: unlike most humans, who needed the angels to reach Theia, Rona knew the Goddess's will and judgment in her dreams. She was beautiful in every way."

He spreads out his hand as he speaks and light bursts from his palm, twisting, and whirling. A face starts to take form, a full bust. Striking wide-set cheekbones, full, proud lips. Her eyes are rich, dark, and deep, matching the dark hair that runs past her shoulders and down her back.

Beautiful. She truly was.

"I was Theia's counselor in the village where Rona lived. Her gift became evident, and we spent endless hours walking and discussing Theia's Order. Even living at Theia's side, I had never understood some of Her mysteries the way Rona could. Over time, I came to love her deeply, and she loved me."

He pauses to take in her image before he continues.

I cut in, my question refusing to stay in me any longer. "But what does this have to do with me?"

He jumps and closes his hand into a fist. Rona's face disappears. He looks back to me.

"Patience, golem. I am getting there." He sighs. "Other angels also came to care more deeply for certain humans. It was impossible not to, they were all so different. Some of them started to couple with human mates. Theia was furious at this and forbade the angels to continue. She placed them in different communities far from the ones they loved. The angels were heartbroken. With Her Will planted in our hearts, we angels had no choice but to obey."

"But humans, with their free will, were not so easily stopped from seeking out the angels they called their own, and the angels' hearts were helpless against such powerful feeling. Their love for their humans set a wedge between the angels and Theia. As the wedge grew, some of them began to find they could choose for themselves, and were no longer bound to Theia's Will as strongly. She was furious at her angels' straying."

"Is that why She called you back?" I find myself

absorbed in his story, in spite of myself. The Texts don't give a reason.

"Yes."

A tear waits to drop at the corner of his eye. "She called us back to the Host and set barriers between the realms so we could never return. But there were some angels so consumed with their love they could choose their own will, and they resisted. They fought back."

Barriers. Suddenly the red-haired woman is at the front of my mind. And the boy, too. So close, every day, just outside my window. Yet I could never break free and be one of them.

But that's not important right now. I pull myself back to the moment.

"The First Realm War."

The Texts warn against straying from the Three, tell stories of the terrors of the First War. But they don't speak of this, of why the First Creatures fought against them.

"Yes," he says. "When we were called back, my heart ached for Rona so strongly I was sure part of it had broken off and stayed with her. She also suffered greatly, and I watched her from the Host with no way to comfort her. But I did not fight. I was too bound to Theia to fight against Her, and too consumed in being separated from Rona for anything else."

He pauses. I search my mind for something to say, but the silence is heavy between us. Thankfully, he starts again.

"We all watched over our beloveds from the Host. Angels' hearts are made to be constant and unchanging. The angels loved their human mates until their dying day and will continue to on until forever. But men," Kythiel's tone deepens into a growl, darkness clouds his eyes. "Men move on quickly. They mourned losing their angel lovers at first, but eventually they forgot them and found comfort elsewhere. Many despaired and lost their connection to Theia altogether, wandering away to Terath or the Underworld and never finding their way back."

I've seen it myself, how quickly men can change. How quickly they forget old ways, old friends, wars, even the Gods.

"But my Rona did not forget me. She cried out to me in her prayers, and I heard her pain. She left for days, wandering, trying to find a way into the Host, but Theia had left no gate unsealed."

Kythiel's velvety voice rings with pride.

"It hurt me to see her in such suffering. Each day was worse than the one before, and finally, my desperation helped me discover I could reach her in her dreams the way Theia did. The first time I found her in her sleep, we were filled with ecstasy. But she was unhappy in her life, and we longed for each other every moment she was awake and we were apart. Our love grew so deep that the hours she was awake and I could not be with her, I felt half of myself was missing."

His eyes hollow with desperation. I instinctively step away, resisting their pull. Why is he telling me all this?

"I came to hate my ties to Theia, for while others slipped away to Terath, they bound me to the Host. But at least my Rona was loyal. Some humans were happy to see their angels again, but others had already forgotten, or would not leave their new partners, or were too old to start over again by the time their angels broke free of Theia's hold. When this happened, the angels fell into despair. And in their despair, they lost their way and were unable to return to the Host. They were trapped in Terath, alone and heartbroken."

Lost in Terath? Locked out of their home? It's no wonder some of the First Creatures turned so bitter toward the Gods.

"The angels felt all the bitterness of this cruel trick, and they rebelled. They sought other human companions to ease their loneliness. They wandered the land and led humans away from the Three with promises of other great ones, usually themselves. Because they could harness magic, which humans do not understand, they had no trouble gaining followers. Some even taught magic to their human followers. They became free and wild and no longer cared about the Three's Order."

Kythiel's eyes are large and tense. He stares past me a moment, then drops his gaze to the ground.

"I spent all the time I could in Rona's dreams, and the rest of it thinking of her, content with what I had for myself. So much so I didn't see how Rona was slipping away, the toll this double life was taking on her. Not until it was too late. She grew weary, then strained, then desperate. I realized after, she had become trapped in her own mind. Finally, she could bear it no longer. She shut herself off from the Host and, unable to reconcile her worlds waking and asleep, she killed herself."

Kythiel's voice wavers and he bows his head, rubs

his eye with his palm. The abrupt end of his story leaves a dead weight through the empty cellar.

He wants my help? With this?

"This all passed long ago. There is nothing I can do for you."

"No! You're wrong!" The marble figure steps toward me, comes forward until his face is inches from mine. His perfect features crinkle into deep sadness, his eyes churn wild. "Golem, bring her back to me."

My hope for freedom snuffs out. I step away from the great creature, my head shaking slowly side to side.

"You would need your Goddess for that."

His great inky wings ruffle. "Theia does not disrupt the Order she set," he scoffs. "She is not a Goddess of mercy, but of rules."

I take another step back. A pit twists in my stomach. "This is not my quest. Go and find her yourself."

Kythiel's fist slams into the wall and rattles the temple's foundation. I flinch, remembering the humans just above. Are they still there? I try to listen for signs of them. But then Kythiel roars at me, "Don't you think I've tried? Do you think I would be here if there was any other way? I have been searching for a way to bring my Rona back ever since she left me. Centuries. But I am as bound to Theia as you are to that box. Even coming here to you was a struggle. And even if I could break that bond, even then—angels are all soul. Souls cannot free themselves of the Underworld. It has to be you. You're a golem, you have no soul. You can enter the Underworld and bring her back from it."

The Underworld. He wants me to break into the Underworld. Steal a soul back. He must be mad. "Find another golem."

"There are no others like you," his words are rushed and tight. "Do you know what most golems are? Dull and misshapen, hardly more than the dirt they were made from. But *you,* I watched you for almost a century before I managed to break free tonight. In all that time there has been nothing close to what you are. It has to be you, you're my only hope."

His wild eyes empty to a dire hollow. I know this look. I see it often. When the Silencers take a child from a mother, a wife from husband. Humans do wild, desperate things when they look like this.

It only lasts a moment. He straightens up, smooths out his face.

"I'm your only hope too, golem. Has anyone else come to you offering freedom?"

No. In all my centuries, they only came to destroy me, to take the box. It's been my whole life. All I've known. Protecting it. Trying to destroy it. Now here it is, a way out. Dropped from the sky right into my hand.

But the price. It is more than I am capable of. I don't know if it is even possible. I study the pain etched across his face. Could he bear it if I failed?

"I don't know —"

He abruptly collapses into a gleaming heap at my feet, dark wings sprawled at his sides.

"What is it you want? I will get it for you. Anything, anything you ask. Just please save my Rona. Bring her back to me."

What do I want?

It's an easy question. All I want, all I've ever

wanted, is for the hunt to end. For the killing to stop. To be free of the box.

To be free to live.

And here it is.

For the first time, in all those dark years, I see beyond the box, beyond my small prison. And all I find there is more darkness. More empty corners. More nothing. I could never fit among the humans. Not like this. That would take more than freedom.

"I want to be human."

I jump at the sound of my own voice. I didn't mean to say it aloud. But it throws from me loud, angry, and packed with endless years of splintered emptiness.

Kythiel's head snaps up to me.

"What?"

Now that I've said it, I know it's true. This ache's festered in me all these years. This is what I want. No, what I need.

"Make me human."

Kythiel shakes his head. "That requires a soul," he says.

"Then I will help you for a soul."

Silence. It drags on like a stick in setting mud.

Finally Kythiel speaks, his lip quivering. "I cannot give you that. Souls come from the Three, and the Three alone."

No.

"This is my price."

"You do not want a soul. A soul is pain. A soul is weakness. A soul is death."

A soul is life.

"You said anything. A soul. Make me human."

The need for it burns through me as a hollow tree set on fire from within. I cannot, I cannot go on without it. Now that the idea has caught within me, nothing can extinguish it.

The angel droops. His wings, his shoulders, his head.

"I can't give you that."

Silence buzzes between us. Despair pours out of his eyes. My hope hardens and turns to anger.

"Then we're done." I turn to the stairs.

"Wait!"

His exclamation is wet, almost a sob.

The air hangs heavy. Kythiel paces the cellar, rubbing his neck, his mouth half forming the words as he mumbles to himself, wrestling, weighing.

I use all my bulk to become immovable. A soul. Nothing else.

Nothing else can give me what the humans have. The love, the passion that fills their short lives so fully, fuller than all I could muster from my hundreds. The connection to each other.

To be free of the box and have nothing to go to, it would be even worse than now. It would be nothing. But a soul...to be one of them...

I would try, risk anything for this.

Kythiel's pace slows as he turns toward me yet again. He stops an arm's reach from me.

"You will have it. After you retrieve Rona."

His words are like magic. Something in me lightens until I feel I am floating. Under it, something nags at my gut—something not quite right. Something too easy. But in my chest, there's a burning, craving hole where my soul will go. I shove the caution away into the shadows, take a deep breath, and let the tension break away into the air. A soul. My very own. Just thinking of it loosens my shoulders and sends tingles up my neck, like I am floating.

"Then we are settled? I must go," Kythiel says. And he begins to turn away with finality.

"Wait!"

A million doubts cloud my mind, a tangle of eagerness and fear. He turns back to me halfway, watching me with defeated disinterest.

So many questions. I pull one out as quickly as I can the one closest to the surface. "How do I get to the Underworld?"

"Walk to the sea. Row out on the water until the sky touches the water on all sides. Swim West. It will be easiest to break through on the new moon," he says. "When you have her back on Terath, I will come to you."

He begins to turn away, and then looks back to me. "And hear me — Trust no one and nothing. The realm of the Underworld is strange and inconstant. Abazel is ruthless and deceptive. He will say anything to confuse, hurt, and hold you there, anything to prevent you from bringing her back to me. Do not believe his lies. Many have been lost to him."

Abazel, the demon king. The name turns my stomach. The myths of his wrath, his destruction in the Realm Wars, were once the stories that kept children up at night. The Texts say he started it all. That he is the root of the brokenness that still has the realm in chaos.

Kythiel releases a soft sigh, his pearly, brooding

forehead tightening into troubled creases.

"You are my only hope, golem. Don't fail me."

Then he turns and walks away, his glow bursting into blinding light. And then he is gone, and I am alone again in the temple cellar.

CHAPTER 5

I STAND ALONE in the empty dark.

My mind is disordered and confused.

In the silence, Kythiel's promise clouds with everything else that he said. Too much information buzzes through my head for me understand.

But I can't just keep standing here until I do. Too much time has passed. Day is surely coming. The Silencers will claim the streets any minute and begin their guard, pacing, policing, seeing everything. I need to get back to my tower now. Shove all this aside; decide what to do with it later.

I walk through space where Kythiel paced, confessing his story to me.

Ascend the rotting stairs.

I pause at the door and listen—nothing. Look past it into the sanctuary. It's empty. I hope the woman was able to finish her ritual, even if the gods aren't listening anymore. Kythiel said he used their prayer to cross over, so maybe someone bothered to listen.

Past the sanctuary to the winding stairs to my

tower. Just get to the tower.

Golem.

A word I thought I'd escaped long ago. A word that burns through me like hot coals on flesh.

Kythiel's request taps at my mind and begs to be let out. But I can't. Not yet. Get to the tower. I move quickly up step after creaky step.

Golem.

The thoughts leak out over everything, oozing, dripping the truth I thought I'd escaped.

I am nothing. I am less than nothing. Dirt.

It's why I hide, why I stay in the shadows. I never fit with the humans. It didn't take long to learn to stay separate from them. To stay alone.

Gritty grains of dirt cling to my feet and between my toes. I faintly sense the return of the thick, dusty air as the rotating stairs take me higher. I breathe it in.

I wouldn't have to live like this anymore. I could stop being alone and be one of them. If I can hold up my end of this deal.

If I can do the impossible.

The enormity of Kythiel's request hangs around me. Is this something I can do? Is this something I want to even try? The Texts warn over and over against breaking the Three's Order. There are legends. Myths. Stories of men who have tried to raid the Underworld. Tried and failed, all of them. And paid the price.

Men who spend eternity suffering for their efforts, trapped in the Underworld never to return. There's no way to know if they are true.

But maybe it doesn't matter. Those are human myths, human attempts. Maybe Kythiel is right.

Maybe, without a soul, I can do what they cannot. He must believe it, to hunt me down as he did. Reeking of desperation.

If he's right, if I succeeded, I could leave all this. Just place the box on the mantle and walk away. Find a people somewhere far from here, if there are any others left outside the wall. Find a home. I could live out the rest of my short, free life until finally, finally I leave this world.

I've reached the top of the tower. Except for the light breaching the window, my comfortable prison is just as I left it.

****

The sun is starting to come out, and so are the Silencers. They stride through the street, eye the shopkeepers as they roll out their carts and set up, wobbly wheels stuttering on the cobblestone. Then, the laborers come again for their morning meals and other errands.

Every day is the same.

Every day except this one.

Because I watch and watch, aching for distraction from Kythiel's looming request, but the redheaded boy and the woman aren't there.

I'm not the only one watching for them. The Silencer from yesterday is out again, pacing the street near the cart she goes to most, craning over the crowds and grinding his sharp jaw. I look around. There are more Silencers than usual today. They're hovering in corners and against the tower walls and next to carts, standing stiffly as the morning crowd draws around them. Their eyes flit to the one from yesterday, the jaw-clencher, as if waiting for a sign. *Waiting for the woman to show up.* Each glance, each shift of their feet pierces through me, and I search the crowds for their gleaming red hair.

But they don't come.

The morning crowd dies down into quiet and I find myself in a puddle of relief. But where are they?

In the street the Silencer kicks at a shopkeeper's cart, narrows his eyes at the tall towers where the laborers sleep. They're somewhere inside Epoh's walls, they have to be, and the Silencer will find them eventually. When he does, they'll pay for all of this.

The other Silencers leave, but the jaw-clencher stays through the evening when the market closes. Finally, the shopkeepers are rolling their carts away. Only when the streets are totally empty does he finally trudge down the street toward the city's center.

Dark falls, and I am left with only Kythiel's words lurking around me, waiting for me to choose.

Now is the time to decide, but I keep staring at the street, unable to look it in the eye.

It should be easy. How many times have I thought about how I would give anything to break free of this life? But can I bear to leave this place after so long? What is left out beyond the wall since the last Realm War? Is it worth the chance of being trapped in the Underworld forever?

The security of my temple clings to me, won't let me go.

Outside on the street dark figures scurry through the shadows. They're going to the only place that operates in the dark: the Hush, Epoh's own black market.

I let them distract me, their hunched figures darting through the night. Their faces covered with scarves and masks to hide their identity. They could be anyone.

At least, most of them could. Another one scurries across the dark street, a bright tuft of red escaping from under a gray and black dotted scarf.

I let go of my thoughts and snap to full attention. What is *she* doing out there?

I move toward the door without thinking, a dense thudding in my head.

I'm following her. Kythiel and his promises — and the doubts they raise — can wait.

CHAPTER 6

MY FEET RACE down and down and around the dark stairwell. I rush halfway across the sanctuary, halt, and turn to face the doors.

Huge iron panels, tower high. They are rusted shut as if the temple were closing itself off from the hate that grew around it.

This place has been good to me, secure and isolated. It has kept me from committing more damage than necessary, swallowed me within itself. Kept me safely locked away.

Thick clouds are pasted across the dark sky. No moonlight breaks through the colored glass tonight. The sanctuary is dark and dull, aged in its hollowness. More like the empty place I've come to know.

I'll lose her if I don't hurry.

I reach for the rusted handle. The large knob is cool and rough against my palm. My fingers clench around it. I hold still as it washes over me, waves of caution, anger, and fear. They course through me in wild vibrations. Then, with a deep breath, I twist the knob and push against it with all my strength. Its achy joints screech as it slides open, filling the sanctuary and calling out a warning to the city.

Fresh night air rushes around me. Soft. Cool. Caressing my skin. The blank light of the streetlamps' flickering flames invades my eyes and greys my dull skin. My head throbs. I feel naked in its glare.

I haven't been outside this temple in ages, hardly outside my own tower room even. Blank days, white noise bustles from the market. Black staring nights of creeping shadows greet me. My feet hesitate in the doorway. I never move. Not until I have to. It's the rule I've followed forever. Ever since I stopped trying to pretend I belonged among the humans. The rule has always gotten me by.

I don't have to do this. I don't have to go after her. There's hardly reason for me *to* go after her. The dense musky air clings to me, begs me to stay. But the thudding in my head is hard, anxious, and loud.

So I ignore the knots twisting through me and head off into the night. My hands sting with floating awareness. The box presses into my chest from its pocket. No time to lose. She's got a head start on me, but at this time of night, there's only one place she could be going.

The only sound in the dead of night is thick clouds rustling over the withering steeples, wind creaking through the tired city towers. Habit keeps me in the shadows as I make my way down the ghost town streets. It's where I belong. Even without a single other being in sight, it feels safer here.

I hear it before I see it. A vague rustle of muffled

voices darting haphazard in the night.

I follow the sound around a corner, and in a blink, the night turns from empty to overflowing.

Just another dark alley in the center of the holy district. Except in this one, the darkness is filled with vague shapes covered in dark clothing. Someone extinguished the streetlamps' flames, and the colors all run together into a dull blend as if wet. A live pumping heart at the holy district's center, darkly churning.

This is the Hush.

Thugs. Whores. Dealers. Priests. The disturbed and the devout. Epoh's sludge. This is what the Hush holds. The darkness rustles with these outcasts, nowhere else to go within the walls, safer in the dredge than in the daylight.

The Silencers turn in at dark and leave it alone. This one outlet keeps the always-mounting pressure from exploding. It turns the angry into addicts, makes them forget. Its chaos keeps the rest of Epoh locked in at night in fear, and it helps them weed out the ones still trying to follow the Gods. Priests give up their sheep to save themselves. Anonymity is precious, the only protection.

So desperate. So reckless. Maybe deep down the Silencers leave it alone out of fear. Not even the Silencers dare do anything that might disturb the Gods.

No one shows their face here. A flood of scarves and hoods and masks bob through the street. When they talk they lean in inches from each other. I've never seen so many humans so quiet. Just the rustle of fabric and vague curling whispers swirl the night. They are a hidden pocket of dark people in a dark street in a dark part of the city. A Hush.

I stop at the street's opening, search through the mass for the woman. There's no sign of her. The idea of pushing through this strange crowd makes my muscles twitch. My hand drifts protectively to my chest pocket where the box lies. I step back...I shouldn't be here. This was a mistake.

But then I see it.

Among the masses pushing through the street, I catch the same flash of fire-red curls escaping from under a gray and black dotted scarf.

I am pushing through the crowds after her before I can think about it, a tense fluttering in my chest pulling me after her. Something that ties me to her and the boy.

Next to the humans, I'm a little too tall, a little too bulky, my skin a little too dull. Most of them never notice. Even fewer would in this horde, in the crowded darkness. But I do. I pull up my hood and tug it close around my face as I push through them.

Even the air in the Hush is tight and crowded. Dingy. Dust floats through it, kicked up from the bustle, twitches in my eyes. It smells of mingling mold, spices, sweat, and smoke.

I push slowly though the shoving silent mass, wary of every move, keeping one eye on the woman as best I can. She moves fast, and the humans swarm like a hive around me. My ears hum with fragments of low conversation, wisps that invade the silence and evaporate fast as the steam of their breaths. Why is she here? Where is she going?

At the other end of the alley, a haggard hooded form in tattered clothing weaves wildly through the crowd, grapping at arms, and his long scraggly beard leaning in close to anyone he can reach. Against a brick wall, two forms hover over a scale, carefully measuring out a white powder that glows with brightness in this dark place. Low chants rise from a group of hooded figures bound together with rope in a circle. A woman in a featureless mask and priestess' diadem makes eyes at me from across the alley, her hands trailing down a tight dress. Her undulating movements captivate me before I can look away and for a moment, I am caught in her gaze.

By the time I regain my balance and look back to where the redheaded woman was, there is no sign of her. I scan the crowd, panic washing over me.

Cold fingers wrap around my wrist and jerk away my focus. I flinch with a jolt of terror — *the box*. I twist toward it and am met with bloodshot eyes.

The small haggard man I saw darting through the crowd is at my side, his face just inches from mine, most of it protected by the shadow of his hood. He straightens his hunched back as much as he can, craning up to me. So close, I can see the crumbs and debris caught in his mangled beard. His breath stinks of stale liquor. I cringe and pull away, but he tightens his grip.

I hear his whisper this time, twisting up to me, "Choose."

I try to pull away. "Choose what?"

I have to find the woman, and every second he keeps me here, she is slipping away. But his fingers tighten, jagged nails digging into my arm. "*Choose*," he hisses. His arm points through the crowd, deeper into the alley. I crane to see what he does, but he's so small there's no chance he can see past the few figures right in front of us.

And then I see it, it's her, the tip of her red braid slipping away behind a corner, and I know it is what he meant me to see.

My muscles seize in angry bursts.

"Choose," the strange man demands again.

I have to get to her. I have to follow her, make sure no harm is done to her. I'll —

Before I can take a single step, a small warm hand slips into my free one. I flinch at the unexpected touch.

"Leave us, Archuus."

The voice is a smooth, cool breeze. It is not afraid; it does not hide in the night like the others. The hunched man bares his teeth in a grimace, glaring past me, but then loosens his grip on my arm, turns, darts back into the crowd. My skin quickly closes again where his nails dug into me.

My other hand remains enclosed in gentle warmth. I turn to it and am met with a piercing blue-green gaze. An uncovered face that stands out sorely here in the crowd of the hidden. It is worn, weathered, creased with great burdens. A body small and lithe like a child's, too skinny. His clothes hang off him, matted down rags.

I fight the calm he gives off, turn to walk away, to catch up to her.

But his voice reaches to me again.

"Come. Before you break into the Underworld, there are things you must know."

Prickles run down my spine. He can't possibly

know.

He turns and walks off, my hand still firmly in his. I have no choice but to follow.

CHAPTER 7

DESPITE HIS ROUGH looks, he moves light as air.

My head throbs.

The woman, I have to turn back to her. I have to stay with her. She isn't safe, she needs me. She shouldn't be out here, risking herself. She should be with the boy. I twist to find her as he pulls me farther away and into the dark alley. I could help them; I know I could, if I could only get to her. She shouldn't be out here, I must find her, I must—

A thick cloth drops down in front of my face, cutting me off from her.

I've been led into a tent. Its walls are mismatched cloths, a dizzying intricacy of once-bright colors.

He sits cross-legged on the cement ground. A series of powders in bowls to his sides, arranged around a blackened pit chipped out from the street's cracks, topped with small branches.

He watches me. Careful. Intent.

"Sit."

My anxiety bursts out in roars. "No! I have to go

back. I've got to—"

But I glance down and his eyes lock to mine again. Steady. Clear, so clear and strong. Something about him...

"Who are you?" I ask.

"I am Ceil," he says. "There are things you must know, things you must understand before you go on this quest."

Suddenly the walls feel too close. I lunge at him, trap him against the back of the tent. My fist seizes his shirt. "How do you know?"

He is still and calm, letting my growling voice roll over him. "The Gods showed me."

A prophet? A real one? My anger clouds into confusion. Is it even possible? Do the Gods still speak to anyone in this realm? Surely not.

And yet. If I do this thing Kythiel asks of me, I will need any help someone like him can give. I relax my hands and drop them away, stumble back a step.

"Be still," he says, "Sit."

My head still pounds, but I place myself across from him, the powders and branches between us, mystified.

Ceil pulls a tray with piles of powders on it in front of him from the side of the tent. He starts pinching at them and smashing the powders together into his thumb.

"The First Creatures can see and hear in ways we cannot. There are things you must know, but I cannot speak of this plainly, or I will draw his attention. Do you understand?"

He pauses and looks up from the powders like he expects something of me. MMy mind goes blank.

No. I don't understand.

But he's still looking at me, his eyes pleading, insistent, and overfull, like he's trying to pour what he knows into me.

I nod. He goes on.

"I'm going to try to give it to you in a vision," he speaks in slow quiet syllables, but his hands work fast, still smashing powders into his thumb. "It's the safest way. But understand, this only works if you hold strong to the question. You have to focus."

What is the question?

He hunches forward, tight and tense. A bead of sweat on his brow despite the chill outside. *He's nervous.*

Suddenly, I am too.

I follow his nimble fingers at work, smearing more and more from the bright powders into his thumb until it is dark as a deep pit.

Something strange and uneasy trembles within me.

Before I can say anything, he thrusts his stained thumb into my forehead, and my vision goes blank and I am thrown back, back, back, back, disappearing down a well, deep and dark and empty. My stomach drops out and my hands prickle with helplessness. Just when I start to think the fall will never end, it lurches to a stop, dropping me onto cold hard ground. For a moment, I lay there, my check pressed against crisp snow, catching my breath.

Then I push myself up. I've been hurled into empty wintered woods. The only sounds are the rustling wind in the trees and the crunch of my steps in the stiff, frozen ground. As I turn to take it in my mind is accosted in flashes of vision.

Dark hair.

Flushed cheeks.

A boy stands against a tree, staring out at something ahead.

I'm not alone. A glimpse of relief but then something else begins to settle within me, darkness. It reaches out to me from the boy and curls up in my chest as if it were my own.

No. Don't let it in. My throat tightens and constricts and I strain to shut it out. But something tells me it was always there, already a part of me.

And then suddenly the image scratches and rips and there is nothing but cold where he stood.

My panic is flat and tasteless in my mouth like ash. *Who is he? Where did he go?*

Wisps and pieces of him fly around me like lost pages from an old book. I reach to a tree and cling onto it for support, digging my fingers in as tight as I can. I try to catch the cast off pieces of the boy's image.

What did Ceil do to me? Why am I here? My fingers press into the tree so hard my skin is beginning to rub away against the bark. I force my hand to relax and let go. I turn again, trying to find the boy. As I move I am caught in a storm of apparitions — the rumble of carts wheels, a cheerful rabble of voices. It is a town, somewhere close by. The jovial community fills the boy with quivering anger, and his anger is inside me.

I stop. Try to hold onto the feeling long enough to understand it. To find the boy again. But wind blows through, the pages shuffle, the moment is lost in another rush of flashing moments shuffling past. I scramble to catch what I can—a high laugh floats through the forest branches—a bouquet of spring wildflowers, curling in on itself as the buds rot and blacken—a necklace around a girl's neck, a simple gold chain with a large uncut emerald dangling from it— and I don't catch the rest because the box quivers in my pocket, a wild trembling pull toward the girl with the necklace. It's twisting, crying for her.

I clap my palm over it through the pocket. Trap it tight in my fist and try to force it into submission, my hands trembling. And there is an urgency in my gut, something telling me I need to understand. But it is too little, it is too much, I can't put it together.

"Do you study magic?"

The voice is warm and inviting like honey, whispering just over my shoulder. I whip around to face it, but there's nothing there.

My temples buzz with a rapid *thud-thud-thud-thud* too loud to think. I strain for more, but the vision leaks at its edges like a blurred watercolor. Like it's all about to dissolve. But it can't, I don't understand yet.

The forest floor rumbles, the stones rattle against it, begin to rise.

From behind me, I sense a soft rosy glow, the flutter of gentle wings.

The voice again, *"What is your name?"*

I whip around, almost catch it this time, but my foot snags on something and I fall, down, down, down past the ground and into darkness.

****

I'm thrown back to the tent with a hot rush of smoke and biting embers.

When I open my eyes, Ceil is waiting.

"Did you find your answer?"

The question ignites a sudden anger in me. I found nothing but wisps and bursts too thin to hold.

"Who is the boy? And that girl?" I growl. The strange floating laugh plays back in my head. "Why did you send me there?"

Ceil looks down. Shakes his head. "You held onto the wrong question."

The rage swells in me. I whip out the box. "My box. It was connected to them somehow. What do you know?"

Ceil darts backward as far as he can while sitting. "Put that away," he snaps. "By the Gods, keep that thing away."

Something in the sharpness of his voice makes me look at him closer. His eyes are tense and his hand is outstretched to shield himself, fingers trembling.

He knows what it is. At least, as much as I do. And he is right to be afraid.

But as I study him, it comes back to me like a bud emerging from the earth. Ceil had something to tell me about the Underworld. And the woman is out there somewhere. The box is not what matters right now. I will be free of it soon anyway, if I do as Kythiel asks. And this man can help me, he says.

I slowly pull in my arm and tuck the box back into my cloak pocket. Ceil relaxes and leans back in toward the fire.

"We must try a different way," he says. He pauses, pursing his lips in reflection. Then he looks back to me. "Do you know the parable of the Three Trees?"

I have to shut my eyes to search my mind, block out the tent. The Text comes to me.

"In the Beginning, the Three Gods planted three seeds. From them grew three trees. Each tree was different, but they grew together in harmony.

"The first tree was a tree of true light. To it came the first creatures of Theia. The second tree was a tree of shadow and sanctuary. It offered rest and refuge to Gloros' sprites, and the strange things of the abyss beyond. The third tree lay between the first and second, changing often like the temporal mortal creatures it sheltered. To it also came Shael's daemons. The three trees grew together for many years. Their roots and branches intertwined and their creatures kept company together beneath them. Until one day—"

"Very good, that is enough," he says. "But there's more the Texts don't say."

My throat tightens. The Texts' story is a dark one. All was well until one day a creature of the first tree asked for a fruit from the middle tree. When the Three denied him, he took the fruit for himself. He told others how delicious it was, and boasted of how he had defied the Gods and gotten away with it. Many of the others began trying other fruits too.

Soon the craving for it consumed him, and the others. The trees were depleted by the increased demand, and could no longer sustain the needs of their own creatures. The trees began to wilt away. To save them, the Three ripped the trees from the ground and separated them, and build great walls around each so the creatures would not break free to steal fruit from the others. Some creatures fled to another tree before the walls were up, but the other trees' fruit could not sustain them, and they went mad from the hunger.

I've never liked this story.

But what more could there be to tell? The Texts are everything. That's why it's the Texts.

"What do you mean?" I ask. I'm not sure I want to know.

Ceil glances away. Small lit ashes float through the tent's thick smoke, snapping and hissing. He leans toward me on his hand, almost touching the flames.

"There was a creature of the first tree who followed the Three's orders when the trees separated, but could not forget the sweetness of the middle tree no matter how many years passed. His desire for it made him forget all else. He never stopped trying to break free of the wall, and finally he forced his way through. The divide between the first tree and the middle tree was weakened by it, and it threatens the peace."

The fire is filling the enclosed tent with smoke and flecks of ash. Ceil's eyes cut through it, sharp and bright and focused. He shoves his words onto me.

"If the walls suffer more breaks, they will crumble. If the walls crumble, it will all begin again." He leans toward me over the fire. "Do you understand?"

The rhythm of Ceil's voice lulls into silence, the only sound the crackling of the fire. Smoke crowds around him and the fire's angry light shifts across his face in harsh dancing streaks, hiding, and attacking him in strange pieces. His eyes lift and lock with mine, hold me captive.

No. I do not understand. There is something behind Ceil's words that I am not grasping.

I shake my head.

He purses his lips into a thin line. Presses further.

"There is another. A creature that belongs to none of the trees and none of the Gods. This creature holds the power to contain the discord. But if he is not careful, he could tear the walls down and unleash the chaos."

Smoke fills my lungs and sways the walls. The small white flames swallow me.

"Adem."

The force of Ceil's voice snaps me back to myself. Did I tell him my name? I look across to him. Small beads of sweat collect along his lip and run from his brow.

"You were not seen in this. One thread can alter the entire tapestry. If you disrupt the Order, not even fate's masters know where it might lead."

The fire reflects off Ceil's eyes and makes them a whipping torrent, dark pits hollow beneath them.

"Do you understand?"

Smoke swirls around my head. Distorts the room. Flecks of ash bite at my cheeks. The ground still spins and dips. Ceil's eyes plead with me as if the fate of the world is in my hands.

"Do you understand?"

I don't. I'm wracking every corner of my mind, but every time I hit a wall.

Anger clouds inside me, words shoot out from me like lightening. "What did you bring me here for?"

I was just following the woman, just passing through. And now he's held me back and weighed me down with meaningless stories and strange visions.

Now my mind is clouded and confused, and I've lost her. It's like a gaping hole right through my middle, a hole that was almost filled and now never will be.

Ceil's eyes are still on me wide and desperate and unblinking, unfazed by my rage. He stares at me as if he is planting his words in my head, begging me to understand. But my mind is barren and cannot make anything of it.

Ceil shakes his head. "I cannot give you any more. There are ears and eyes everywhere. Think. Who is the creature of the first tree, Adem? And who is the creature outside the walls? *Think.*"

The creature of the first tree? How could I know? What could it matter? The Texts say nothing of *who*.

And this creature on the outside. What could I possibly know of him? A creature that belongs to nothing in these realms. Walled out in the darkness while all the rest are enclosed with their trees. Never once is such a thing mentioned in the Texts. And yet this creature pulls at me, tugs at my chest, clings in my brain.

Then it clicks.

"It's me."

I'm the thing trapped outside. All my life, just outside it all. Locked out from all that surrounds me. Somehow, I am this creature, and I can't bear it.

I look back to Ceil. "You've got to help me. I have to get in. How do I get in?"

As I speak I reach out to grip his shoulder, but he flinches away.

"Yes, but—that's not—"

The heavy smoke presses around the very walls of

the tent, crowding, squeezing, and smothering. *I have to get in.* Ceil takes a deep breath. He tries again.

"Kythiel is not—"

But before he can finish he starts to cough. It grows and grows until his entire body is convulsing, and he is forced onto his hands, slouched forward over the fire.

It stops as suddenly as it began; Ceil's body whips bolt straight. His eyes are glazed and white, his face slackened.

"Did I tell you to consult the prophets, golem?" It is not Ceil's voice. It is strange, twisted, and somehow familiar. Despite the fire's heat, it turns my skin cold.

It's Kythiel.

"Our pact does not concern him. It does not concern the gods. Do not meddle in these things, for you cannot understand them. Get on your way to the sea. Try this again, and he will not survive it."

Ceil's body drops to the ground in a heap. My chest hollows, a vacuum of panic. In a heartbeat, I am at his side, pressing my ear to his chest. I listen. The tent spins and the dull thudding of my brain is growing, but under it, a soft steady rhythm. His heart still beats. He will be okay.

I stand, stare down at him. I should leave before any more harm comes to him.

I turn and lift the dizzying pattern of the tent's door. A cool breeze accosts me from out in the night.

"Wait."

He's awake already. I stop and turn back to him. He forces himself up.

"One more thing," he looks at me through strained eyes. "The boy must live."

My mind clouds, an impenetrable fog. Again, I do not understand. But I can't afford questions. I must go. Already I've wasted too much precious time.

I nod and leave, dropping the dizzying pattern of the tent door behind me.

CHAPTER 8

THE HUSH'S DUST, soot, and dingy desperation cling to me. It weighs down the cloak on my back, sticks in my eyes, and clings to my skin. My thoughts are becoming clouded and constricted by it.

Ceil's words twist in my head. I shove them aside.

Where did the woman go?

I should never have let Ceil stop me. I should have kept following her. All he gave me was a knot of strange images I can't untangle. Now Kythiel is angry, my time running out. And, I've lost her, with no way to catch up this time.

The night is old and the Hush is thinning. The sky isn't lightening yet, but it will start soon. As I weave through the covered faces, my eyes dart to each of them, searching for a hint of her red hair, though I don't expect her to still be here. Something in me aches to see her again, reminds me of the empty hole that cuts through my core.

I pause at the cross section where the hoods and masks turn back in toward the city. I turn the opposite direction, toward the wall, unsure where I am headed. She must have returned to her quarters by now like all the others. Beyond the Hush alleys, beyond the temples, up against the horizon, the wall dips in and out of sight between the towers. I wander without thinking, weaving through the streets and side alleys until I find myself in front of it.

The wall. The divide between Epoh and the wasteland. Between torture and freedom. Order and chaos. Between a life in the shadows and a soul.

I wonder what's left out there now, beyond it. Do I dare find out?

I reach out my hand and run my fingers over it. Smooth concrete, at least three stories high. If I were to do this, where would I even start? I turn and look up. The tired buildings here aren't close enough or tall enough to make the leap. But the towers ahead, the ones the laborers sleep in, are the highest. Tightly packed cells, stories and stories high. Perhaps one of these would get me over. If I choose to try.

I'm already out of my temple. What harm is there in finding out?

The moon is sinking and the sky is beginning to lighten, but the sun isn't showing itself yet. The quiet between the Hush and the Silencers falls, the emptiness of dampened twilight. Epoh sleeps.

It's a long walk to the residential district. I try to take smooth, fast strides. Still no sign of her. Not that I expect to find her now, so close to morning. As I walk, I drag my hand across the cement wall behind me. The friction releases a tense whisper in my wake. Dust and grime that has packed in over the years loosens and sticks to my skin until my fingers are smooth with fine debris. The sharp rocks that line the ground against the wall crunch under my feet.

As the towering buildings of the laborers' district get closer, I can see some of the buildings have stairs snaking up their backs to the roof. One near the edge must be five, six stories tall. Plenty for me to clear the wall.

I trudge on, keeping my eye on its dark silhouette against the graying sky.

The night is silent except for the rustle of my steps. Shadows lie in wait at every corner. Though the shoddy apartments are dark and quiet, I jump at every brush of the wind. I've become too comfortable in my one-room world. Maybe I should just go back to it. It's not too late.

But then, *tap, tap, tap.*

It is clear and crisp in the dull dusk. Silencers' boots on the pavement. Far away, yet. But coming closer. And from the cluttered rhythm of it, there's several of them.

Panic shoots through my gut like cold metal and I freeze in my tracks. For a moment, I am sure they are hunting for me — *no one escapes* — before I remember they don't know I exist within their walls.

Somewhere a sharp whisper pricks at my core from out of the fading darkness, the opposite direction from the Silencers. It washes over me in a forceful wave: I am not the only one thinking about escape tonight.

****

Silencers are on the hunt, and they're getting closer.

I need to get out of sight. The escapers are close too; I could hear it in the whisper. Between the Silencers and the escapers, I'll take the escapers. I pick an alley, dark and narrow, and duck into the shadows.

Just in time—the tapping of boots and the swoosh of a Silencer's cloak pass by my alley, striding down the street I was just on.

I press against the cool stone of the building behind me and let out a slow, relieved breath. That was close. But I have to keep going. I glance around, try to figure out my next move.

And that's when I see it: at the other end of the block, a hooded figure flinches, and ducks behind a pile of crates. No, not a hood, a scarf. A gray scarf with a black dotted pattern. A tuft of red escapes from the side.

Relief floods though me. I can't believe it, I found her.

I am pulled down the alley toward her like I'm caught in a current, weaving through the darkness, across another street and into the alley she's hiding in. Behind her shadowed figure, a second pair of eyes flash at me like sparks—the boy is with her.

In the back of my mind, I track the tap-tap-tapping of Silencers' boots all around us. One is rounding a corner, turning down the street toward us, again just on my tail.

I move slowly to keep from scaring them too much; my hands up and spread to show I mean no harm. All the same, they tense and start as I approach. The woman jumps to her feet but the Silencer is just steps away. I push her back down and crouch next to her and the boy. I press my fingers to my lips. They stare at me wide-eyed, but then the Silencer passes by, and they stay put.

They each have a pack strapped to their backs, pressed tight against the side of the building. The boy's face is clean of the blood that poured from it yesterday morning. Dark, swollen bruises have taken its place under each eye and across his nose.

Heat rushes to my cheeks. So long I've watched them from so far away. And now her eyes lock directly with mine as we listen for the Silencer's steps. The Silencer's steps fade as he passes by, and we all relax a little.

How were they going to get over the wall? Could they even survive the jump down? The woman has a thick coil of rope rolled around her shoulder. Suddenly it all makes sense. She must have paid sorely for this in the Hush, even more to ensure the seller's secrecy. Though it seems fear won out over greed tonight.

Is there anything to secure the rope to on top of the wall? I doubt it. Surely, she's thought of this. Then desperation is a strange thing.

The boots are getting closer, a clutter of stern taps just a few blocks away. They're heading toward the wall.

For a moment, I imagine myself creeping behind them, snapping necks, and bashing skulls. These Silencers are coming for them, my humans, and I am their only protector. But the blank eyes of a thousand dead Hunters are on me as soon as I think of it, cold and accusing. My skin clams, my stomach tosses. Shame burns through me. Maybe I should take these men down, but I can't, I just can't. I can't bring myself to do it.

But we can't stay here and wait for them to find us, either. Our only protection here is the shadows.

I signal to the woman, pointing to the next street down. We need to keep moving. She gives a nod and takes the boy's hand. I run past them to the edge of the block and out into the open street. Their soft steps trail just behind me, the rustling of their packs in my ears. We make it into the cover of the next block's buildings. The woman presses against the rough brick right next to me, and I can feel the tense heat radiating off her skin, the soft exhalation of each quick breath. Beside her, the boy pants. His wide eyes stare up at me. I've never seen him so quiet.

It's only seconds before boots crunch on the sharp rocks by the wall. I twist around the corner to see. Five of them. Just a few blocks away at the wall, they hover in a circle, listening as one gives orders from one with a jutted brow and sharp, square jaw.

The Silencer from the market.

I turn my body, widening my shoulders to create a barrier between him and my refugees. He can't see them. I won't let him.

He stops talking. They split up.

One treads this way.

The boy must live. It rumbles through my brain without permission. Ceil's warning. And the strange small man with the mangled beard — *choose.* I clench my fingers into the wall behind me and squeeze my eyes shut tight. It can't mean what I think it means. They can both make it. I will make sure of it.

The woman's hand is braced against the brick right next to mine. Strong, rough, hardened by years of difficult work. I lean out to check the Silencers again — my hand shifts, our fingers touch. It quivers all the way up my arm and down my spine.

One of the Silencers is coming this way, checking each side road as he moves closer and closer. There's no time to think. I take her hand in mine and pull them along the building wall and around the next corner.

A close miss. I hear the Silencer's tread just as we settle against the new wall. But we can't move building to building all night. They have to get out of Epoh, and the sooner the better.

Will I go too? The question tugs at my mind. Kythiel's offer is the only chance I have to break free, but even thinking of going beyond the wall into the unknown is enough to make my mind go blank. I shake it back into focus.

For now all that matters is that none of us can afford to be out in Epoh's streets when the sun rises, and the sky's darkness keeps fading more and more.

I can't fail them. I have to do something.

Straight ahead, my eye catches the shadow of a winding staircase against a tall building. The one I was heading toward when I found them. It's only blocks away, right ahead of us.

We could at least see better from up there. Make a plan. And the Silencers aren't looking for them on rooftops. It'll be safer there, at least for now.

I nudge the woman and point to the stairs, then up. She squints, and then nods. I take her hand again, and her other hand holds tightly around the boy's. I pull them after me and we weave through the dark street to the next cluster of shadows.

As I flop against the wall, there is a throbbing in my temples and my ears and my neck. Beside me, the woman and the boy are hunched over, stifling heavy breaths. Did they hear us? I brace for the fast tapping of boots on cement as Silencers start running our way.

It doesn't come.

I allow myself to breathe again. One slow, deep exhale.

One block down. One, two, three, to go, it looks like. I can hear at least one Silencer wandering through the streets somewhere ahead of us. I strain to listen, try to figure out where he is, but it's impossible. We need to keep moving.

Soon as their breathing steadies, I take her hand again and pull them another block. Two more. Then one more. I can smell the rust on the stairs reaching to me. Still the Silencers are unaware of us. But his steps are getting closer. His steps hit my ears still fresh from the pavement. He can't be more than a block away.

All the more reason to keep moving, and fast.

I look out around the corner to make sure the street is empty — it is, at least for the moment. The woman and the boy are still panting but even so, I take her hand in mine one last time, and the world rushes around me as I break for the stairs. Behind me, a stiff tug on my hand, a sharp gasp. I twist around as I run — the boy. He's fallen, is sprawled in the street, still as stone.

The woman fights my grip, pushing back madly to get to him, but I hold her hand tight — we're in the middle of the street, caught in the light of rising morning. I push her toward the alley's shadows and then I run back to him, stop to scoop him up in my arms. His eyes are closed and he is limp in my arms, but I hear the padded thump-thump of his heart and am filled with relief. He's only unconscious.

But something else is wrong. A new kind of quiet has set in around us.

The Silencer stopped walking.

I lift my eyes from the boy and there he is, the Silencer, his eyes hooded and dark under his heavy brow. The square jaw locks into a smiling grimace. We stand there frozen for half a moment before he kills the silence with a yell. The rage takes over, wild and hot and out of control. The boy is back on the ground and I am racing toward the Silencer, grabbing his throat, squeezing, squeezing, squeezing to stop the sound.

The Silencer thrashes against my arm and kicks at my legs. His pulse races, and then subsides, and for once, the Silencer's jaw goes slack as his eyes roll back into his head.

Then I feel the sagging weight in my hand. I realize what I have done, and drop the lifeless heap to the ground. The panic and rage leaves my hands and pools into my core in a heavy knot. My fingers shake. Can I do anything but kill? I turn away.

Behind me, the boy is awake again, and he gawks up at me, shaking. *He saw.*

But there's no time to calm him. The other four guards are responding to the Silencer's yell and their footsteps are closing in from every direction.

I scoop the boy over my shoulder and run.

When I round the corner, it is already too late. I'm only half a block from the woman, but the Silencer running up the other side of the alley is even closer. He grabs her wrist and tears the scarf from her head, sending her curls flying. The scarf drops to the ground as he twists his hand into her hair and tugs her head back. She doesn't make a sound. Not until she sees us does she cry out, fight against the Silencer's iron grip, reaching out for the boy.

He twists in my arms when he sees her and bursts into hysterics, screaming and reaching for her, desperate to be freed from me.

I hold him tight.

Another Silencer rounds the corner at the far end of the alley, and I hear even more footsteps behind me. Surrounded. There's no time. I feel a dull tug at my chest. If I put the boy down to free her, he will be captured in seconds.

The boy must live.

"He's alright," I call to her.

What else is there to say? We both know it's too late now. A futility behind her eyes echoes inside, me, too. I tried to help them, did all I could. It wasn't enough.

She gives me a last frantic look. "Protect him, angel," she says. It's as much a command as it is a prayer.

Angel. I nod. Yes. Anything. My chest hollows into a heaving empty vacuum.

But there's no time to think about this now. I have to get the boy to safety. Another Silencer rounds the corner and races toward us. A hard clatter of boots tells me the others are getting close.

The only escape is up.

The old stairs cry out under my weight as I race up them three at a time, twisting through its slithering turns. The boy screams in my ear, struggles, trying to get back to her. His teardrops absorb into my shoulder. It goes against everything in me to leave her, stings bitterly through my chest, but it's the only choice.

We're only a flight up when the Silencers start clamoring after us, a stampede of echoing, shuddering clangs rushing toward us.

I wind round and round and round until finally I am on the roof. I gained on them in the climb, their human muscles weakening with use, but I still don't have long. Behind me, the sun's first rays graze over the wall, stretching my shadow across the roof like a giant.

I rush across the roof's edge on all four sides. There's nowhere to go from here. Only down. We must be six stories up, at least. Can this small boy even take the fall? I have only seconds before he will be taken by the Silencers and suffer an even crueler fate. And me, what would I do on the other side of the wall? There's only one thing I could do.

The boy must live. Choose.

And finally I do. Suddenly my choice is so clear I can't remember what was holding me back.

Of course, I go over the wall. Anything else is a dead end, an endless loop I've already lived over and over again.

And the boy is coming with me. At least into the wasteland. He can't stay here. The rest I'll figure out later.

The Silencers' footsteps are getting close.

I back up to the opposite end of the roof, my eyes locked on the wall, the one thing that can get us past the Silencers. I wrap my arms around the boy as tight as I can, and then I run across the roof and straight into the sky. A last second thought makes me clip my final step, and I aim to land on the wall instead of over it. Maybe I can at least cut the fall in half.

I slam into dusty cement and my foot skids across the ledge. I bend low to absorb the force of the landing and scramble to bring us to a stop, holding onto the boy tight, tight, tight. But I can't balance fast enough, and we roll over the wall's edge. I twist around and grip the ledge with my hand.

We dangle off the outside of the wall. My head pounds, *thunk-thunk-thunk-thunk-thunk,* drowning out all thought.

I squint toward the ground, a shimmering blur. It is shorter than the leap we just took. I still don't know what it could do to the boy, but there's no other way.

I release the wall and wrap myself around the small, young body above me and wait, praying I take all the impact.

CHAPTER 9

THE CRASH OF our landing thunders over the landscape. Neither of us moves.

My splintered limbs sprawl over rough shards—glass. They put glass down outside the wall, one last little way to hurt anyone crazy enough to try to escape. My skull pushes back out into shape, twisting with echoed distortions as the impact tears through it. I must have hit it on something. Somewhere beyond it, faint voices and the shuffle of boots headed back into the city. They probably think the fall killed us. It probably would have if I were human.

All I can see of the child on my chest is a limp tumble of his bright curls, the top of the pack on his back bulging over him. His heart beats weakly against me. I wait anxiously for my broken bones to pull back into place so I can see how much harm I've done to him.

Finally, I am back in one piece. I slide out from under him, shift him gently to the ground, trying to move him as little as possible. How much damage can his small frame take? How much pain?

With the dark bruises from yesterday under his eyes, his slack expression is haunting. I softly check over his arms and legs for breaks, then his head, a knot twisting through my stomach. Nothing appears askew or broken. His chest rises and falls.

He's unconscious, but he will be okay.

Relief mixes with anxious churning and the flat taste of clay.

But what do I do with him now?

Protect him, she said to me. Her deep eyes burned into mine. *Angel.*

But he can't go where I am going. He can't cross to the Underworld. And even without that, staying with me is anything but safe. I am no angel. I wonder what the woman would think if she knew what she'd really left him with.

I've tried it before, living with the humans. I look enough like them to pass, mostly. They accepted me, for a short time. But they asked questions. I didn't have answers. And when generations passed and I did not, they changed toward me, grew suspicious. As they should have. I started moving a few times a century. The hard accusing looks in the eyes of those who had been friends were worse than the sad goodbyes, the questions I could not answer for them.

Even then, there were incidents.

Humans are strangely curious things. They are drawn to beauty as wasps to a flame. If they saw the box, they reached for it. It called to them.

What happened next was unstoppable.

I was unfit for life among them. I knew what I was.

Something wrong. Something missing. *Golem.*

It didn't take long for the guilt to outweigh the loneliness. I left them. Locked myself away the best I could. In the centuries since, the only lives I have taken have been those of the Hunters. No matter where I hide, where I wander, they find me. All others I left behind long ago.

So it is impossible for me to stay with the child.

But how can I leave him behind? Alone, here at the doorstep of those who would destroy him. Alone, out here in the unknown? Who knows what's out here. He might not last until sunset. I promised to protect him. I can't leave him here.

I look to the horizon. It is broad, blank, and endless. It is overwhelming. Before it, the wasteland. A wide stretch of debris, hints of the lives that used to be lived here—hints of buildings, shattered ceramic and glass, patches of cement—all crumbled, weed-infested, and fading away. The debris of the Second Realm War. Even after all these years, it's still as barren and devastated as it was the day the gods banished the rebels from the realm.

I crouch down, taking the boy in my arms. His arm rests across my chest, soft, warm, and trusting. So close to the box hidden in its pocket. I push his hand to his side and try to forget the trembling that is taking over my body.

I hold him close, and I walk.

The wasteland extends on and on and on. As I make my way through it, my mind settles into its blankness. The child is soft and warm in my arms, his head gently resting on my shoulder. Light catches in his curls, like the sun reflecting back at itself. A hard seed of anxiety forms in my stomach. What am I leading him to? He's been unconscious all day. What if he never wakes up?

Finally, he stirs and I am filled up with relief, overcome with anxiety. He jolts his head up and pushes away with a gasp.

"Miriam!" He squirms in my arms and it is all I can do not to drop him. A thread of panic quivers through me and I put him on the ground as carefully as I can, wait for it all to fall apart. He looks around.

"Miriam..." he says again. This time the tension dissolves from his face, leaves behind only a deep sadness. He turns slowly, taking in the empty wasteland that surrounds us. He stops when he is facing me.

Just like in the temple tower, he is not afraid. His stare wrenches my shoulders tight.

The guilt sinks deep within me. "She...I...I tried, I tried—"

But he is not paying attention to me. He stares at the ground. Tilts his head, as if listening intently. "They got her, didn't they?"

Such certainty.

"Yes."

He nods his understanding.

The guilt piling on my shoulders is too much. "I'm sorry, I failed—"

He stares at the dirt between his feet. "No. You're the only reason we had a chance."

I struggle for a response. "She would have done anything to protect you. Made me swear to do the same. She is a good mother."

"My mother is dead. Miriam is my sister."

I close my mouth and bite my lip. He really is alone now.

All I want is to fix it for him. To hold him tight until it all dissolves. My chest contracts with the ache reflected in his eyes. "We cannot go back for her. It's too dangerous. I promised her I'd — "

"I know. She wouldn't want us to."

He turns away and rubs the tears away with his palm. Takes in the blank horizon again. "How long has it been?"

"Since sunrise." The sun is high over our heads now.

"Where are we headed?"

"West. The sea."

He nods. "That's what she wanted."

What she wanted? But there's nothing out here. Did she know something? Was there a plan? My mind crowds with questions, but I look at him and his eyes are wet with pushed-back tears and I let them go.

"We should keep going."

"Not yet."

He scavenges the ground, picks up small sticks and other pieces of debris. He keeps going until his arms are full.

Crouching, he arranges his collection into a careful pile. He tosses off his pack and digs through it, pulling out a piece of flint and steel. Sparks begin to fly as he hits them together. He continues until the pile catches. As the fire crackles across the debris, the boy kneels before it and prays to the Three. A prayer for a safe passage into death to Gods who left their people behind. Something long ago forgotten in this realm. Whether it is more shocking he knows this ritual, or that he dares perform it, I can't decide. Could They really deny him this small thing? Do They even hear him?

There is a pause when he is done, both of us staring into the flames. Then he stands and extinguishes the fire with a kick of dirt.

He pulls his pack back onto his shoulders and rubs his eyes with the edge of his sleeve. "Okay."

I want to know how he learned this, hear some kind of explanation. But his head is tucked down to his chest, his gaze locked on the dirt. Again, I make myself stay quiet.

We walk on in silence.

Every swing of his arms makes me flinch, my muscles tense and strained. I try to keep myself still, not to show it to him. But what if he tries to reach for the box? So many before him have stumbled onto it one way or another, as if it calls to them. The fear is all-consuming, it drenches every step I take and sloshes in my mind. Pointed corners press tensely against my chest through the pocket. I keep my distance from him.

Eventually he stops again to dig through his pack, pulls out a canteen and a folded cloth filled with crackers and dried meats. He counts out a few of them and hands them to me, along with his canteen.

He hardly has enough for himself.

I shake my head.

He frowns. "You must need it."

"No," I tell him. "You eat."

His eyes are hesitant, but he sips from the water a

few times and tucks it back into the pack with most of the food. The crackers and meat he set aside he nibbles at as we walk.

Ahead of us, the sun sinks away. It is not long before the boy's steps begin to stumble, and the bruises under his eyes darken with weariness. But before he will let me take him into my arms to sleep, he lights another small fire and utters an evening prayer. He stomps out the flame and bursts into sudden movement.

"What are you doing? Stop!"

Every inch of me is overtaken with a shudder of confusion and I flinch away — *don't let him touch the box.*

But he doesn't come at me. I look back. It's not an attack for the box, only series of pushups, jumps, and combat exercises. I try to take a breath.

He stands, panting. "These are my drills."

Another slow breath out. Drills? He's only a child.

"You're going to hurt yourself." He's still weak from the fall and the Silencer's beating.

He peers up at me over the dark bruises that streak his face. "I always do my drills. No matter what. That's just how war is."

He's not making sense. It jumbles my brain and anger leaks out the cracks. Already he's dropped back to the ground and is huffing away.

"What war?"

"Don't know," he pants. "That's just what my mother always said."

"Your mother had you doing this?"

"Yeah." A sharp breath. "And then my sister. It's important that I'm ready."

"But," I bend over and grab his arm, make him be still. "Why? Ready for what?"

He forces his breathing to slow a little and looks up to me. "I don't know. She hadn't told me yet," he says. His brow pulls together and he looks away. "I guess now I won't know until it's here."

My fault. Guilt knocks away my words. Jordan may not believe it, but that doesn't stop it from being true. I watch silently until he finishes.

After, once his body quiets again, I take him cautiously in my arms and walk for both of us. His head slowly sags until it is resting on my shoulder, his hair tickling at my neck.

The sky is wide and crisp with clarity tonight, speckled with stars well beyond what could be seen in Epoh. Well beyond what I could ever remember. Crickets chirp in chorus all around — at least one thing has survived out here.

In the dark, in the quiet like this, thoughts start to push their way to the surface of my mind. Doubts.

Ceil. He was trying to tell me something. Something I needed to know before my quest. Why would Kythiel stop him?

But the more I mull on it, the more tangled the knots get.

"She's still alive."

I jump at Jordan's voice. I thought surely that he was sleeping by now. All my other worries dissolve for the moment.

"We can't know that," I tell him. "Perhaps if she is lucky, she is at rest."

His head nods against my shoulder. "I do know."

"No. You couldn't," I say.

"But I do," he insists. "I can feel her. Everyone has an energy. It's all connected. If she was gone, I would know."

His certainty unsettles me, prickles in my spine. But he couldn't know. Could he? I hope his mind isn't where mine is, considering the tortures she is likely facing even this minute.

"What is your name?" he asks.

The question gives me a chill — how long as it been since anyone asked me this?

"Adem."

"Adem," he repeats. His words are starting to get lazy with sleep. "I'm Jordan."

Soon after, his breathing slows and deepens and it is only the wasteland, the night, and me.

CHAPTER 10

I WALK THROUGH the night. As we move west, the cold eases, the sun gets stronger.

Jordan sleeps and sleeps and sleeps. He lies still as a rock, collapsed into me all through the night. He's taken a lot for so short a time. But the swelling of his bruises show the earliest signs of healing under his skin, easing away into purples and blues and yellows.

Finally he wakes, squinting into the day's brightness, and slides to the ground. The first thing he does is kneel down, bend his body to the earth. He pulls his hands in and folds them under his chin. A morning prayer.

Then the drills. The questions rush through my mind again. But I stay quiet—he's been through enough for a small boy these past few days. And I've already done enough to contribute to it, leaving his sister behind. With a painful twinge, I wonder where she is right now. How much she's suffering. If she's still alive.

When he is done with his drills, we push on.

The farther we get from Epoh, the more we leave behind the ruin. Plants have started to regrow out here, healing amidst the destruction from the War. As we walk, Jordan studies them, pulling leaves from some and storing them in his pack. It makes it easy to keep him a safe distance from me. When he stops to ration out more of his crackers and dried meat, he eats some of the plant leaves too. Again, he offers some to me.

"Why don't you eat?" he asks.

"I have no need," I tell him. I quicken my pace, moving a little past him. I'm exposing myself.

"And you do not tire. You walked all through the night." He starts skipping to match my pace.

I say nothing. Tension is clenching up my chest. He sees too much. For a moment, we trudge on in silence. What can I say to him?

He bounces high toward me in another skip, and swings out his hand to me. It flies up near the box in my pocket, and I can feel it, the box, it's restless, crying to be held, stretching for him, always, always hungry to be discovered, to find someone to lure in. Someone for me to kill. Jordan's skin brushes my arm, and I jump away, a shudder overtaking my whole body, a loud gasp escaping me.

His face scrunches, surprised and sad.

"What's wrong?" he whimpers.

Anxiety pounds through me. "What were you doing?"

He cautiously steps toward me, his eyes wide and cautious, carefully studying my face. In the sun small flecks of orange glow in them like sparks. He slips his hand into mine.

This is all? My ears rush with heat and shame. Of course, he is not trying to take the box. How could he even know of it?

"Okay?" He still watches me, brows pushed together.

"Okay."

I close my eyes and tighten my hands into fists, then relax my muscles and feel the tension break way. When I open my eyes again, he is watching me, his eyes wary. A small, careful smile spreads over his lips. We walk.

He forgets the moment quickly, and soon our quiet is comfortable again. He kicks a pebble along as we go.

Night eventually falls. Jordan carefully counts out his crackers, leaves, and strips of meat. He sips from his water. He does not offer me any this time. Then he bends to the earth again, folding his palms together under his chin. Evening prayer.

"Where did you learn that? The prayers?" This time my questions won't stay in me.

He finishes his prayer before answering.

"My mother taught us. We've always done it."

"In Epoh?" It doesn't make sense.

"Yeah. Lots of us did."

But that doesn't make sense.

"But Zevach banned anything to do with the Three."

He shrugs. "We did it anyway. Just not where they could see."

Suddenly my confusion hardens into a tight seed of anger. Why are they endangering themselves over something so pointless?

"But the Three are gone. They left."

He just shrugs. "Some say that. But I don't think so. I feel Them sometimes."

"No. They're gone," The words come out of me in hard, bitter shards, like something settled so deep in me I forgot it was there. "After the Second Realm War, they left."

The remorse doesn't come until I look at Jordan's face, somber and flat. He doesn't say anything. He just reaches up and takes my hand.

The dark settles in, his eyes begin to droop and his steps begin to drag. Again, I take him in my arms, and he curls against my shoulder and stretches his arms around my neck, pressing against my chest. His warmth seeps into me and the angst, the tension begins to disperse in response. I hold on to just a little of it, a tight knot in the middle of my back. I can't afford to become too comfortable. That's when it all goes wrong.

"Why is your skin so cold?" He pulls his head up to look at me. "I've never met anyone so cold."

He knows, he knows, he knows. My shoulders tighten with discomfort. What will he do? Will he leave me? Maybe he should.

"I told you. I am not like you." I swallow the great lump in my throat before adding, "You should fear me." He needs to know.

"Fear you?" he frowns. "You saved me."

It's no use. He almost sees me for what I am, but he doesn't understand.

I hold him to me in my arms and say a pointless prayer to whoever might listen. I pray for somewhere safe for him.

Then as his breathing slows and the dark stillness

settles in, the questions start to creep back into my mind. The fears.

What was Ceil trying to say? That look in his eyes as he spoke, trying to pour it all into me. Their glazed-over iciness when Kythiel overtook him—so angry. *Why?*

The strangeness of it, the inconsistency of it with the desperate beautiful creature I met in the cellar, it nags at me.

If only I could understand what Ceil was trying to tell me, maybe it would make sense. I roll it over and over with each step through the night, but it is useless.

****

By morning, we have come far enough that most of the chill has left the air.

Jordan wakes early. I place him on the ground and he eats, prays, does his drills, and we get moving again. It is not long before he stuffs his cloak into his pack. He runs circles around me, trails behind me, and leaps between my footprints.

His speech is as active as his body, a rapid flow like the crackling of a fire. He covers everything from his friends in Epoh to the plants we come across.

And later, more questions.

"Were you part of Epoh? I mean. I know you lived there. But were you part of it?"

Knots squirm inside me. He's looking at me as he looked at me in the tower. Studying.

"What do you mean?" I know what he means.

"I just...I never saw you out before that night." We both know which night. The last night. The night I failed Miriam. "Why did I never see you?"

"Epoh is large."

"Epoh is small," he counters. "And I would notice you. You are so big. You look..." He squints up at me. " You're just different."

We go on in silence for a time, the only sound the crunching dirt below our feet.

Until he starts again.

"You killed that Silencer."

The words slam into me as if I'd walked into a wall, and I stop in my tracks. I thought after the fall maybe he'd forgotten.

I turn to him. Remember the panic that stretched over his face, the way he gaped up at me after, when I turned back and scooped him into my arms.

"What you did saved me. It almost saved us both."

The guilt rises and spreads within me like hot air trapped in a tight space. I remember the rage that took over as I squeezed at the Silencer's neck, and I am not so sure saved is the right word.

"I shouldn't have. I should have..." But I don't know what I should have done. I should have kept the rage in check. "And even so, it was not enough."

"It was. It was enough for what the Three have in store."

"The Three are gone." The words are out of me before I can ask myself if I should start this again.

"They're here," Jordan says.

"You have not seen what I have over the years." The suffering, pain, and violence. My voice is a feral snarl, but it doesn't faze him.

"I can feel Them."

He said that yesterday, something about feeling the

Gods. "What does that mean?"

He shrugs. "I just feel Them. I've always been able to. It's like...it's like heat. The same way I can feel Miriam is still alive. The same way I can feel the magic in you." My ears perk at the words. He stretches his hands out toward me; his head tilts to the side, pensive and curious. "There's so much of it."

How does he know, how could he possibly know?

His hands drop. But he is still watching me.

"Adem, what are you?"

I stop in my tracks. Stare at down to my feet. Dirt sticks between my toes. I grope for words, anything to say, just not the truth.

"I'm not like you."

Pieces of each word stick in my throat like splintered wood.

"I know you're not." He steps up next to me. "You're..." for the first time he pulls his eyes away, the first time in our three days, and scuffs the ground.

My ears burn. It was wrong to bring him with me. He sees too much. When he flees from me in fear out here, there will be nowhere for him to run to in the wasteland.

"You're a golem. Aren't you?" he asks again.

Golem. It digs into me like a shovel forced into packed earth.

"What do you know of such things? A small child like you."

The full bitterness of my words hits me as soon as they are out, pungent and awful, a taste that seeps into my tongue and won't leave.

His soft serious face and wide eyes don't waver.

"Just what's in the Texts."

The Texts. It's not much. The first mention I found, I'd thought I'd finally found my answers. But what the Texts had for me was less than a handful of dust. Just what I already knew, and myths of men who had created them, men who may or may not have been anything more than stories. No matter how many times I read them, I could not get anything more from them. It was like trying to squeeze blood from stones.

Jordan keeps talking. "There was one man a long time ago. The Forger. He made a whole army of them, making them over and over until the magic drove him mad. He made more golems than anyone else, ever."

I know it. "That's just a story. It's not in the Texts."

Just empty words. Lies. If so many golems were created, where did they all go? I've never found another in all my ages of being.

"Did the Forger make you, Adem?"

"He is not real," I growl.

Quiet.

"But someone made you. Who is your maker?"

My cheeks grow hot. "I don't know."

"Oh."

Jordan's eyes dart away. But he's not done asking questions.

"How...how is that possible?"

How can I explain what I don't know? "It was many ages ago. Everything that far back is blurry. Whoever it was, I don't think he wanted me to find him. He sent me away."

Jordan stares at his steps through the dirt. "So you've just always been alone?"

"Yes."

The word hangs there, empty. Bare.

"It is better that way," I add.

He looks back up to me, frowning. "Why were you in Epoh? Why did you leave?"

So many questions. They build up like a wall around me, pin me in. My mind is weary with them. Loud. It is crowded and crammed with this new information.

"Adem?"

No more. Not now. I can't. I don't look back to him. I keep my gaze locked on the ground in front of me.

"Adem?"

Suddenly pressure bursts inside me and I turn on him. "Why didn't you run like the others?" I roar.

I feel a twinge of remorse at the way his curious expression flickers out, but the pounding anger quickly drowns it out. "What?"

"In the temple. You were with the boys that found me in the tower. They ran. Why didn't you run?"

Jordan's eyes stay on me a moment before dropping away.

"You were so sad. I just wanted to understand why."

My rage flattens out, swallowed up into itself. Sad? I suppose I am. I stumble through my mind for something to say, but it's like fumbling through the dark. Finally, I turn away and trudge on ahead.

It's a moment before I hear his soft steps rustling behind me.

We push on in silence.

But all he said is trapped in my mind. With each step I pick it apart, examine each piece. A quiet anger simmers over my skin.

We walk on like this until the sun drops.

"Adem?"

Jordan's voice is soft in the twilight, but it jolts me out of myself. I'm still not used to hearing my name.

His face is creased with caution. I was too harsh to him before.

I grunt reluctant acknowledgement.

"What were you made for?"

My foundation lurches as if the ground has dropped out from under me.

"What?"

He retreats half a step, looks down. I hear how my voice sounds too late. Rough. A snarl.

"Golems. They're made for a purpose. What were you made for? Do you...do you know?"

The box. The curse always on me, clouds around me, a constant fog of inescapable burden.

"I do."

Its charge bursts out from my pocket in waves. It cries to be let free, to be held, to be known and used.

Jordan skips with excitement, pulls in close to my side. "What is it?"

"I don't know."

His nose crinkles as he tilts his head in confusion.

"Whatever it is, my maker hid it even from me. It's locked away in a box that will not open."

Those wide trusting eyes brim with awe. "Can I see it?"

"No!"

He jumps away, startled. Again, I hear the violence in my voice, and my chest clouds with guilt. It was an innocent question. He doesn't understand my burdens. How could he?

The box strains to freed, claws at my mind. I push it away.

We trudge on.

Jordan's head droops low; he keeps back and away from me. I try to ignore the prickling in my hand, the hand he would be holding right now if only I'd kept the beast inside me in check.

It wasn't fair. If I had told him, he would have listened. I know he would. He's listened to all the rest, and he's still here.

And deep down I know, it's not just the box. It's something else in me aching to get free. Something I'm desperate to let out and too scared to release. Something that craves what Jordan feeds me. To not bear this alone anymore. Something to fill my emptiness.

I stop walking.

"Alright."

"Really?" Jordan skips to my side with a bright yelp, his whole body reenergized.

I reach into my pocket and pull out the box, hold it tight in my fist, the corners digging into my palm. Up by my shoulders, where he could never reach. Thorny vines twist within me, pierce me all over from the inside.

I will show him. But he has to understand first.

"You cannot touch it. Not even by accident. I will kill you. I will not be able to stop myself. Do you understand?"

He nods, a slow solemn nod, his eyes round and serious. He folds his hands behind his back. "I swear."

I lower my closed fist to his eye level and slowly curl my fingers back. The gold paint sparkles in the sunlight. Jordan gasps with wonder. He leans in his face for a closer look.

My whole hand shakes with unease.

Then it all starts tumbling out of me, all the things I never say.

"You're right, about not seeing me in Epoh. I hid there. I've killed, I don't know how many, because of this box. It makes me. I'm bound to it, I have no control. I tried to get away from them. But they followed me. They always follow me."

The shaking has spread to my shoulders. I feel so vulnerable, so naked, so empty the ground could swallow me up.

Jordan frowns. "Who follows you?"

"The Hunters. They keep coming. For the box. And I keep killing them and I can't bear it." A dry sob chokes my voice. "There's something in me, something dark. Something that likes it. If I don't break free of this, I'm afraid it will take over."

Jordan isn't looking at the box anymore. He's watching me. His eyes well over with feeling — anger? Fear? Sadness?

My shoulders feel light, floating, as if a great physical burden were taken from me. I want more, I want to unload everything, drop it all and forget it in the wasteland, lift Jordan close and pour it all into his ear.

No, no, no, enough. I have no right to put such risk and burden on this child, just for my own relief. I snap the box away. Secure it back deep in my cloak pocket, fasten it away from the world, from Jordan. Neither of us says anything. I turn and keep on walking into the setting sun.

Jordan stands a moment longer, staring, and then trails behind me.

He eats, he does his drills, and soon he is in my arms for the night.

The noxious doubts and questions creep back again with the darkness. But this time I'm ready to fend them off. There's no telling what a desperate soul in the Hush might say, might do. I have no reason to believe Ceil's cryptic claims. Kythiel and I made a deal. It's simple. It's clean. What's there to be hidden?

Besides, he's an angel. He could not deceive me even if he wanted to.

CHAPTER 11

OVER THE NIGHT, my stirring thoughts give way to salty warmth that fills the air.

Soft earth between my toes, the breath of the sea skimming over a sandy bluff, it wraps around me in a friendly embrace.

The ground here is softer. I crouch, shift Jordan in my arms so I can reach down, and roll a handful in my palm. A silky, powdery dirt rolled with large grains. Sand. It sifts through my fingers with a soft slither of friction. Cool pebbles bounce and roll as they hit the ground. So unlike the rough broken pavement of Epoh. As it falls, it releases its smell into the air: a rich dusty cloud of earthy musk. I breathe it in deep.

Ahead, an old well creaks as a dangling bucket swings in the breeze.

And then, dancing on the turns of the wind, I hear laughter.

I stand in a flash, soil still enclosed in my fist.

It's not possible.

Is it?

I step up the bluff to investigate. When I reach the peak, I can hardly believe what I see. A small grouping of humble houses, arranged around an open center. Quiet. Still. They are not many, not like the thousands of Epoh. But more than I imagined it possible to escape. How did they survive out here? How did they find each other?

What else inside Epoh's walls was a lie?

A man passes through the town's middle, shoos two small children through the door of one of the small shacks. Another peel of laughs, soft as chiming bells, bounce out from one of them as they duck inside. The man scans the horizon, and then walks out toward the shore.

I duck back behind the bluff, dribble the rest of the soil from my hand, shift Jordan in my arms. This is no place to stop.

The wide flat vastness of the wasteland spreads until it fills everything. I pull my cloak around me tight and cling to it. Now, with a whole community right over the bluff, I remember my aloneness.

Because I know immediately this is where Jordan belongs. With the humans.

But I can't let him go, not yet. I place him slowly, softly onto the ground and settle into the side of the bluff, just high enough to peer over it. I've seen too many times what men are capable of in broken times like these. Before I can leave Jordan here, I must to be sure he will be safe among them. *Angel.* I promised.

Inside the village, more of the humans are coming out to its center, still stretching, yawning, and rubbing sleep away. A young woman and boy catch my eye as they come out. They're a matching pair with richly tanned skin, the same tousled brown locks. The woman reaches down and squeezes the boy's shoulders lovingly, then roughs up his hair. He squirms away laughing, looks back and sticks out his tongue at her before running down to the shore to join some other children. She smiles and watches him go, beauty and peace radiating from her.

I can see Miriam being just the same, if she had been a place like this, and not under Epoh's shadow. Is this where she meant to lead him? How could she have known it would be here?

The woman turns and joins a group of the villagers lining up around large pots with hot coals glowing beneath them. Others begin to line up, each holding a bowl. They greet each other with cheerful calls, outstretched hands. At the front of the line, the pot-tenders scoop something into each person's bowl in turn. Buckets of water are lugged out from behind the huts and passed around. They disperse throughout the open center, forming small, lively groups as they consume what they've been given.

The sea breeze blows away my fear. All will be well for Jordan here. And now I must let him go. Before I can't bear to anymore.

I do not wake him for goodbyes. There is no point.

I hold his sleeping body close, climb back to the top of the bluff and over. I creep up to the closest hut and let him go, placing him on the ground against the hut's wall. I brush the wild red locks from his closed eyes. I stand there watching him sleep, unwilling to move on.

But the village is bustling and I can't afford to stay

and be discovered. I turn to leave, but his small hand flies out and grabs my wrist. I turn back to wide eyes and trembling lips.

"Where are you going?" he pleads. Sleep is still heavy across his face.

I press my finger to his lips to quiet him.

"You can't come with me any further," I whisper. "You're staying here. With other people."

He shakes his head repeatedly as I pry his fingers off my arm. When I am free, he lurches forward and wraps his arms around me. "You're coming back, right?"

I hope so.

"I'll come back."

If I do, I'll have a soul, and everything will be different.

My throat stiffens and I can't say anything more. I place one hand on top of the bright red hair brushing against my neck.

"Hands up."

The voice comes from behind me, sharp and commanding. My body snaps into full alert, ready to fight. I let go of him and hold my hands up by my head as I turn around, trying to stay between the voice and Jordan as much as I can.

The man is large, muscles thick and bulging. He stands just out of reach, wielding a spear. He should never have been able to sneak up on me. I've gotten too comfortable in the wasteland's isolation.

"Who are you?" he asks. "Do you have the key?"

"No one," I tell him. "But this boy, he needs—"

"Do you have the key!" he yells.

A key? Key for what? "Listen," I plead. "This boy needs—"

But Jordan wriggles past me. "Marcus 30:16!"

The man blinks, his stance wavers.

I pull Jordan back in to me. What is he doing?

"Marcus 30:16! 'And all who seek shelter shall be welcomed, and the Three shall never turn them away.'" His eyes are wide and dilated.

The man clenches his spear tighter. His expression grows dark with suspicion.

"How do you know that?" he demands. "Who sent you?"

More of them are coming, men and women bearing shields and swords, forming a circle around us, backing us against the hut. My jaw tightens with tension, my hands ball into fists. The rage bubbles under my skin, ready for a fight. I'll kill every last one of them if I have to. But don't make me, don't make me, don't make me.

"I asked you a question," the man says sharply to Jordan. "How do you know that?"

He still holds the spear tight in his fist, its point tilted Jordan' way.

I step between them, ignoring the spear's blade just inches away.

"Leave him alone!" I growl. A hot urge to smash, to hit, to get out of this now, no matter what, rushes over me.

Jordan's voice reaches around me. "My mother. She told us."

How can he be so calm?

"She said it was the key to the new world. But I

didn't know what she meant."

The man steps closer. I shuffle to stay between them.

"Who gave it to her?" he demands. "No one has come to us with the key in over ten years."

"I don't know," Jordan responds. "She never explained. She never said what was out here."

A gentler voice calls out from the collecting group from the village. "And where is your mother now?"

It's the woman—the one with the dark hair. The one that is so like Miriam.

Jordan glances toward her, something flickering over his face, and then drops his gaze to his feet. "She's gone. It was many years ago."

The woman walks past the man, past me, and kneels down next to Jordan. "Why have you come to us?"

"They found out we still worshipped. My sister said she had a plan. She said we needed go West," he responds.

"And where is your sister?" The woman's voice is calm and still like the breeze.

"They...they got her when we were escaping." His voice quivers as he says it. The woman reaches out and caresses his cheek, and then stands back up and faces me.

"And who are you?" she asks.

"I am nothing," I mumble, but Jordan is talking over me before I can finish. "He helped me escape. He fought the Silencers to protect us. I wouldn't have made it here without him."

The woman nods. Then she turns back to the people

from the village, who are murmuring quietly to each other and giving us cautious glances.

"They have the key," the woman announces. "We haven't had anyone come to us with the key for many years, but the rules are the same. We swore safety for all who came to us with the key."

The others nod. The spears drop.

I force my fists open and stretch out my fingers.

"Food," the woman commands. "And water." One of the others nods and turns into the town. Another heads back where we came from, toward a small rounded structure behind the town—a well.

"Come with me," the woman smiles. She turns to lead him into the village. "You must be exhausted."

And just like that, the tension disintegrates. The man relaxes his stance and steps away. The people disperse back into the village. The tension in my arms releases.

Yes, he will be safe here.

A bowl is pushed into my hands. The woman motions back to me to follow her. Jordan grins.

Me? Come into the village? No. This wasn't the plan. My heels dig into the sand. A knot twists in my gut. I can't.

The sea breeze brushes around me with soothing salty air, tells me all will be well. But this is just what I've avoided for so many ages.

The woman watches me, waiting. So does the guard and some of the others. They may be welcoming us, but they're still suspicious.

I follow. For Jordan.

The woman leads us to a large log and urges us to

sit. A bucket of water with a large ladle is placed between us. I look down into my bowl — steaming chunks of fish and rolled grains, the smell of salty sea rising from it. Jordan sits on a long log fashioned as a bench. He drinks and drinks, takes in the bowl's contents in just a few oversized bites. He glances my way. A small group of villagers is gathering near us, watching, curious.

If I don't eat too, I'll give myself away.

I shove a spoonful into my mouth. It tastes lumpy and thick, the same flat way all food tastes for me. But I force down every last grain. I even take some water.

"More?" the woman offers. Jordan takes it eagerly. I shake my head. It's not until Jordan's third bowl that they start talking to us.

The woman sits in front of us on the sand.

"What happened in Epoh?" she presses. "What brought you here?"

Jordan launches into story, firing out fast words and waving his arms between heaping spoonfuls. He starts with the market, the game, the Silencer, Miriam's slip. How we met up trying to get out, and our walk through the wasteland. He doesn't tell them what he knows about me.

The woman listens intently. As he talks, several others come closer to listen, surrounding us from all sides. My stomach twists with fullness from the food, and unease from their closeness. Why do they come so near? The woman ignores them and listens patiently, lets Jordan tell it all without interruption. When he is finished, she leans toward him with a comforting smile.

"My name is Lena," she says. "And this village is

Haven. As far as we've found, we're the only free people left since the Second Realm War. And we've looked. A lot."

"Of course you are. There's nothing left. There's just Epoh," Jordan responds.

"Oh no," Lena says. "They want you to think that. All of them do. But there's many other cities still out there among the destruction. Most are much like Epoh. Some are worse."

Other cities? Out in the wasteland? All this time since the Second Realm War, and still they each live apart, in isolation from each other?

Jordan tilts his head, busy thought reflected in his eyes. "Do they know about each other?"

"We believe each might know of a few of the others. But we can't know for sure. We can't even know if we know of them all."

"But why would they lie? Why would they tell us we're alone?" Jordan asks.

"Ah," she responds. "Don't underestimate the fire a single spark of hope can start. You got out. More might try too, if they believed there was anything to go to. Leaders like Zevach guard their power zealously."

The young boy she was with earlier comes to her side, hands Lena two large blankets. "Thank you, Avi." She stands up.

"Soon we will build another hut for you. For now, you'll be on the floor of others' huts."

Huts? With the others? My chest twinges where the box presses against it. I bolt to my feet. "I have to go."

"Go?" Lena exclaims. "Where is there to go?"

I bite my lip. I have no way to explain.

"I—I didn't leave Epoh to come here. I'm looking for something. Someone."

Lena's smile fades. "Whoever it is, the chances of finding them are little to none, if they're still alive at all. There's nothing out there. You've seen it, what it's like."

Eyes are on me from all sides. A thudding rises in the back of my head. There's no way to explain it...Kythiel, the box, the beast lurking inside me. I stand with no words, shaking my head slowly side to side, again and again.

"At least stay a few days," she coaxes. "Regain your strength."

I shake my head harder. But then a small familiar warmth, Jordan's hand, slips into my own. He gives my hand a soft squeeze, a quiet plea not to leave him just yet.

"Okay."

But even as I say it, every particle in me cringes against it. My hand lets go of Jordan and drifts toward my chest, rests uneasily over the box.

He skips over to the boy who brought over the blankets, now playing with some of the other children. "Hey. Avi, right? I'm Jordan."

Soon it is as if Jordan has always been among them.

CHAPTER 12

WE SPEND THE rest of the day recovering and watching. They set us up next to a hut with more food and water. When they are all done with breakfast, the bowls are piled into the pots. The children drag them to the sea, scrub and rinse each one, splashing and laughing as they work. The rest arrange themselves on the ground, facing toward the sea. When the children are back, one man stands and leads them in the old daily rites and prayers of each of the Gods. They meditate in peaceful silence.

There is no fear here.

Then they rise, fresh-faced and relaxed. The religious leader steps down from the front and joins the people now. Another man steps forward, burly and brusque—a warrior.

As soon as the new leader's voice charges into the air, everything snaps to order. They form into orderly squads in sharp, focused movements, shouting responses in unison to the commander's calls.

He directs each group and they set to work.

Scattered groups spar in hand-to-hand combat, build, and test weapons, practice with a bow and arrow.

"What are they doing?" I murmur.

Jordan is studying their moves and exercises, absorbed in following their circuits. "They're training. Like me."

He's right. This isn't just a village. It's an army. My mind clouds with confusion. "But what for?"

It carries on for hours, the groups rotating through the stations at the commander's call. Not until the sun is past its highest point does the commander put the groups at ease.

The pots are pulled out again. Then some stay with the pots and tend to fires, while others walk out to the boats, take them to sea, and dredge out heavy nets. When they pull them in, they are flooded and flailing with fish. The children meet them at the dock and help bring in the haul. The cooks prepare the fish and cook them. Then they all come together again at the village center and eat. The rest is set aside for the next meal. The meal is a calm pause in the action, a collective deep breath.

And then they are back at it, doing drills and exercise until the sun touches the horizon. A final time the pots come out. They eat with weary satisfaction, filled with their day's work.

Both times, a bowl is pushed into my hands. Lena sits with us, doing more explaining than eating.

Haven started with just a few people. People in a city much like Epoh, who saw what was coming before it happened. When their warnings were not heeded, they got out. They wandered for many years before they made it to the sea, and found there were other cities that survived too. Once the community stabilized, they looked for ways to tell others of the village. Helped them escape, too. The village grew.

But that was all many years ago, Lena says, and the old ways died off as leaders tightened their hold on their cities. Now they focus on the war to come. The Third Realm War. Their prophet says it's coming soon.

Jordan asks question after question on each piece she gives us. But eventually I stop listening, my focus diffusing into a deep-seeded anxiety. I was all right when the humans were separate, doing their work. But now, all these humans surrounding me, open and free and crowding. They don't know the danger they've put themselves in, letting me be here.

Any moment one of them will sense the box in my pocket, I know they will. Knots twitch in fraying threads through my neck and my arms and my legs, waiting for it to happen. They're too close, too many. I can't stay here.

But there's a peace in these people. Something that seeps in under the fear and settles into my core. I hate to leave it, hate to leave Jordan.

When they are done, they bathe in the sea. As in the morning, the children scrub and rinse the dishes. Jordan goes with them, splashing and laughing with the others.

And then when it is dark and they make their way into their huts for the night, Jordan follows Lena and Avi to theirs to sleep. Two men in the hut next to them wave me in to roll out my blanket on their floor. There is hardly enough room for me to step into it, the doorway brushing against my shoulders as I bend down to fit through. When I lay down between their cots, we are almost shoulder-to-shoulder. One could rise at any moment forgetting I'm here. Roll over and fling an arm toward me. And that could be the end of it. I lay between them with every muscle tight and tense, my arms crossed over my chest, flinching every time they shift. Waiting for them to fall into sleep.

Once their breathing is slow and deep, I slide between them and out into the night. The relief of the air and the quiet is immediate. The hushed waves soothe my mind. I look up to the sky. It still hangs high in the dark sky, a thin sliver. Soon it will slip away completely and I can leave. Maybe tomorrow.

And then a slew of new dangers wait for me. Unknown ones.

I stand outside as long as I dare, let the stillness seep into me, until the moon is close to sinking over the horizon. Then I squeeze back into the hut quietly as I can, the layers of strain and burden piling back on.

I lie on my back and stare at the roof, waiting for Haven to wake up. My fingers trace the outline of the box over and over and over through my cloak until the quiet harmony of morning greetings wafts over the roofs as the village comes to life.

Past the village, cattails bob easily in the breeze. They roll out of their huts as softly as the waves roll onto the shore. I step out as soon as I hear them stirring. But now with the others all around the anxiety edges in again. My feet won't take me over to the line for food where they stand in a drowsy line with their bowls. Instead, I head away, out to the bluff. Where it is safe.

I sit, and I watch.

Then Jordan comes out from Lena and Avi's hut, stretching, his bright hair illuminated in the sun's rays. Then he runs over to Avi and the other children in the town's center and quickly, easily, laughing and running with them.

Already he is at ease among these people. It's incredible, this gift he has.

Soon the morning meal is handed out. And soon after that, they are looking for me. Jordan sees me first. He runs up the bluff to me with a bowl. He holds it out to me, panting slightly.

"They wanted me to bring you this. They want you to come join them."

I look down at the bowl, study the fish and grains. I'm shaking my head before I even look back at him. I want to be there for him, I do, but I can't, I can't do another day of the strain, another day risking all their lives. And he doesn't need me. Not anymore, not here.

I push the bowl back toward him. "The box." It's all I can say.

Lena is trailing up the bluff behind him. Jordan nods, then turns around and sees her. He runs lightly down the bluff to her, stops her from climbing the rest of the way up.

"He needs more time," he says. She glances back to me hesitantly, but they walk back to the village together.

I stay on the bluff all day.

The town continues its routine. From this distance, I am free to soak in as much of this peaceful place as I can, as much of Jordan as I can, wave by wave, savor every second. He's so easy, so carefree, and open. He settles into Haven as if it was always his home. Even his bruises are almost completely faded, the last signs of Epoh disappearing. And me, and our journey here.

It's better this way. I ignore the hollowness in my chest and accept what I knew all along—there is nothing for me here among the humans, not with Jordan. Not now, not while I'm like this. I focus instead on the unknown dangers ahead.

As twilight closes in, I soak in all I can with a last look to the village. Jordan has taken over its open center, teaching the other children his kick-the-pebble game. Their calls and laughter stretch through the cool air, free and open. No danger. No Silencers. No binds.

I look and look to the horizon, wait for the moon. Some distance up the shore, the waves splash against small clusters of dark rocks. In the middle of them, the rocks rise into a small cave.

Dark. Secluded. *Safe*. Like my room in the temple tower. My body aches, craves the solitude it offers. But I can't, not now, with the humans watching.

The moon never shows. This is it, I have to go tonight.

Eventually the dark settles in and the adults call the children in from their game for bed. Jordan lingers in the village center, staring out toward me, waiting. But I can't bring myself to go back down, take on the layers of fear and burden again, to say goodbye to him. Not again. Finally, Lena calls to him, and he goes in with a final look up to me.

And then I am left alone to face the dark and the

great task it brings for me.

Night closed in too quickly. The sky is a moonless vacuum, hollow and empty.

It's time.

CHAPTER 13

THE WAVES POUND against the rocks, impatient and queasy. Hours pass. I wait long enough to be sure that all the village is deep in sleep. Finally, I must accept it is time to make my move.

I stand up and go back down the bluff, through the village all the way to where the sea touches the sand. My feet are heavier with each step as the dark water soaks into them. Even so, I stay in the waves all the way to the boats to hide my footprints. Anxiety edges into my vision and twists the darkness.

It is a short walk. Too short. The dock waddles and creaks as I trudge down it, all the way to the edge. The boats look smaller now, as I stand over them, than they did from the village. I lower myself into the very last one, bobbing against the dock's wooden boards. It seeps low under my weight, but it holds afloat. Paddles lay on its floor by my feet. I lift them into place, running my hands over the handles, worn and smooth with use. I untie the boat from its post and break free from the dock, rocked by the sea's uncertainty. Doubt tosses in my stomach.

I row.

The paddles push me forward with a soft *splshh* as they hit the water. Each splash mingles with anxiety and magnifies in my head. The waves feel rocky and uncertain below me, and the darker things in my mind that the shore kept away are coming back out. The impending immediacy of Kythiel's charge surrounds me.

Splshh. Splshh.

It's dark out here, a strange kind of dark that reflects back at itself from the water below, a dark that disorients, confuses, and makes the shadows seem more threatening. A tight ball of fear grows between my shoulder blades, gets bigger with each pull of the oars. The repetitive motion lulls me into an uneasy drifting quiet.

Splshh. Splshh.

But there's no need for the fear. Is there? Kythiel made it sound simple. Easy. Swim over the barrier, get Rona, and come back. But Ceil's face floats into my mind, creased with heavy lines of tense worry. The story he told me, the Parable of the Three Trees. The creature trapped on the outside, the one that was somehow me. *I have to get in.* And the way Ceil choked, coughed, and fell to the ground of his own tent, the strange way his eyes lit and his jaw contorted when Kythiel spoke through him.

A thought passes through my mind for a second time, unwelcome — *Kythiel is hiding something from me.*

Splshh. Splshh.

But what?

It doesn't make sense. What could there possibly be to hide? He's an angel. Bound to Theia's Order. I shake these dark thoughts out of my head. It's not true. It's not possible. It doesn't matter. What matters is my soul. My way out. I'd do anything for that.

Splshh. Splshh.

Splshh. Splshh.

How long have I paddled?

My body took over the repetitive motion while my mind drifted. Where am I?

My dazed eyes stare out into an unbroken horizon. I pull them back into focus. All around me, dark shadowed hush of waves, flecked with echoes of stars as far as the eye can stretch.

I'm nowhere.

My destination.

I pull in the paddles. Stand up. The boat creaks with worry beneath me. The endless dark overtakes me, attacks from all sides. And for the first time in all my bottomless past, I feel small. Impossibly, foolishly small.

What am I doing?

There is nothing below me but water and salt, sand and seaweed. The sea cannot pull me over the edge of the world, across realms, to the resting place of the souls. I've allowed a desperate creature to lure me in. Angels? Prophets? Gods? This all ended for this realm long ago when they abandoned us here.

I could still turn back. There's nothing to keep me here. I could go back to the village, to Jordan, and forget all this. A trembling emptiness in my chest yearns to.

But.

The box.

I could never live among the humans as I am now. I already know how that ends. And soon the Hunters will come. Over and over into forever. They always do.

My soul. Without it, I am nothing. Ruled by something I cannot stop, pinned to this existence with no death, no escape. *Golem.*

The thought of it drops in my stomach like cold lead. I can't stop here, not when I've come so far. Not with so much to gain, so little to lose. There is nothing I have not already tried thousands of times to be free of it. Kythiel's promise is my only hope.

The time for questions is past. I step to the boat's edge and leap toward the horizon before I can do any more thinking.

The water is thick and heavy, tugging me downward. It seeps between my particles, loosens the specs and grains of my body, makes my limbs heavy. My cloak mats to me, tangles my arms and legs. I fight to stay afloat, taking a moment to adjust to the new sensations.

Then, I swim.

I pull on and on, the boat shrinking behind me each time I look back. Finally, it disappears completely. The waves grow larger, tossing, pushing, and pulling. Dragging me under in dark foamy heaves. They are strong and sudden, and each time one forces me under my chest throbs like it will burst and I wonder if this is it, if it is pulling me through to the Underworld. But they keep coming.

I push against it as hard as I can, and harder still,

the blunt edge of panic pressing into my mind. But the faster I swim, the stronger it pushes back, until I can't tell if I'm moving forward at all. I thrash against it harder and harder, a rapid pulsing in my ears, but still I slide backward against the current's pull. It tips steeper, steeper, steeper, until it seems I am swimming up a wall. The pull is too strong, too steep for me, the panic presses deep into me with a swelling dark vacuum, but I don't dare slow, for fear I will fall away into the depths. The tilt slants more and more, until I am sure it will fold on itself and swallow me.

Then it lurches, the sea relieves itself in a swell and forces me over. I fall up, up, up, away from the sea and into the murky depths and my stomach drops out in the sudden free-fall.

Up becomes down. The current thrusts me into murky rushing waters. I am blind, I am deaf, I am lost to it, overwhelmed and helpless. An undertow catches me, shoves me along, rolls, and tosses me until I cannot tell which way it takes me, and I give myself to the churning waters. With a thud it rushes me into something hard, pins me against it.

I stay there, the water rushing around me, embracing the steady stillness. Then I spread out my arms to feel out my situation. One of my arms bursts beyond the water and finds a ridge. I grasp it and pull myself up, straining against the torrid current.

CHAPTER 14

AT THE SURFACE, the water is quiet and still.

My head sloshes with the pull of the water as I try to take in my surroundings.

It's dark. Dim light throws between the water and a gray starless sky, hard and rough like a cave.

I made it. I'm in the Underworld.

The realization rushes my mind with a dizzy lightness.

But there's no time for anything more. Just in front of me, my hand clutches to pulpy splintering panels — a boat. A long iron staff points at my head, clutched by a hard, wiry figure towering over me. Under his cloak's hood, the man's face is screwed into a frown.

"What are you doing?" His voice is tense and prickly. "Get in."

No point causing trouble if I can help it. I strain against the bottomless waters to do as he says. The boat gives way under the pressure of my weight. The man watches my struggle still and stern, keeping his staff's rough point at me. The boat rocks as I roll in, sends me tumbling across its floor before settling. My mind teeters with it, a mix of relief and disbelief and confusion.

"Sit." The man nudges me with his staff.

His body shows great wear, but his movements are strong and gruff. His face hangs from his skull, scrunched into a scowl that runs deep in its crevices.

A bench runs the length of the boat's side, and a second figure is perched near the helm. The man's staff and eyes follow me, his muscles tightly wound.

I sit. Slowly. Stretch my hands out to show I mean him no harm.

Salty water is sloshing out of me and pooling around my body on the boat's floor. As it leaves me, I can feel my elements collect and tighten. And then, as I begin to dry, something new. Heavy. It's the air — this realm clings like cooling wax.

The man leans in to me, staff still poised to strike.

"What are you?" he demands.

"I am nothing." *Golem.* I cling my secret close to me on instinct and habit.

"Do not lie to me!" He lunges toward me violently, leans over, inches from my face. "What are you? What brings you here?"

My thoughts slosh through me with the pull of the river and I cannot come up with an answer.

He presses again. "I am the keeper of this realm and its gates. I know everything that is here, everything that passes into it. And you are not of it. Nothing enters the Underworld without going through me. Nothing. You reek of old magic. What have you brought here? What do you come for?"

The Keeper's hot breath blows on my face with his words and I smell fear on him, a tense, tight waft all too familiar to me. He holds the staff steady, aimed at my head. If I want to pass through without conflict, I have to tell him something.

"I come from Terath."

He leans away and stands upright, still charged.

"Of course you do. That's where they all come from. But you are not one of them, you are not a soul. How did you get here?"

"I swam."

The deep lines of his face shift, forming into new shapes. His brow crinkles, his mouth balks. "I have never heard of such a thing. It cannot be possible."

"It was not easy."

The angry edge in his voice slips away to confusion. "But you are drenched in the water of the River Lethe. No man could swim here and come out still remembering. The water makes you forget." He gestures to the figure at the front of the boat with his staff, and my gaze follows his direction.

When I realize what I'm looking at, the hairs rise down the back of my neck. It's a soul. A wispy beam, hardly even truly there. At first, its low glow is all I can see of it, but as I step closer, it takes shape, an echo of its form in life: A woman. Her body streaked with bloody gashes. Long red curls.

I stand abruptly, the boat rocking beneath me, and step closer. Could it be possible?

Her face is slack, lacking the tight energy she once blazed with. The fiery eyes are empty now. But it is. It's her.

Miriam.

I rush to her side. The boat lets out a loud creak as the weight shifts.

"What are you doing?" The Keeper snaps.

Up close, I see her more clearly. See her as she died. Clothes ripped and disheveled. Long streaks of brilliant red wherever her skin breaks through. Her face, purple and swollen. Her suffering presses on me like a weight too heavy, flecked with sharp shards of guilt and shame as I look over the signs of the tortures she endured. I failed her.

"I'm sorry," I mumble. "I'm sorry, I'm sorry, I'm sorry, I'm sorry."

"What are you blabbering about?" the Keeper says, his words stern and clipped. "Leave her alone. Sit down."

She stares through me with blank eyes.

"She does not remember?" I ask.

"Of course not. The river washes the soul's memory clean. This is what I was—"

"Do her wounds still hurt her?" This is what really matters. Just let her forget; let her be at peace.

"No," he scoffs. "Those are bodily wounds. Here she is only spirit. Those marks will leave her as her spirit gets used to being free of the body and regains its strength."

Something settles within me, knowing her pain is over and gone.

She leans toward me, peers into my eyes. Strains. Like trying to see through a dirty window.

The Keeper edges closer, his steps vibrating through the floorboards. "Why?"

"What?" I hold her gaze, searching for her within the stupor.

Something flickers over her face. Recognition?

"Why do you ask these things?" The Keeper's voice raps hard against my skull. "Do you know her?"

"No!" I exclaim. "Not really."

"By the Gods. Do you want her in a fit of unrest? Get away." He shoos at me with his staff.

I duck away, lose balance, and tumble right on top of Miriam. Despite how floaty and insubstantial she appears, her body still holds its physical heft—and a piercing coldness I didn't expect. As soon as I regain my bearings, I spring up. But it's too late.

Miriam bolts to her feet, her glow flickering in and out. Her eyelids flutter, and she releases an awful gasp. The boat rocks below us, responding to the shift in weight.

"Now you've done it," the Keeper sneers at me. "Do you understand what you've brought on for this soul?"

Miriam gasps again, her eyes wide.

"Forgetting is a gift. It helps them pass on," he scolds. "Remembering, it is a curse, a punishment for those who must pay for their deeds on Terath."

I rush to her and grab her arms. "Miriam. Miriam. Miriam. Miriam." Her name pours out of me like an endless flood.

"I knew it," the Keeper snarls. "I knew it. The timing of it all. You do know her."

She blinks.

"Miriam?"

Miriam's eyes dart all around, taking it in. When they reach me, they stop and lock on.

"Angel," she breathes. She clutches my cloak. "Where am I? What happened?"

I don't know what to say. I fumble for some way to explain.

I don't have to.

"I...I'm dead." The words are soft. Accepting.

"Yes."

"And Jordan?"

"We got out. He is safe. We found more people, a whole village, at the sea."

She closes her eyes and exhales.

When she opens them again, a crease forms between her brows. "What are you doing here?"

"That," the Keeper butts between us. "Is exactly what I want to know. Did you come to take her back? You cannot have her. You must let her pass on. This is the way of it. You asked before if she felt those wounds. She doesn't now, but she would if you took her back. She would relive her entire death all over again as you dragged her back to Terath. Leave her. She deserves to be at peace."

"She does. I have not come for her." I try to break my stare at her to convince him, to look at the Keeper, my feet, anything else. But I still can't believe I'm seeing her again.

Could I bring Miriam back, too? Oh how I wish I could. I owe it to her, really, after leaving her behind with the Silencers. But I don't think I have it in me, what it would take to bring back both her and Rona. It burns bitterly inside my chest, but it's just no use. I have to do what I came for.

As the Keeper lifts his staff to start pushing through

the waters again, his eyes narrow. "What are you here for then? What are you? You have still not answered my questions."

"I am nothing. A—" I don't want to say it. Not with Miriam right here. But then she has a right to know, the way she trusted me. The way I failed. "A golem." The word pinches in my chest. I glance to her, brace myself for her shock, a sense of betrayal. But her face still holds the same calm expression. "I do not look for trouble, and I will soon return to my realm."

"Oh yes, I am sure of that. And you plan to swim back, I imagine?" he says, rolling his eyes. "You took great trouble to get here. There must be something you are after. Now tell me. Is there a different soul you seek? Are you looking for treasure? Trying to become one of the legends? There's very few reasons you heroes ever try this. None have ever succeeded."

"I'm no hero."

Miriam abruptly reaches to me and takes my hand in hers. It is opaque but somehow also dense. A chill shoots up my shoulder, into my chest, and settles there. But I hold onto her tight.

"Well that's a first," the Keeper retorts. "You will tell me what you've come for anyhow. Tell me or I will send you back right now."

I squeeze Miriam's hand tighter. "I cannot allow you to send me back."

The Keeper slams his staff into the boat's floor with a *thunk*.

"*You* cannot allow? You have no say in this. You think strength is the only thing? Let me warn you now—you may think I look small and old and shriveled, and that overpowering me would be easy, but I was not placed at this post to be bullied by the first thing bigger than me. This realm holds powers you could not possibly understand, and they are at my bidding. What is it you have come for? Tell me, or you will leave whether you *allow* it or not."

The words spout from him with fervor, each one sharp and piercing. It's probably true, what he says. And I'm too weary of fighting to pick another.

"It's a soul. A different one."

"I knew you were here to play hero," he scoffs.

I have no response for him. He wouldn't understand.

"However..." he rubs his bald, wrinkled head, "A golem, eh? If there was ever one that could succeed..." His eyes drift off to somewhere else.

A sudden loud chortle springs from him. "Oh, how interesting," he grumbles. "How tempting." His eyes whip back to me. "How did this soul you are seeking pass away?"

Miriam lets go of my hand and steps toward him, eyes narrowed in suspicion. "What could it matter to you?" She glances back to me, "Don't tell him. Don't tell him anything."

My gut squirms—she's right, the Keeper's questions are strange. But then, what is the harm in telling him? I am not sure I will get past him if I don't go along.

I press my hand to her shoulder. "It's okay," I say. Then to the Keeper, "She stabbed herself. In the stomach."

"Ah, a suicide!" He says it with relish. "When?"

Miriam stares at me as if betrayed. She shakes her

head — *don't.*

But I don't see any other way. "Many ages ago. She is from the Beginning."

"The Beginning?" The Keeper arches his eyebrows. "You have been trapped on Terath even longer than I have been trapped here. She must mean a great deal to you to go through all this to bring her back. Why have you left her here so long?"

"I...did not know how to save her yet." He does not need to know everything.

He considers me, and I am still as stone, determined not to give myself away.

"Was she at peace with the Gods when she passed?"

I grope through the dark crevices of my mind for all Kythiel told me. "I don't think so."

"Then there is a chance..."

The Keeper shifts the boat toward the shore. His eyes drift to me with an unsettling grin. Miriam watches him with fiery eyes, her arms crossed.

We float into the shore with a lurch.

Rigid rocks stretch from the water into the land; dark shards cover the shore like sand. The ground reaches up to the hard, barren sky in stony tree-like pillars, sparse along the shore but thicker as they creep inland. A whole forest. Somewhere beyond them, whispers, rustles, moans, cries punctuate the quiet. I cannot imagine what the forest hides. I do not want to.

The Keeper nods to Miriam. "Come here."

She crosses to him at the helm. He bends over the side of the boat and scoops water into his hands. "Drink."

"No!" She pushes his arms away. Water splatters across the floorboards.

"You must. It's the Order. You will have a much easier passage to the Crossing this way. With a clear mind."

"Then it's good I'm not going to the Crossing," she turns to me. "I'm coming with you. I'm helping you first."

"No—" I start, but the Keeper speaks over me.

"Preposterous!" the Keeper retorts. "What could you possibly do to help?"

But Miriam ignores him. "It was more than coincidence that we've met again here. You helped me get Jordan out of Epoh. Now I'm meant to help you, I know it. Our paths were brought together for a reason."

"This is no divine power," the Keeper scoffs. "It's just the realm's way. Souls find those they know here. They are drawn together like magnets. It means nothing."

And yet I have no soul. What does it mean that we've still managed to come together in this strange vast realm? What is this force that pulls us together again?

The Keeper steps to her at the boat's edge. "If you choose to face the realm fully conscious and take your chances, I suppose that is your business. But you must go. You must make your own way. Every soul must."

Miriam frowns. "And if the way I choose is to follow him?"

They stand toe-to-toe, eye to eye. The Keeper glares at her, grinds his teeth.

"Then I can do nothing."

Miriam smiles triumphantly as the Keeper shrugs away.

"Off. Both of you. Carefully." He shoos at us with his staff toward the helm. We climb over onto the shore. Dark shards of rock and thick sandy grains stick between my wet toes.

The Keeper follows us, then leans over and runs his hand against the boat's inner wall, pulls a dark cloth from along it. A quick swish of his wrists and the cloth flies out over the boat. As it settles on top of it, the boat is replaced by a clutter of dense rock, floating oddly on the river. Then he leans forward and tugs at its helm, dragging it up onto the sand.

I stride into the water next to him and pull at the boat's side. But the stones under my feet are slicker than I expected—my feet slip from under me and I crash flailing into the river. The water's awful chill hits me at the same time as the Keeper's piercing shriek, "What are you doing!"

The rocky silt below me begins a slow rolling vibration.

"I—I'm helping."

"Did I tell you to disturb the water?" the Keeper yells.

Vibrations roll over the water's surface and grumble under my feet, growl and grow into a terrible shake that takes over the entire shore.

The Keeper heaves the boat out of the water and braces himself.

"What is it?" I ask.

"You woke the river's beast, you fool," the Keeper

snaps.

One of the Underworld's monsters. The Texts speak of these beasts, powerful, terrible things that thrive in the darkness, the only creatures that can truly live in this realm.

Just like me.

I pull out my blade and push the Keeper and Miriam back from the shore. I will not let Miriam get hurt in any way because of my failure, not a second time.

The rumbling grows until the river is quivering and harsh waves toss. A scaly head with flat lizard eyes rises slowly from the water, a long slithering neck. The waves toss, splattering shocking cold on my arms and drowning my feet.

A second head stretches out of the water, then a third. As they emerge, I see that all three necks connect to a single body. The beast tilts back onto its thick hind legs and releases a roar that rolls off the sky and shakes the ground. Fangs flash within its stretched mouths.

It storms the shore, takes a swoop at us with a hard whip of its tail. I swing my blade, and catch a few inches of flesh as it tears past me. The beast throws its head back and an angry shriek echoes off the cavernous skies. But when the tail swings back at me a second time, the wound is already pulling back together, leaving only the dark smear of its blood.

A lump hardens in my throat. I tighten my grip on my blade. It's healing itself. This won't be easy.

The beast thunders closer, and the Keeper is forced to fend off swooping heads with his staff. He calls to me over their growls. Something about the heads.

One of the heads rushes toward me, and I swing my blade down on it hard, slice through its neck. Hot dark blood rushes over my hands as its head lops to the ground, flailing and hissing. The two remaining heads let out an angry shriek that echoes off the cavernous skies. Victory courses through me warm and rich.

Above the beast's roars the Keeper yells, "Are you mad? I just told you, don't touch the heads!"

What?

A dark tingling dread rises inside me. I look back to the beast.

The chopped neck is twitching, pulling apart, splitting itself down the middle, stretching and twisting itself into two full necks. Two new heads are now stemming out from where there used to be one.

I freeze, mesmerized, terrified.

A hissing blur rushes by and latches its teeth into me. A hot thrashing sensation sears down my arm and across my back like lightning. And then, just as fast, the teeth release and the head rushes away.

I stagger back. A deep throbbing sets in between my particles, burning its way inside me. I fall to my knees overwhelmed. Somewhere in the back of my mind, I realize I must have dropped my blade.

Pain. This is what the humans must feel. The same primal cry that I have heard from them a thousand times over is now twisting its way out of me. Dumb with sensation, I slump against the ground and catch myself on my hands. It is too much.

As the initial shock of it dies down, questions flood my mind: How can I feel pain here when I never have before? What else is different for me here in the

Underworld? How vulnerable am I here, really? Clearly, much more so than in Terath.

A blurred tangle of swooping necks wave overhead. There are four of them now. Each has matching sets of poisonous, painful teeth. I pull my arm into myself on instinct. How can I overcome such a beast? Fear wells up and chokes me.

But the beast is still angry, and already its heads are coming toward me again.

Move, a voice inside me urges, *you need to move.* I grope over the sand for my blade — fresh, raw shots of pain spindling down my arm from the wound — but I can't find it.

A hissing sound rushes toward me from behind — I whip around in time to see four vicious serpent heads rushing toward me and duck behind my good arm, brace for more thrashing teeth and searing pain.

It doesn't come.

Instead, a great primal shriek does.

When I look back, there is a seething split down the monster's chest, and Miriam is squeezing out from underneath it. My blade is in her hand, covered in dripping dark red up to her elbow.

Already the wound's edges are quivering, beginning to close. She raises the blade again and digs into the beast with intense focus. Blood splatters onto the rocks. All four heads rush toward her with angry snarls, and I gasp and reach for her, then flinch as my wound sends new ripples of pain through me. But the Keeper runs forward and fends them off. She works, the blade moving quickly in and out, in and out, the beast flailing and twisting and screeching. A river of thick blood pours from it, and the wails become weaker, the thrashing necks droop.

Finally, Miriam tosses the blade aside and reaches in with her bare hands. She pulls away with all her might and bursts free, holding the beast's dark, dripping heart in her hands. The creature's roars die to whimpers, its heads twitch and wail, slowly wilt to nothing as the pool grows below it. We all watch until the last head stops blinking.

When there is nothing left but a limp tangle of necks, Miriam drops the heart to the sand. Then she picks up my blade, rinses it off in the water, and hands it back to me.

I stare at it in her hand.

"You...you killed it."

She smiles, still breathing heavily.

"We wouldn't have needed saving if you had listened to me," the Keeper snaps. "What is wrong with you?"

My eyes drop to my feet. He's right. "I didn't know." How could I have? I whip back toward Miriam. "How did *you* know?"

"Oh—well—" She flushes red from her ears to her neck.

The Keeper takes advantage of the pause. "Enough! This is no time for stories," he whips back to me. "Do you know what you've done?"

I blink back at him, uncomprehending.

"Did I tell you to help with the boat? Did I tell you to disturb the water?" His shrill voice rises to a yell, his tightly fisted hand shaking his staff. "No!"

"I thought— You said—" But already the details are

slipping from me.

"The rules are different here than in Terath. Unpredictable," he snarls. "The realm can sense you here. Your very presence disrupts it. Your every word, every move sends ripples through the realm. If you want to want to see the light of Terath again, *don't mess with anything.*"

He glares at me.

My shoulder throbs. It's still not healing.

It's shooting spindles of pain all across my back and down my arm. Pain. And it's not going away; the wound is not closing. Terror leaks into me with slow understanding. It's not healing, and it's not going to heal. Whatever made me so invulnerable in Terath doesn't work in the Underworld.

It's as the Keeper said. The rules are different here.

Will it ever heal? Or will it feel like this forever, the pain slowly seeping deeper and deeper into me? What else is looming out there in the Nethers waiting for us? Can I die here? The possibility sinks into the pit of my stomach like a brick. I'm too close to freedom to let it happen now.

And under this fear is another question, whispering to me with a tingling thrill: *What of the box?* Are its rules different here too? My fingers itch to pull it out and see, but not now, not here, not in front of the Keeper.

"I ought to call the demons to come take you away right now," he says.

I say nothing. It would be better at least than forcing me from the realm.

"They would be quite pleased with me if I brought you to them," he prods again. "It's what I'm here for."

A creaky grin spreads across his face, revealing a spread of yellowed, cracked teeth.

"However, I think I might help you instead."

Help me? Him? Every particle within me resists this idea. But who knows how long it could take me to find Rona without him in this abyss? Maybe it would be good to have someone who knows this strange realm on my side. But still something nags at me.

"Why?" I ask.

"Let's just say I have scores to settle," he says, wringing his bony hands. His eyes narrow. "But if I *do* help you, what do I get for it?"

My hope drops.

"I have nothing."

"Don't lie," he snaps. "There is so much old magic coming off you I can practically see it." His eyes drift, landing again on my cloak pocket.

It twists inside me like a knife. He knows.

I'm caught. I reach into the cloak's inner pocket and pull out the box. "This is what you sense." I hold it out for him to see.

"Oh yes," he eyes it greedily. "Give this to me and I will take you to where this soul is that you seek. Or at least, where she would be, if she is still in the Nethers."

The Nethers? But this is not the point, not now.

"I cannot give it to you." Frustration trembles through my fingers and I feel an urge to crumble the box to pieces. *But can I, here? Could I just hand it over and walk away?* But there's no finding out right now.

Even if I could, something in me snarls at the idea of giving it to him, this strange devious man. This box, whatever is in it, it' powerful. And it craves to be set free. For the first time, watching the hungry look in the Keeper's eyes, I wonder why. My gut says I've been forced to guard it so carefully for a reason. It could be dangerous, and whether I'm still bound to it or not, I'm responsible for it. I couldn't bear to be responsible for any bad that comes from it, too, it I were to hand it over to someone with the wrong motives. All these new things swirl around inside and implode on my craving to be set free.

"Then I cannot help you." The Keeper shrugs and makes a show of turning back toward the boat.

Out in the dark abyss the moans and cries are rising again. Trying to find my way through it alone feels impossible.

"Surely there is something else I can give you."

He walks back, an assured grin on his face. "No. I want the magic." His hand drifts thoughtlessly toward it. I snatch the box away.

"Touch it and I will be forced to kill you." I growl it with dark animosity. He needs to understand, he needs to fear it. He needs to keep away from what is mine.

Instead, he laughs.

"Kill me? I cannot be killed. I am immortal. The one and only immortal man." His pride sputters into bitterness.

Miriam gasps. Her face clouds and she steps away from us. They stare each other down, the Keeper gritting his teeth.

"What?" I ask. "Miriam. What's wrong?"

The small strange man clenches the staff. Miriam's hands ball into fists. I step between them. "Miriam?"

Miriam jolts back to herself and turns to the Keeper.

"We'll do it. We'll give you the box."

The Keeper cackles with delight.

My insides go cold. "But—"

Miriam quiets me. "Not now," she whispers.

The Keeper stretches out his hand for the box. I stare down at his outstretched palm and the words catch in my throat, I don't know what to say, what to do. Miriam steps in front of me and pushes his arm away. "You think we will just hand it over so you can run away and abandon us? Bring us to her. Then you can have it."

"Fine." He pulls his hand away with a grimace. "If this woman you seek is still out here in the Nethers, she'll be in the Pit."

He used that word before, Nethers. This time I demand explanations. "The Nethers? The Pit?"

"The Nethers," Miriam gestures out to our surroundings. "The outer rim of the Underworld. Where the lost spirits roam."

Is that what I keep hearing, the groans of the lost?

"And you'll see what the Pits are when we get there," the Keeper grumbles. "This way."

He points off into the forest of stony pillars. Then he turns and heads into it, without checking to see if we follow. It's dark and oozing with haze. Soon he is swallowed up by it, and the only sign of him is the crunch of his footsteps against the pebbled ground.

I fasten my blade back into the hilt and start after him, but Miriam grabs my arm. "I can't explain right now, he's too close. But, it's better to keep him in our sights, even if it means making false promises. Trust me."

Then she follows the Keeper into the forest.

Before I go after them, I look back to the river one last time. My shoulder throbs. How I ache for my small, safe temple room back in Epoh now.

CHAPTER 15

THE FOREST IS empty, far as I can see. Which is not far with the thick haze that hovers all around. It is darker in this hollow than on the river. No water to reflect the dim light. Just flat earth and bald sky. Miriam's soft glow stands stark against the dim barrenness. Our only light as we follow the Keeper through the pillars.

Every step twinges in my shoulder. And every twinge reminds me the rules are different here, and pulls my mind back to the box. Am I still bound to it as I am in Terath?

Miriam meets my pace and walks at my side. I tuck away the question for later.

"My mother."

Her voice is low and small in the quiet. The only other sound is the soft padded tread of the Keeper ahead of us, that and his shallow panting breaths.

"What?"

"You asked how I knew about the beast in the river. It was my mother. She taught me all the beasts from the legends of the Underworld—both of us. How to identify them, how to kill them."

It fits. The prayers she taught Jordan, the rituals. "But why? Jordan didn't know."

Miriam's nods. "We didn't want to put too much of a burden on him. He's still so young." Her eyes drop to the ground. "And now it's too late, I can't tell him, ever."

"Tell me. I will take your words back to him."

Up ahead the Keeper hums to himself as he weaves through the stony pillars. I try to keep my voice low. Something tells me to keep him out of this.

"You have to understand. By the time Jordan was old enough to remember her, our mother, she wasn't quite right," Miriam shuts her eyes and sighs. "She used to protest against Epoh to return it to its original vision. For freedom. For the Gods."

I remember when Zevach was closing his fist around Epoh. Many from among Epoh's people fought back in those times. Before they understood all Zevach and his soldiers were capable of. Many were hurt. Many died.

"But the Silencers fought back. She'd get beaten terribly, over and over. Once one got hit in the head, too hard, and it did something to her brain. After that, she heard voices. She thought they came from the Gods," she looks to me, her voice gets quieter. "She believed the voices told her Jordan was going to be the one the Texts foretold would lead the Gods' army in the Third Ream War. And she believed them. She started drilling us, preparing us for war. Teaching us the Texts and every legend, she knew. The voices took over our lives."

War? Drills? It's just like in Haven.

I glance ahead to make sure the Keeper can't hear us. He darts nimbly between the pillars without looking back.

Miriam continues, "Jordan was too young to understand. But I heard what the others said about our mother, and I was ashamed and angry. I stayed away from home as much as I could...but then she got very sick. Before she passed away, she made me swear to keep training Jordan. And I did, at first just to distract him from grief...but then I started seeing it. He knew things he couldn't possibly know. I don't know if he's all my mother claimed, but he *is* special."

I remember Jordan, his hands spread out to me, feeling the magic radiating off him. Special.

"I had to get him out. I had to." Her eyes blaze, bright and warm. Her soft wisp of a hand clenches onto my wrist. The frigid tension pinches in my shoulder. "The Gods sent you to us that night. You have a place in their plans, too."

Me? No. Even if the Gods do still glance toward Terath on occasion, they don't see me there among their own creatures. But Miriam stares at me, eyes brimming with hope, a smile on her face.

It's too much. I look away.

"We're falling behind," I mumble, and quicken my pace to catch up with the Keeper. Miriam's soft glow trails close behind me.

****

We walk on and on and on in the quiet, deep into the strange forest. Deeper than I thought possible for it to go. Dirt. Steps. Stony pillars. Maybe for days. Or at least hours. It becomes hard to tell the difference. Always the Keeper stays just ahead, keeps us chasing after his scratchy head bobbing through the pillars.

He acts stranger and stranger the farther we go. Murmurs to himself, counting out pillars, changing direction at random. Doubt begins to creep in, spreads like a weed through my mind. Does he know where he is going at all? Perhaps he has gone mad down here by himself all this time.

Or worse, it occurs to me. It could be a trap.

We can do nothing but follow. Follow and wait.

Meanwhile, the box calls to me, nestled against my chest and interfering with my thoughts. Can it open? Does it control me here like it did in Terath? The questions nag and nag and beg me to answer. Not here. Not so close to the others. I remember the hunger in the Keeper's eyes as they drifted toward it inside my pocket.

But my fingers twitch just thinking of it.

I slow my pace. Just a little. Miriam drifts ahead of me, holding pace with the Keeper. Bit by bit, I let the distance between us grow. How far ahead do I dare let them get? Too far and I'll lose them completely.

I wait until Miriam's light is far away and obscured by the pillars. Until I don't dare break off from them anymore. Then I turn my back to them and pull out the box. Somewhere in the distance, they're already calling for me. My time is short.

Even in this dim light the box shimmers, bursts

with golden magnificence.

Do I dare try to open it? Suddenly I am seized by tingling nervousness, get lost in its hypnotic glistening.

"What is that?"

I jump at Miriam's voice, just behind me. My thick fingers fumble, the box tumbles out of my hand. How long have I been frozen here? Too long. I lost my chance. And now the box is loose, exposed, lying in wait on the ground. Her hand reaches down to pick it up.

"No!" Panic swallows me. *Don't touch it, don't touch it.* I've shoved Miriam away before I realize it.

She's sprawled on the ground. My panic dissolves into stinging shame. I snatch the box away and hide it in my fist.

"I'm sorry." I kneel to her, stretch out my hand to help her up. "Are you okay?"

"She's fine."

The Keeper. I whip around to face him. How much did he see? Was he right there all along? His cold expression tells me nothing. I try to cover it up.

"I'm glad you came back. Thought I'd lost you."

He grins. Stares me down with cold eyes.

"Let's see it."

"See what?"

Too fast. The tense buzz of anxiety rises in my mind. *I said it too fast.*

"The magic you carry. You've taken it out. I can feel it. Now let's see it."

"No."

His eyes narrow.

"Maybe," I relent. "When we get to the Pit."

"Maybe? Maybe next time I don't come back for you." He stares at me, his hand clenched tight around his staff. I stare right back. "Maybe I change my mind and tell the demons you are here."

Hot anger creeps up my back. What choice do I have? I bring my fist to my chest, fingers clenched. "You cannot touch it. Do you understand?"

The box pulls for him, trembles against my palm.

I imagine him snatching it, my hands seizing him and ripping off his head.

It brings warm satisfaction, cold fear.

"Sure, sure," he responds. He leans in close. His eyes are wide and hungry.

I loosen my grip and splay it out in my palm between us. It quivers, sending tiny vibrations up my arm and nipping in my aching, wounded shoulder.

And the Keeper. He leans over it, his mouth hanging open. Closer and closer and closer until his eyes are inches from it, examining the elaborate engravings. I can feel every breath he releases.

With my hand outstretched, he is closer to the box than I am. Every step, every breath, every move he makes, my muscles flinch.

Behind him, Miriam is leaning in, too.

I snap my fist closed and stuff it back into my pocket. "That's enough."

"Yes...yes..." the Keeper murmurs.

But his eyes are still on my pocket.

"We need to keep moving," I push.

He jumps as if waking. Blinks. Gives his head a shake. "Of course," he says. "This way."

And he is off, scurrying into the stony forest.

The dread that rises every time a human gets too close, it drops from me like a cloak as soon as the Keeper steps away. But it doesn't leave. It's always there, pooling at my feet, real and dense. It clings at my ankles and drags behind me with every step. Can I ever break free of it? I've missed my chance to find out. For now all I can do is follow and keep up. Be ready if another opportunity comes my way.

The Underworld groans and creaks around me, shifting its pieces, uneasy and restless. Up ahead, the Keeper forges through the pillars, rambling over his shoulder to Miriam. I hurry to catch up.

"—to point B. There's no straight path, and the way is always different. Always shifting."

I cut him off. "Shifting? The realm?"

He stops on his heel and whips around at me. In my rush to close the gap between us, I almost ram into him. "Yes. Shifting. If we walked back the way we came right now, it would be different. It's in constant motion. Restless. And it knows you're here. It doesn't like it." His expression hardens.

The air behind him twitches—or does it? I squint, stepping closer, but there's nothing there. Suddenly the realm's cavernous creaks and ticks feel hostile, like the realm is whispering angry things at me. Little bumps rise all up my arms.

"Then why are we following you?" Miriam demands. "How could you know the way if it is always changing?"

The Keeper turns to her, rolling his eyes. "Because I have this." He shoves his free hand into his robe and pulls out a white stone, smooth and flat and barely the size of his palm. "Without it, you're lost. Which means without me, you're lost."

Miriam leans it and studies the stone. "And what's that?"

He blinks at her. A slow smile spreads over his face. "Well. That's exactly what I was about to show you."

He takes a few steps away and plants himself. Just behind him, the air glimmers, a faint disruption to the space — there *is* something there. I just can't tell what.

"Now keep close," he says. I look over to Miriam and she glances back, and then shrugs — what else is there to do. We shuffle toward him.

"Closer than that — hold onto me." He juts out his elbows toward us, and we each take hold of a bony arm.

The box quivers in my breast pocket and a twinge in my gut tells me not to trust him. "What are we doing?"

"We're going through the glimmer."

While he speaks, he flips the stone over between his hands, pulls us forward with him toward the glimmering air. Once, twice, three rolls of the stone and we're in it, the glimmer is sucking us in. I'm jerked forward with a lurch, I'm squeezed flat and thin and tight until my very particles are stretched, and as the world starts to fade away to twisted streaks of darkness, I am swallowed into a deep, chilling panic.

Somewhere near me in void the Keeper whispers, "To the Crossing," and then everything drains away into a violent swirl and it's all I can do to cling to the Keeper's arm with all my might.

CHAPTER 16

THE VACUUM SPITS me out and my body skids across hard ground.

I lay there a moment and wait for everything to stop spinning. Slowly, I become aware of the dull throbbing across my back. And the cold. A deep chill goes down to my bones. The kind Miriam gives off, but more, so much more.

Something pokes me.

"Get up."

The voice reaches out and tugs at me with an echoing dissonance. I pull my head toward it. More spinning.

The Keeper blinks down at me in blurry double.

"What happened?" My voice sounds far away and floating, detached from my body.

"Exactly what I said. We went through the glimmer. I didn't realize I'd be dealing with a helpless pile of dirt on the other end."

His frowning face slowly merges into a single form.

He pokes me again with his staff. "Now get up."

Somewhere in the background, high staccato notes poke through the air. Familiar. Miriam. I pull her words into focus.

"No. No, no, *no.*" Her voice crackles like angry embers.

My wounded shoulder is stiff, burns as I push myself up. The pain is spreading, seeping deeper than it was before. The open wounds on my skin where the beast's teeth pierced me feel loose and festering.

"You must," the Keeper responds to her protests with cold insistence.

"You lied! You said I was free to follow, and I will," Miriam snaps back.

My mind works slowly to piece together what is happening. Something is wrong. But where are we?

I squint and look around — it's brighter here. Like the sun bursting through after a long snow. My eyes adjust and I make out the forms of other souls. Lots of them.

"I still have a job to do, bringing souls to rest," the Keeper shrugs. "And your attempt to help will only make things worse. Send more waves through the realm."

"I don't believe you. I'm supposed to help him."

My focus is coming back. The souls are strewn all through the open space we've been catapulted into. They're all facing toward me. Staring. But not at me. I turn around to see what it is.

It's astonishing.

Radiant white marble. A bridge. Right in the middle of nothing. Where it leads to is obscured with glimmers and haze. Swirls of wispy cloud. A sense of quiet wonder wells up within me.

"You're *supposed* to not have a memory right now. You're *supposed* to find your own way here. You're *supposed* to mind your own business and not be such a damn disruption," the Keeper snaps, "And believe me, there's enough disruption in play as it is. Having you with us will only make the way harder." He gestures to her and walks over so he is at the foot of the bridge. "Come. Look. They're waiting for you."

The sweetened eager tone of the Keeper's voice snaps me to full attention. Suddenly I understand and the wonder deflates from me as quickly as it rose, is replaced with cagey anger. He's trying to separate us. My fingers curl into tight fists.

I won't let him.

I already lost her once in Epoh. She should be with Jordan in Haven right now. Safe and alive. The Keeper isn't taking her from me again.

Miriam makes her way after the Keeper warily. I follow, determined to keep her close. When she reaches him, she looks to the bridge in the blank haze and gasps. Her complexion goes white. As I step behind her and look over the bridge straight on, I see it too. *Souls.* They're waiting, beckoning to her on the bridge beyond the haze.

So many of them. Many share Miriam and Jordan's brilliant red hair. My stomach lurches—suddenly I miss him with a deep tugging ache. Like a homesickness. Like a hole right through my core.

One of the souls in the front smiles at Miriam warmly. Bright curls tumble down her shoulders, pale green eyes shine, and soft pale skin gleams like the moon. She could almost be Miriam's reflection; they are so similar. She reaches out for Miriam, an invitation.

"Mother," Miriam whispers. She steps forward, stopping just at the bridge's foot. Her hand reaches out and then abruptly pulls away at the shimmering film. Instead, she drops it to her side and just smiles back.

"Go. Join them," the Keeper nudges.

But I need her. I *want* her with me. My shoulders clench with resistance, sending bolts of pain through me.

She stares longingly at the figures on the bridge a moment longer before tearing herself away.

"No," she turns back to the Keeper with a glare. "Not until this is done."

I breathe out my relief.

"The Nethers will eat away at you," the Keeper warns. "It will tug away at your mind, unravel it like a ball of yarn. Don't you feel it? I know you do. You're more vulnerable this way, conscious, carrying all your memories around. You might never find your way back."

"Don't worry about me. I will be fine," she says.

But she's not.

Now that the Keeper says it, I already see it in her, wearing her down. A weariness clouds around her eyes, the same weariness the Keeper carries.

And now that I see it in her, I realize, it's in me too. Creeping, creeping, creeping, and polluting my thoughts.

If the Keeper is right about this, maybe he's right about all of it.

He urges her again. "You're lucky to be here once;

some take ages to make it here. Go. Cross. Take your peace while you can."

The realization sinks into me. The guilt piles up. I may want her with me, need her even.

"No," she insists.

But I owe her this.

"You should go," I say. A knot tightens in my gut.

She turns around, looks at me with sharp eyes, as if betrayed. Takes in a breath to speak. But I don't let her.

"I feel it. The realm wearing down on me, like he said. Can't you?" She glares at me, silent, arms folded over her chest. "What if you don't find your way back? You deserve peace, Miriam. Don't walk away from it. Not for me."

But she clutches my arm and chills shoot up into my shoulder as she pulls me close.

"Don't you get it? This is exactly what he wants, he wants to split us up," she mutters, glancing back to the Keeper. "We can't let him."

Behind her the Keeper shifts on his feet impatiently. She stretches up on her toes and presses her hand into my shoulder. Her hand sends a blasting freeze through me.

"He's Cholem," she says.

I look back to him again, look him over hard. "Who?" As the chill settles into my shoulder, it numbs away some of the pain.

"Cholem," she repeats, "The immortal man. He sold his allegiance to the demons in the Second Realm War in trade for his immortality. He has no loyalties beyond himself. Don't trust him for a second. If he wants us separated, that is a sure sign we must stick together."

I want to argue with her, to insist she cross over. But a fear of being alone, of not making it out, keeps my tongue still. Besides, what if she's right?

Miriam turns away from me, glares at the Keeper, and then strides off into the forest.

"I'm coming!" she declares, shouting over her shoulder.

"Good luck out there in the abyss alone," the Keeper calls back. "You won't last a hundred steps."

I look to the Keeper and then back to her glowing figure, growing fainter through the stony pillars. If I'm choosing one, I chose Miriam. I turn and follow her.

"Wrong way, fools," the Keeper croaks.

But I hear his hurried steps behind me.

CHAPTER 17

MIRIAM WEAVES THROUGH the stony pillars nimbly ahead of me. We push on and on and on.

Was it wrong to let her come? The question nags at the corner of my mind. She could be at peace right now.

I'm not sure I could have stopped her. But I could have tried harder. I should have. What is it to save one soul from this realm if I doom another? I was too weak, too afraid to give her this one thing, a final peace.

The Keeper has gotten us this far. Fought beside us against the beast in the river. Even tried to bring Miriam to the Crossing. Could he be all Miriam says? Maybe he's not as shifty as he seems. Maybe it's just the toll of the ages he's spent in the Nethers, the realm tugging away at his mind. If there's anyone who knows what it means to be trapped, to watch the ages pass by around you as you lose yourself to the years…it's enough to make anyone unravel.

As we walk, I look around at the dim strangeness of it all, this peculiar realm. A gilded shimmer catches my eye among the dark pillars. *Gold?*

I stop and look back again. Just to see if it's real. Because it can't be, not here in this dark, strange barrenness that is the Nethers.

But it is.

The pillars are growing small golden nubs. Like the earliest beginnings of fresh branches on a tree. As I make my way through them behind the Keeper, I can't help but slow down and stare. The thicket of pillars begins to lighten, and ahead, even more shimmers of gold. The little ridges become buds. And the buds are growing something. Round golden leaves, shiny and thick like wax. I reach out to touch one, and it's cool, smooth, metallic. Still soft and growing.

I look to Miriam. She raises here eyebrows.

Ahead, a soft sound: *chink*. We follow it through even more pillars, thick buds of gold dripping off them. One drops to the ground next to me, landing in a pile that covers the ground around the foot of the tree. *Chink*.

The Keeper has stopped to admire it, too. When he hears our steps, he looks back at us. For the first time since I came across him, he's smiling—a real smile, a smile of happiness instead of wry bitterness. A smile that spreads wide across his lips shows his broken, crooked teeth and crinkles his eyes. He sighs, "By the Gods, how I love this place."

He drops to his knees, leaning over a pool of the gold droplets at a pillar's trunk. I look around—all the pillars have them. Piles and piles of gold. I lean over and run my fingers over them. Unlike the growing bud, these are flat, hard, and round. They're coins.

Smooth and unmarked, but coins all the same.

The Keeper jumps back to his feet in a flash.

"This way," he says, bright-eyed. "It gets better."

"Wait," Miriam comes to a halt. "This is one of the realm's traps."

The Keeper whips around, rolling his eyes. "Well aren't you just the little scholar."

"We have to get out of here!" she exclaims.

"Realm trap?" I don't understand. "What's a realm trap?"

"It is of no consequence!" the Keeper cries. "This is our fastest way through."

"No consequence? The consequences are huge," Miriam retorts. She turns to me. "The realm creates traps like these to prey on lost souls. It offers whatever it thinks will tempt you most. Tries to lure you in so that you can never leave. Souls get lost to these traps for ages."

"I knew you'd be trouble," the Keeper says, glaring at her. "Trap or not, this is the way."

Miriam narrows her eyes. "It is the only way?"

"It is the best way. The other way takes much longer. And time, that is something we do not have." He leans toward us, leering over his staff.

Miriam gives him a long stare, and then turns to me.

"He's right, the time would hurt us," she says. "But you have to understand — whatever you do, don't take anything. Or eat anything, for that matter. Or drink anything. Better yet, don't touch anything. The realm knows what you want, and it will use it against you. It will draw you in and you won't be able to leave. You might not want to. Ever."

Who could ever wish to remain here, in this terrible in-between?

"Do you understand?"

"Yes."

We follow the Keeper in. The opulence is too great to take in, piles of gleaming gold that get bigger and bigger, crowd the pathway and spill into it, stretch beyond what I can see. Some of the pillars sprout colors. Blues, greens, reds — sapphires, emeralds, rubies.

The further in we go, the more elaborate it gets. Elegant golden statues, rings, necklaces, crowns. The piles of gold grow into mountains. Great chests overflow with treasures, too full to close. A soul has claimed one and tries to lug it away, but it won't budge. He's caught in the trap. *Leave it*, my head screams. *Forget this. Run. Run to the Crossing and find rest.* He's trapped, I realize. Just like Miriam said.

The Keeper slows our pace, lost in the treasures. As if he's forgotten we're even here.

The thought rises through me like steam. *The box.*

I was too eager before, but this is my chance, I can see if I'm still bound to it here. I have to do it now, while he's distracted.

I drift behind him and Miriam, carefully widening our distance. The Keeper takes his time, savors each bejeweled piece. The box calls for me, my hands ache to reach in and free it from its pocket. I hold them to my sides in tight fists. Wait. Wait. Wait.

My pace slows gradually to a stop. I give the Keeper one more careful sideways glance. His back is to me. In front of him a grand golden statue. Miriam trails behind him. I lift my hand to my pocket and bring out the box.

It's strange. I've always considered the box such a treasure, so hatefully lovely, with its golden shimmering paint and elegant patterns. But here among real treasures, it seems tired and worn.

Slowly, slowly, slowly my trembling fingers wrap around its base.

And then—*whoosh*—a shadow rushes past at the corner of my vision. I jump and whip around toward it, every particle of my body humming with alarm.

There's nothing there.

But I saw it.

Didn't I?

I stand still as stone, hairs raised and prickling down the back of my neck, waiting for another whoosh of motion to give it away. My fingers strain with needles of pain where they dig into the box's edges. My eyes dart all around, searching every crevice, every shadow of the massive golden piles. The endless treasures twinkle back at me.

Nothing.

I'm more on edge than I thought. I slowly fill my lungs with air and then let it out. There's no time for these distractions. I push the paranoia away and loosen my grip on the box. My other hand slowly takes hold of the top. My head buzzes with anticipation, fear. *What is in it?* Am I truly about to face the thing at the root of it all, the deaths, the curse, the reason for my very being?

I pull on the lid.

Its seal sticks, then releases with a quiet *pop*.

My chest flutters. I can hardly believe it worked.

The hinge creaks as I push it open, my fingers shaky with nerves, and I peek hungrily inside.

Within lays a large uncut emerald, rough and sparkling, attached to a glistening golden chain. It is simple and unassuming, should pale in comparison to the treasures surrounding me. But I stand transfixed, staring blankly at its strange, seductive beauty. My entire body pounds with pulsing delight. This is it, the thing I've guarded so long, the thing I've fought for, killed for.

I want to hold it.

It's like a craving, a deep desire that was in me all along, and I am just now recognizing. I reach out to pick it up. But before I can, there is a *zing* of rushed steps through scattering coins and something rushes toward me.

Miriam gasps. "Look out!" she yells.

A rushing blur, a tug at my fingers, and the box is gone. My chest drops out and I wait for the force to take over my body and reclaim it.

The force doesn't come.

Panic fills the vacuum where my chest should be, ice cold and dark as pitch.

It's gone.

The box — the necklace — is gone.

I process what has happened just in time to catch the Keeper's low cackle, the *swoosh* of his cloak as he turns away from me with the box in his hand.

It's gone and there is nothing tethering me to it anymore, nothing keeping it from disappearing forever into the abyss of the Nethers.

I should be relieved, should be happy to let it go, just stand here and let the box leave my life forever. But wild panic claws against my ribs until I feel they will burst. A sinking realization builds inside me that this was the only thing that was ever certain in all my years and years just, and it just left me behind with nothing but questions. The useless too-late understanding that I never could have really left the box here, because even if the magic does not bind me to it here, I would not have been able to. That I am bound to it in other ways.

And now it is gone and the Keeper is getting away. I have to stop him, without the box's help.

And now he has a head start.

The panic inside me burns into seething rage.

Mine.

I thunder after him with a feral growl and leap for him, my fingers grasping onto whatever they can, tangling into his cloak, and we go rolling across the gilded ground. Mingled with the clinks of disheveled treasures, the Keeper releases a sharp gasp. He squirms and writhes to get away, is already pushing himself back up. But while he is fast, I am stronger, and he can't shake my grip. I won't, I won't, I can't let go. I pull him down again, we both scramble for the box, my hands hardly aware of what they do as I battle his lightning fast moves.

Finally the rage bursts in me and I grab for his neck, and I've got him, I've got him, I've got him and I lift him tight in my fist as I stand, pulling him off the ground, and his feet dangling and my chest throbbing a hundred miles a second because if he gets loose he will be gone in a flash, faster than my mind can tell my feet, *go.*

And there it is, locked into his flailing fist. The box. *My* box.

His eyes are fastened to mine. His face turns red.

"Let it go!" I cry. "Let it go or I will kill you!"

The Keeper grimaces. "Does anything stick in your muddy brain? You cannot kill me, you fool. I am immortal." His words are thin and choked, but still soaked with pride.

His face is turning from red to purple. His struggle turns sluggish. He should be going unconscious by now.

"How about we make sure?" Miriam has caught up to us. Her voice comes from just behind me, contempt leaking out the edges.

Purple to blue, blue to white, as his face drains of color.

The strain of his weight pulls at the wound in my shoulder. It bites like a fresh blade twisting inside it. Splitting. Widening. Deepening. I clench my fingers tighter. He coughs and gags against their pressure.

"Why?" I demand. "We had a deal. You were already getting it."

"Guess...I don't trust you." He somehow squeezes the words out. They sound broken and lost, each a separate piece, spit out like a loose tooth. "Looks...like I...was right."

Helpless fury bursts inside me, and I punch him. Partly because the pain spreading over my back is too much, partly because I can't stand watching the life draining from his undying face.

His flailing turns to convulsions. His eyes turn flat

and hollow. Each shake of his body shoots bolts of pain from my wound across by back and down my arm.

"Let it go!" I hear my own words as if they came from behind me. They are small in my head, but they come out in a roll of fierce thunder.

Throbbing blue veins stand out against his sallow skin. His eyes are bulging.

"Put...me...down. We...can neg...ho...tiate." Each syllable raw like guzzling gravel.

And then he smiles. That awful crooked grin, a taunt.

"We'd never negotiate with a traitor like you," Miriam bellows. "Why do this? You were already getting the box. You just had to do your part."

"Mud brain might have," the Keeper coughs out. "But...you, don't trust...*you.*"

His face twists and darkens as he gasps for air he can't force down. He can't die, but he feels the pain, the struggle of the life he should be losing. And he's weakening from it. I squeeze his neck tighter.

Miriam steps closer, folding her arms over her chest. "I keep my word!"

"Maybe. But with realm creeping into your mind?" He gasps for air again with a strange rattling sound. "Already picking away. Creepy...crawly. Know you feel i—"

But before he can finish Miriam dives under my arm punches him in the gut. "Put it down!" she screams.

"No."

She wrestles against his arm, struggling to pry the box loose from his grip. With every flinch or twist he makes, the pain digs deeper into my shoulder, the desperation settles deeper into my chest. It's too much. It has to stop.

Something in me erupts. I hit him. Then I do it again. And again. Because I can think of nothing else to do.

He writhes from the pain. My heart races, and with every throb a haze of red edges in, closing in on all sides of my vision. I dig my fingers in harder, bring my other hand to his neck, and I shake. Miriam steps back. I shake him hard, with all my might, rattling every bone of his limp form, a desperate guttural cry escaping from me as I do it. The sharp pain shoots through my back, reminds me of the pain I'm causing him, and it is deep, terrible, and satisfying. I shake. I shake until finally, his grip loosens and the box drops to the ground, lands among the golden coins with a soft *chink*.

Miriam rushes to pick it up, cups it gently between her hands.

I toss the Keeper aside like a heap of rags.

Relief floods in. The pain in my shoulder subsides to a dull ache.

But the Keeper isn't done yet. He rushes at Miriam, coughing and gagging, and claws at her arms for it. She hits him square in the jaw and he keels back and tumbles into me. The struggle is a blur of fists and kicks and tearing cloth, splashes of gold. This time when he breaks free, he runs, darting back through the mountains of treasure we came through. I grab for him, but even now, he is quicker than me. He ducks away, and instead I get a fistful of cloak and hear the tear of threads as I try to yank him back.

He's gone.

I'm left kneeling on the ground, heavy limp cloth from his cloak in my hand. Too late I remember how desperately we need him. I've only my blade for protection, and no idea where to go.

"Oh Gods."

I start to rush after him.

"Where are you going?" Miriam calls to me. Her cheeks are flushed. She clutches the box close to her with both hands. My hands itch to snatch it away — *the box is mine* — but I press them against my sides instead, resisting the angry beast inside me.

"We need him. We've got to get him back."

"It's no use," she sighs. "We couldn't catch him if we wanted to, he's too fast. We'd only get lost looking for him. Even if we did, what then? He'll only try to take it again."

She hands box back to me. Just like that, as if it were nothing. As if it were any other object. I close my fist around it tight, tight, tight, and its pointed corners dig deep into my palm. I trusted her before, but now I'd let her hold my very life in her hands.

She's right. Going after the Keeper would just lead to another struggle.

As always, the box's curse has infected everything. I tuck it back into the breast pocket of my cloak. Take my time, give extra care, and make sure it's secure. Because the Keeper could come back for it. Because once I'm done putting the box away, I have no idea what to do next.

Finally, I look up to face her.

"We need to get out of here," she says.

"Yes."

Miriam turns around and starts walking back the way we came.

"Wait," I call to her. She stops and turns to me. "The Keeper was taking us the other way."

And the gold. It's strange and utterly dazzling. Mesmerizing. Something in it calls to me, invites me to go further in.

"No. We need to get out of here as fast as we can. Who knows how deep it goes. Who knows if he was even leading us toward the Pit or not," she says.

But I dig in my heels. "No backtracking. I need to get to the Pits." And we are losing time. Miriam is slipping away. I see it edging in around her eyes, the realm tugging away at her. The gold shimmers, whispers to me that I am right. We need to keep moving. We need to keep going deeper.

"You *will* get to the Pits," Miriam snaps. "But if we don't get out the trap will lure us to stay. Then you'll never find her. Don't you feel it?"

The gold whispers that she is wrong, don't listen, don't listen. But that's what it is, it's the trap. Through the pounding fear of the shadow-thing, the gold's call winds through me with a stillness, a desire to sit and watch it forever. I force it into the back of my mind, and the fear rises again.

A dark fluttering shadow rushes at the corner of my vision—the same as whatever I saw before.

I whip around toward it, a thick panic pulsing through me.

Nothing.

I try to pull its image back up from my mind and take a closer look, but all I get is a dark blur. A shadow. Hardly even that.

It could be anything.

Or nothing. Maybe it's the realm getting in my head, like the whisper of the gold. I stand locked to the spot, staring, straining, searching for any hint of movement.

"What are you doing?" Miriam demands.

"Did you see that?"

"See what?"

I turn back to her. "That...that thing. That shadow."

"I saw nothing," she shrugs, scanning the horizon. "Just piles of—" She gasps. "Over there!" She points behind me, and I spin around to see, but I'm too late.

Something bursts in me, red—alarm red, panic red. It bursts from every particle of my being. I can feel it settling into the creases of my fingers, behind my ears, along my spine.

We're being watched.

"You saw it? What is it?" I ask. My fingers drift to my blade.

But she isn't listening. She twists side to side, her eyes darting up and down, searching.

"We need to get out of here," she says.

Another whoosh of movement. I turn to it and catch just a flash of wispy shadow like the swish of a tail in the corner of my eye. By the time I'm facing it, it's gone, darted off into the abyss.

We're exposed and vulnerable out here in the open. My lumbering dullness surely stands out against this endless glitter. Whatever is out there, we're an easy target for it here.

My mind drifts to my room in the temple. My body craves the safety of enclosure, of the darkness. I want to be tucked away, for the earth to swallow me up and protect me.

"We will figure out another way to get to the Pits. But right now we just need to get out," Miriam says. "Follow me."

She turns again to go back the way we came.

I almost follow her. But I can't stand to go back, farther from Rona. I take one last look around. And that's when I see it. My chest swells with relief.

"Wait!"

Miriam turns again with a heavy sigh. "We have to get out."

"I found another way." I point to show her.

Beyond the mountainous coins, the roughness of rocky wall. Coated in shimmery gold that blends into the coins. It's no wonder we missed it before. But there it is. A mountain. And tucked into its side, an opening. A dark gap in the bright gold, an escape.

It's just what we need. A place to hide. A place to shield us from the strange looming things of this realm.

She nods. "Go."

We break off from the path and wade toward the cave, our feet dragging through the coins. The piles grow deeper the further on we press, and we are all but drowning in the heaps of gold, pearls and gems.

Finally, we reach the cave's mouth. I stretch my hand out and touch it. Cool and rough. The gold flakes away on my hand, revealing its truth underneath, earth and rock. It releases the flinty smell of stone. I want to press into it, wait for it to grow around me and make me a part of it. Instead, I push myself up into the cave, grab Miriam's cold arm and pull her in after me.

The release is immediate. Even as I set Miriam down, I feel the gold's hold over me dissolve. The cave's enclosed darkness wraps around me and I am home, I am safe.

Miriam stands next to me panting, her face flushed. A twinge of worry quivers through me—she wasn't like this after fighting the beast in the river. She was strong then.

And her eyes, a distance is creeping into them. *Creepy crawly.* Like the Keeper said.

I'm huffing a little too, the gash in my shoulder biting deep into me. I've never been out of breath before.

"What's that?" she asks. She nods to my cloak's side pocket. I look down to it.

A torn piece of fabric. "It's from the Keeper's cloak."

This stray fabric is of no use to me. I take it out and am about to toss it aside when I notice its unusual weight. I hold it up to examine more carefully.

I didn't just rip off a piece of the Keeper's cloak. I ripped off his pocket. I reach inside and pull out a smooth white stone.

"It's the glimmer stone!" Miriam exclaims. "If we can find another glimmer, we can get to the Pit. We just need to find a glimmer."

She laughs.

I've never seen her laugh before. It's airy and free. It lights up her face and suddenly she looks so much like

Jordan. It tugs at me and makes me homesick for the shore, but all the same, I feel the corners of my mouth pulling up into a smile back to her.

Maybe not everything is against me.

CHAPTER 18

WE PAUSE AT the cave's mouth before moving on.
Miriam pants, bent over and leaning on her knees. My
own breaths heave, too. It gnaws at me, to think what it
might mean. How tired we are from such a short climb.
But I can't do anything about that right now.

At least we're safe. For now.

Safe and enclosed in the cave's cool darkness, I let it
all fall away. Tuck away my defenses and ease into the
cool cloak of the shadow.

This is right. This the way we need to go. I can feel
it.

Miriam pants, "We need to keep going."

Weariness and cold are seeping deep into my bones.

"Rest a little longer. Catch your breath. Then we'll
go on."

I lean against the wall and pull out the box. Open it
up—the top lifts so easily now—and stare at the
strange green jewel inside. What is this necklace, that it
demands such protection? That it causes so many to
want it so desperately?

More questions, nothing but questions. Even here, where I am unbound from it, it has brought nothing but troubles. I almost wish I'd never opened it at all. Almost wish I could disappear back into my temple tower, before any of this started. Back into its shielded protection, I crave. It feels so far away, so long ago.

But no. That was not real security. The Hunters kept coming and coming. The box kept me from any kind of happiness.

But even that was so much more than what I have now. The bottomless unknowing of this realm, the surprises and twists. The gnawing pain.

I ache for that simplicity again. I ache for the shore, for Jordan.

I close the box and put it back into my pocket, where it belongs.

What is he doing right now, I wonder. Playing with the other children along the shore? Training, maybe?

My eyes drift back to Miriam. Can I really leave her, after all this? She turned down eternal peace to be at my side. Maybe I can at least help her back to the Crossing.

And there's only one way back to Jordan. Only one way I could stay there. Not Miriam. Rona. She is the only way this will ever stop, the only way to any sort of end for me. Bring her back. Get my soul.

I close my eyes, and I can almost feel the warm breeze caressing around me. Almost hear the soft waves brush the sand. The sun on my skin. Almost hear his voice calling for me, waving to me to join them.

My eyes whip back open. My ears twinge.

I *did* hear him. No. It's impossible.

But then it comes again.

"Adem!"

His laugh bubbles in echoes from deep within the caves. With it my spirits float and the pain, the weariness, the cold is forgotten for a fluttering moment. My mind brightens, as if a warm light were swelling within me.

"Did you—" I start, but Miriam is already on her feet.

"Yes," she says. "It sounds just like him."

We listen intently. Nothing.

I step deeper in toward the tunnel. "Jordan!" It echoes away without response.

The quiet leaves a vacuum behind, a craving that must be filled. Frenzied thoughts flood into it. He shouldn't be wandering this strange realm by himself. He could be in danger. What is he doing here? Fear edges in on me from every side. The light tugs at me, urges me to race down into the tunnels.

"We've got to go find him!" I exclaim.

I start to run, but Miriam lunges at me and grabs my arm, dragging me back into the cold. "Wait!" she cries.

For a flash I am flooded with a feral anger, a rabid desire to lash out against her. Doesn't she understand? Jordan is here. We have to get to him. The light tugs at me again, begs me to follow Jordan's voice with a frantic urgency.

"He needs us!" I growl.

"He sounds fine," she says. "And we don't know that it's him."

Her words won't process. Of course, it's him. It sounds just like him, she said so herself. Boiling frustration mixes with the light and my head starts to spin. There's no time for this.

"Adem!" Jordan's voice bounces through the caves to me again. He's calling me.

"We have to go! We have to find him!" I yell at Miriam, pulling away from her.

She grips my arm tighter. "Wait! Listen to me! Doesn't this seem strange to you? Don't you think — ?"

"It doesn't matter, he needs us!" I shrug her away and run down the path toward him. My steps unsettle the ground, filling the air with dusty earth. I hear Miriam's footsteps trailing behind me, hear her call for me to come back, trailing farther and farther away. But the light washes over me and I feel strange and lightheaded and it tells me I have to, I have to, I have to get to Jordan, and Miriam can wait. I can come back to her once I have him, and she will see. We will all be together again.

Jordan. I'm coming.

****

"Jordan?"

I race through the cavernous tunnels, determined to find him. Miriam's voice stretches after me, her voice the only sign of her left through the twists, turns, and dark tunnels. Dim bands of light seem to travel with me as I move through them, helping me to see ahead. The light comforts me — I will come back and find Miriam once I have him, and she will see. She will be glad I went for him. And so I press on, deeper and deeper into the cave.

Until I reach a split in my path. Jordan is down one of these tunnels. But through the rocky twists, I see nothing, and the echoes of his laughs have floated away. I need him to show me the way.

I call for him, listening, waiting. Desperate to hear him again.

I must be going mad.

But he sounded so real. So close. And I have to find him.

I will.

I must be deep below the ground by now. The air is tight and pressured, buzzes against my skin. I take another hesitant step forward.

"Jordan?"

The dark ahead breaks down my call to nothing. The air inflates with hope. But it is too still. Dead.

I wait.

And then, "Adem!"

It twists down the tunnel and runs through me in quivering thrills.

He's here.

"Jordan!"

I chase after his echoes down the path. The light still runs with me, keeps my way lit, as if it were part of me. It spreads through me and reaches in thin strands, mixes in with my eagerness and excitement, and a sweet warmth spills through me. Tells me this is right. This is the way. I'm getting closer.

Again, the tunnel splits, and I have to pull to a stop. Wait for some kind of sign. "Jordan?" The light nudges at me, wants me to go on. "Where are you? Jordan?"

A pause, and then there it is again. Jordan. Calling

for me.

I go to him, let the light guide me closer.

How much farther? Already I've come a long way and still no sign of him. Too far. Even I could not have heard Jordan from the cave's mouth if he is this deep in its depths. Maybe I should go back and find Miriam.

But the light pulses within me, reassures me, stills my mind to a warm hum, basked in the promise of Jordan just around the next corner. His voice is close. The light surges and my head gets light and giddy. I don't care how he got here, I just need to get to him.

"Adem!"

His laugh spills out in bubbles and bursts over the rough cave walls and I want to catch them, I want to hold them in my hands and stash them in my pockets.

The light swells. I break into a run.

Closer. I'm getting closer.

I am drenched in the light like a soaking sponge. It's rooted deep within me. My anxiety stills as it quiets my doubt and loosens my shoulder's ache. It is so strong it practically pulls me forward.

Jordan calls again and it is like a beam of sun stretching out to me, so real I could reach out my hand and hold it. I've never felt so warm, so light, so full and giddy.

I burst into a large opening, a break from the tight tunnels. Wide stretches of rough rock reach over and around me. The light surges over the walls and dissolves away, leaves just enough to see through the darkness. The kind of darkness that wraps around me like a blanket and tucks me away from the world, the kind I could pull around me and hide in for years and years and years.

"Adem!"

The sound is sweet and familiar. Like home.

I turn to Jordan and he races toward me, leaps into my arms. He is warm and solid, alive. Not just a soul. And safe, safe and happy. My chest all but bursts open with relief.

"I knew you'd find me."

"Always." Always, always. The rumble of my voice skitters up the rocky walls. "How did you get here?"

"Get here?" He cocks his head questioningly, a little wrinkle forms between his brows as he pulls them together. "I live here."

"But..." I look around the cave again. Barren rough stone. There's nothing, no food, no bed, no sign of life here at all. "How?"

Even as I say it, I hardly care. Light and intoxicating warmth pulses through me. He's here. Here in the Underworld. It's impossible, but here he is, not two feet from me, beaming his Jordan smile that is just the way I remember it.

And the box no longer has its hold on me here. No threat looming, a constant barrier between us nagging at the corner of my mind as I stand here, close enough to touch. Deep in my core, I was sure I'd never really reach this.

I laugh.

For maybe the first time.

I just wasn't made for this elation.

But isn't it strange for a human to be so comfortable in this darkness, this cold? Yet he doesn't seem to mind.

"You must be hungry," he says. "Eat."

He pushes a small silver platter to my face, overloaded with juicy berries. I take in their sweetness from the air, dense and rich. It is unlike anything I have ever smelled. I lean into it and breathe deep.

I shake my head. "I am not like you. I do not eat." And then I realize. "You know this." Where did the plate come from? Just a moment ago, I could have sworn—

I kneel to him. Look into his eyes.

Innocent and wide, flat and stormy gray like the caves.

Something deep in the back of my mind scratches at the door, begs to be let out. From the corner of my eye, the rustle of darting shadow.

Answers begin to creep forward like dusting off an old book, but the light swells against it and tells me I'm home, this is right, and I can't remember the question.

"Try one anyway." Jordan shrugs. "They're so good."

He holds a handful toward me. I stare at them. Their richness squeezes in juicy streams over his fingers, pollutes the air in a burst of ripeness. A burst of light inside me, an emptiness growls in my stomach. Is this what hunger feels like? Perhaps in this realm I do need to eat. Perhaps one would not hurt.

Don't eat, don't drink. Miriam warned me. The light throbs against it. The emptiness stirs angrily in my stomach. The berries are full, juicy, and rich with color.

The faint scratching again at the back of my mind. What am I thinking?

I shake my head.

Jordan pulls his fist to his mouth and devours the rest himself. Juice dribbles down his chin and sweetness explodes into the air in a thick, fragrant cloud.

When he is done, he licks the last of the sweetness from his fingers.

I wish I'd taken one.

"Oh!" His eyes widen with excitement. "Have you seen outside yet?"

Outside? In this secluded pocket deep within the mountain?

He takes my hand in that fearless way that only he has ever done. "Come with me!" He playfully tugs at my arm. Leads me to the back of the cave.

His tugs send bolts across the wound in my back and deep into my muscle. The pain calls me back to myself. Who knows how much time has already passed, where Miriam has wandered while I've been gone—how could I leave her out there in the Nethers alone? I fumble through my mind for the words to explain and break away.

As we get closer to the rocky walls, my perspective shifts, and I see it. The back of the cave is not the back at all, but a crack in the mountain's side. A breeze stretches out to me through it and blows away everything else.

A breeze that's soft, warm, and salty and feels like...it feels like...

"Jordan, where are we?"

But I already know where we are. I just don't understand how. Did I give up and return to Terath? The light keeps growing and filling and pushing out all else, replacing it all with its warmth and tingly bliss, and I can't remember. Stinging confusion drowns underneath its warm buzz.

"Jordan, how—"

"Come!"

He slips through the cracked wall, turns and waits for me to follow.

It is too tight. I will not fit.

But Jordan is waiting, expecting me to follow. Something in the warm sea breeze reaches to me, sweet, calling me home. I shut my eyes and press into the crack. Rocky ridges hug against my back, my arms, my cheek. Cool and rough. And then I am past it. Somehow, I got through.

Another gust of breeze. Soft and salty fresh. It eases its way through my hair and over my aching back. I realize suddenly just how cold I was. How the chill sank deep below my skin and settled into my bones. It warms me from the inside and rests within my chest, mingling with the bursting light already throbbing within me. The familiar whisper of waves floats to my ears.

But how did we get here?

The light expands, relaxes my mind. Tells me to stop questioning. To accept this incredible gift.

"Look," Jordan tells me.

I open my eyes and look.

It is just how I remember it. Even better.

Sandy grains tickle under my feet. Rolling waves topple to the shore. Not far off, sits Haven. Its people for once aren't working for survival or training for battle. They are out on the beach with us. They're playing. Their heads turn to us, and they beckon to us to join them.

Jordan is at the sea's edge, jumping waves.

"You see?" A familiar woman's voice from behind me. A hand lands on my shoulder. "You belong here. You are safe here. With us."

Wild curls bounce in the breeze.

...Miriam?

It is and it isn't a trick of the light, something familiar but not the same.

She's smiling, hair tossing into her flat gray eyes, so like Jordan's.

She is standing too close. Something is clawing at the crevices of my mind. Something trying to scream, trying to tell me something. My mind floods with questions, trying to find the one that will unlock it.

If we're back on the shore, will I be forced to protect the box again? It quivers in my pocket and I feel it calling to be held. I know what will happen as sure as if it has already happened. She will reach for it. I will kill her. And then I will have to leave. For good this time.

I couldn't bear it.

But she just keeps smiling. Easy, free, simple. She stands too close, too close, too close and it twists in the pit of my stomach.

How is she here?

"We know your secret." Her words are like a plunge into a lake in winter. Her eyes are wide and earnest. "It is safe with us." She reaches out to me and her hand is on my chest. Resting right over the box. Alarms scream in my head. I brace myself for the inevitable. Nothing happens. "*You* are safe with us."

I try to slow the throbbing panic coursing through me.

Safe.

And then at the edge of my eye, a darting shadow. I whip around. Nothing. Just soft breeze and open sky and warm sun. The light latches into me, expands, and expands until I am blinded by it, until it is too loud to listen to anything else. *Quiet,* it demands, *Stop questioning. Be happy.*

The sun dances in sparkles over the waves. Birds sing a sweet, lazy tune. The light bursts, makes me dizzy and lightheaded.

It is all I ever wanted.

"Here, eat," Miriam says. More of the fruit. Suddenly a whole plate of it is in her hands.

"No." Something in me still resists, even now.

Where did the fruit come from? Like before it seems to have come from nowhere.

"Oh, but they are so good," she says. She brings a few to her mouth and bites into them, releasing their aroma into the air. "You must try it." She lifts my hand and drops some into my palm. I lose myself in their rich sweet smell.

No, Miriam warned me. One bite and I will be trapped here forever.

But this is Miriam. This is just where I want to be. Isn't it? Isn't she?

What was I doing?

I have to stretch deep into my mind to pull it out. A name.

Rona.

I was looking for Rona.

I try to remember why. The image of a bright, beautiful creature with wings rises to my mind. I grope for more. But it is too far away. Like a lost dream.

"I should go."

My words float aimlessly in the air. As if they came from someone else. The light fights it, tries to push them back.

"But you must rest. Look, you are injured." Her soft fingers press on my shoulder. The touch softens the pain, courses through me like a healing elixir. It rises to my head and buzzes with a peaceful lull.

"You must heal first. Then you can go if you must."

Everything in me hungers to yield to her. The berries are plump and rich, still in my hand. And yet still the clawing at the back of my brain. Why fight, why resist something so good?

Jordan is splashing in the waves. The sea stretches behind him wide, open, limitless. He calls for me to join him. "Finish your berries and come play with me!"

The sun is behind him, putting him in silhouette against its splashes of color as it sets. His hair flies around his face in the breeze like rays of sun.

I remember leaving him here, the way my core clung to him as I walked away, how I promised him I'd come back. The way his deep brown eyes darkened as I tried to explained, set sparks through those flecks of fiery orange.

And suddenly the door slams open and I recognize the gnawing thing clawing at my mind.

His eyes.

This boy is not Jordan.

The real Jordan's determined face rises to my mind,

MUD

his soft brown eyes with bright orange flecks, and my chest sinks, sinks, sinks like a rock in a pond.

Finally, I understand.

I do not have to die to be trapped in this realm.

And that's exactly what this is. A realm trap. Set just for me.

CHAPTER 19

THE SUN STRETCHES across the sand, warm and bright. The waves wash soft on the shore. A bird floats overhead, singing. But it's wrong, it's all wrong.

A sickening knot twists in my stomach. Adrenaline charges through me like an avalanche.

"I must go."

I hear myself say the words, but they do not feel like mine. Small. Distant. Impossible. The light is still in me, stretches its beams down my arms and my legs, filling me with dizzy warmth, stealing my focus. How could I ever leave such a place? It's everything I've looked for all these years. Already it has started to mend the holes inside me. Must I rip myself away?

Stop, I snap myself back. *This is not real.*

The thing that is not Miriam is smiling. A wide, relaxed smile that pushes a dimple into her check. Where is the real Miriam now, wandering the dark caves alone? How could I abandon her like this? She tried to warn me.

"Of course you must," not-Miriam responds. Her

ease sends prickles over my skin. "But please, not yet. You must rest. Let us take care of you just one night before you go on your way."

She takes my hand. It is warm and gentle. Real. What's the harm in enjoying this peace for just one night?

No.

This is not real.

If I do not go now, I will never leave.

A muffled sound catches my ear from within the cave. I turn to look back. "What was that?" Almost like someone calling out.

"It's nothing." Not-Miriam pushes the plate of swollen berries to my face again. They are bright, ripe, and red. Red like rage, red like poison. "Please eat. It will help you stay strong in your journey."

She puts a hand on my back, gentle and kind. Right by my gaping wound. The pain has loosened and eased while I've been here. It is hardly anything now. If I leave, the pain is bound to return.

When I leave.

Because I must leave. I owe it to Kythiel to keep going. More importantly, to Miriam, to the real Jordan. To myself.

This is not real. This is not real.

The thick waxy air is crowding in on me. My shoulders are pulling in tight, tight, tighter every second.

I want to run away as fast as I can.

I want to curl up next to not-Miriam on the sand and listen to the waves' whispers forever.

Not real, not real, not real.

What does it matter? Why shouldn't I stay?

The words rush into my head, as if shoved in from the outside. I could rest here forever on the shore. Never again fear the box, what it will make me do. Never again feel the sinking dread of the Hunters. I could join these people and sit on the shore, watch the tides rise and fall forever. What is the difference, really, between going back to Terath and letting myself be happy here? What could it possibly matter to anything? Whenever will this come my way again?

So long I have lurked the shadows of Terath, without a moment of peace. Here in the realm of the dead, I find my first true taste. And now I will rip myself away?

No, I will never leave it, never.

My hands are balled in determined fists. Here I already have all I've yearned for. If I go back, I may never find it again. Even with a soul. My mind floods with thoughts I'd locked away, did not dare think before. What if the humans still never accept me among them? What if the soul does not work as we expect, and I am still bound to the box even after? If I've learned anything here in the Nethers, it's that anything is possible.

Not-Jordan runs to me from the waves, takes my hand, panting.

"What's wrong? Come! Play in the waves with me."

I look down to him and something else's eyes meet me. I remember the boy I swore to protect. The real one, the one waiting for me back in Terath in a real village by the shore.

This is something I cannot let go of. Not for

anything.

Again, a call pierces from within the cave. I whip around. This time I am sure of it.

I let go of not-Jordan's hand, turn from him. I walk quickly back toward the crack in the stony wall. I do not stop.

Not-Jordan pulls on my arm, says something to me with a wide smile.

But I am not listening now. Not to him. My ears are focused on the shouts coming from inside the cave. A voice I know, a voice I hardly believe I'm hearing. It's Miriam. Real Miriam. Could I be so lucky?

I must get to her, get away from the shore as fast as I can. Not-Jordan tugs harder, but I avert my eyes, not trusting what's in front of me anymore. I focus on the bare rocks of the cave walls ahead of me, Miriam's calls beyond it.

Not-Miriam rushes next to the child, pulling at my other arm, her voice a high-pitched buzz in my head. I struggle against their weight, an impossible weight for two humans, as if they're made of lead, anchored into the ground. But my legs push me forward, forward, forward, and the sand sinks under my feet with each step as they drag dense and heavy behind me. Their knees drag and scrape on the rocky ground, they cry for me to stop. The pain in my shoulder is back, a fierce piercing sting that digs all the way through to my chest, raw and sharp.

This is not real, this is not real, this is not real.

They get heavier and heavier, until the pain in my back is unbearable and I do not think I can move forward another step. I am almost there, just feet from the opening back into the mountain. Miriam, the real Miriam, shouts for me clear as day, "Adem! Adem!"

"Miriam!" I call back.

As I shove back through the crack in the mountain, it seems to be tightening, fighting against me.

"Miriam!" I call for her again.

I turn to the strange figures clinging to my arms, unclenching their fingers from me one by one. They cry, whimper, beg me to stay — not real, not real — and when I am done and stand upright again, I find changed creatures before me.

Creatures like fury embodied.

Their skin rots down to their bones, turns ashy gray and withers into the realm's darkness. Blood red eyes glow out of grimaced snarling mouths, revealing feral fangs. Thin dark wings twitch from their backs.

"Oh Gods."

Miriam is rushing toward me. I try to fling the horrible creatures away, but they will not release me. Miriam is quickly at my side, swinging at them with her fists, but each dissolves into shadow and darts away as she makes contact. I don't try to understand. We turn away and we run, run, run.

The creatures come at us in whooshes of shadow, re-form at our sides to grab, claw, and bite. More start to join them, and more, and more. The whole beach of villagers must be after us now. A flock of shadow and fury all around us, whooshing and snapping, scratching and shrieking, and I can't push them away fast enough. As soon as my arms reach for them, they dart away again, nothing but shadow.

We trip and stumble our way across the open cave.

They swarm us, clutching at my heels and clawing my head, a blurred rush of darkness swirling all around. I can hardly see the ground ahead of us to get away.

We're almost at the opening back into the mountain's tight tunnels. I grab onto Miriam's arm, her deep cold shooting back into me through my palm, and pull her through it with me. The shadows' shrieks echo, darting after us. The pain is sharp in my shoulder, even worse than before. The light collapses within me like a vacuum, cold, empty, and leaving behind a raw, naked longing. It begs me to turn back.

But I dare not stop, not again. Not for anything.

Keep moving. Wherever we end up, it will be better than this.

CHAPTER 20

WE RUN AS hard and as long as we can. Until we can no longer hear the awful echoes of their shrieks twisting down the tunnels after us. We run until Miriam is gasping, and my back is seizing with pain, and we're forced to slow to a walk. The steady, slow pace quiets my body and the adrenaline starts to wane. My ears prick at every tick of the caves, every rolling pebble. Behind my eyes, my last look at those strange creatures still burns. Were those demons? I understand now the Keeper's fear of them.

I break the silence. "I'm sorry," I say.

Miriam stops. Whips around at me. There's a bloodshot twitchiness in her eyes, her expression edgy and strange. My gut twists. Her expression loses focus and her lip trembles. I am afraid she is going to forget everything again like when I first found her, but then something else takes over. Her brows pull down and her eyes turn fiery in an expression that is not hers.

"By the Gods, you worthless pile of mud." Her voice is wild but her words are stiff, as if coming from somewhere else. "You can't do anything right."

A sick feeling twists in my stomach. This is not Miriam. Not like the Not-Miriam creature in the realm trap. It's really her standing in front of me this time, but something else is using her to speak. It's the realm working its way into her again. It's getting worse.

Hot shame wrestles through me. I try to tell myself that these aren't her words. But it doesn't matter.

"You're right."

By now, my guilt is settled deep within my cracks, like dust between the pages of an old forgotten book, entrenched in the biting cold and the searing pain and the weariness.

"Of course I am. I'm the only one getting anything right. *You* can't be trusted. *You* shouldn't have it. We should."

We?

I'm nodding along, but I don't understand. Have what? Then she stretches her hand out expectantly, that cold empty blankness on her face. "Give it to us."

I eye her carefully, the stiff way her arm hangs, the blankness filming her eyes, and take a step back. "What?"

"The box. Give it to us," she snaps. "We should have it, not you."

A chill prickles down my neck. The realm is inside me as much as it is in her. It knows just what to say. I am so full of guilt and shock I almost do it.

But what would the Underworld want with the box? Was it the realm in me all along, whispering to me to open it, to leave it behind here?

"No."

She lunges forward and tries to snatch at it within my pocket, an unnatural growl pushing from her. I take a step back and her momentum throws her to the ground.

"Miriam?"

I'm afraid to get any closer, afraid to leave her on the ground in this crumpled heap.

But when she lifts her head, she is herself again. I can see it in her beautiful eyes.

"What happened?" She brings herself to her feet.

I'm afraid for her, for what happens if the realm takes her over again. If it takes me over. In the back of my mind, I hear the Keeper's cackling laugh. The realm will always win. It's too strong. It has too many tricks. Already I see the edginess creeping back into her eyes.

"The realm."

If only we could find a glimmer and slip through to the Pit. If only the realm would lead me as easily to Rona as it did to the shore.

But wait.

Suddenly, like a landslide crashing over me, I have an idea.

Maybe it *would*, under the right conditions. Something inside me breaks through my fear and soars like a bird — finally, a plan.

It's so simple. And impossibly difficult.

"Miriam." I press my hand to her shoulder and feel the piercing freeze. She's getting colder. "It used Jordan to trick me before because it's what I wanted most. Right? That's how the realm traps work?"

"Yes," she says.

"But Jordan isn't here. So it had to use an illusion."

"Yes."

"But when it can use the real thing, it does. In the Keeper's treasure trap that was real gold."

"It certainly seemed to be, yes. But—"

"What if I wanted most was to find the soul I'm bringing back, would it bring us to her?"

She considers it, pulling her brows together, and crinkling her forehead. "Possibly. Probably. Why?"

My chest prickles with a thousand nervous pins. "So if I can just change my desires, I can lead us right to her."

She shakes her head. "It's not that simple. You can't just change what you want most. It's too ingrained," she says. "Even if you could, what if it didn't work? What if it led you into another illusion instead?"

I don't know that I could break free from the realm's lure a second time. I almost didn't make it out this time. But I don't think it will. I think if the realm can use the real Rona, it will.

"I have to try."

What else is there to do? We can't keep wandering blindly, easy prey to the realm and its shadows. Miriam seems weaker every time I look at her. We're running out of time.

I stop walking. Focus hard. How does one change their deepest desires?

I drag them out, lay each of them down for inspection in my mind. The ache to rid myself of the box. The craving to live with the humans. Exposing them like this makes me realize just how deep they run, fueled on all the desperation of ages on ages. Also, how flimsy they are, rooted in nothing but my emptiness.

I dig through my mind, reach back to the temple cellar, back to Kythiel. It is so far away from me now. I pull it to the forefront of my thoughts.

Rona. How very little I know about the woman I came to save.

I pick up the pieces and scrutinize them, cling to them, try to make each one bigger.

Her love with Kythiel, deep and unshakeable.

Her face, the glowing image Kythiel pulled for me from his memories. So lovely, so proud and unstrained.

How she died, a cold blade through her stomach. Her world torn to shreds by two men who she could not find it in herself to leave.

And with these sparse threads, I've run out of pieces. This is all I know of her. I hold them close, try to force them together and make them a full person.

I can't.

Find Rona, I command. *Find Rona. Find Rona.*

I try to push down my other desires, let them go. My cravings for freedom, for a soul, for life. What's a little more time after so many years? But they fight and cling to that place I've let them fester so long. It hurts, a deep longing ache, splitting through my core.

Find Rona, find Rona, find Rona.

I wrestle against each of these desires, fighting to sever them and keep them down, until finally, limp and raw and tired, I drag off all my wants, lock them away in a corner and hope they stay hidden there long enough for this to work.

Find Rona.

Something else settles into place, fills the raw aching gap where my dreams lived. I slump against the wall, suddenly breathless. My muscles ache, my chest heaves. Everything in me fights for stillness. The cold has seeped through to my core, a cold that settles in and makes its home in me, threatens to never leave. My shoulder throbs. The skin at its edges is hardening, ragged, and rough.

The realm is wearing away at me. How much worse will it get? How much can I bear? I could get lost here, trapped in the realm's madness, locked away from everything and everyone. If that happens, I fail Kythiel. I fail Miriam. I fail Jordan. This could be my last chance.

"Is it...is it working?" Miriam asks.

Find Rona. Find Rona. Find Rona. It pulses in me strong and steady. Like a heartbeat.

And yet I can feel the realm's haze winding through my mind, weakening it, slowly tugging and unraveling it. I slump against the wall and down to the floor under its weight.

"What's happening?" Miriam asks. "What is it?"

It's everything.

It's my longing for the security of my temple in Epoh, the realm I turned away from, where I could not be harmed. It's the box and its rules that have abandoned me now, leaving me vulnerable and aimless. It's Kythiel and his dangling promises. The cold ache keeps seeping deeper, deeper, and deeper into me through the hole in my shoulder. It's Miriam, the way the realm keeps chipping away at her. It's Rona, how impossible it has become to reach her. It's how vulnerable and broken I am here. All of it. Like an avalanche crushing me into the ground.

It's too much.

It was hard in Epoh. But at least it was clear. No choices, no risks. Just the waiting and the killing and the waiting again. Only what the box commanded. I should never have stepped away from that temple into the night.

And I'm so empty I could crumble.

Find Rona.

Something soft and muffled interrupts my thoughts.

And before I can pull out of my thoughts enough to look up to see what it is, Miriam calls to me. "Adem?"

Her voice is thin and wary. I look up to her, and she points down the tunnel, toward the sound. I turn, and I see why she is afraid.

A large dim light is making its way toward us. It's taking its time.

"What is it?" I ask.

She shakes her head. "I don't know."

Her voice trembles. Reminds me that this Miriam, the one with the realm creeping deeper and deeper into her, is not the fighter she once was.

I step between Miriam and the glow. I pull out my blade, ready to put it to use. It's time I fought for myself anyway. We stand and wait as it stumbles closer and closer. As it nears, the light breaks, becomes several small lights trudging on together.

Miriam gasps. "It's *souls*."

I squint to look closer. The lights take form. Their light is soft and glowing. It is souls. A whole horde of them.

The relief pours out of me in a sigh that's almost a

laugh. "We just need to let them pass."

We press against the wall to let them by. Rock presses into my back near my wound.

As they near I can make out more — dark cloaks wrap around them, red cloaks. My throat constricts. Every muscle tenses. My blade falls out of my hand to the ground.

They're all Hunters. Men I killed.

There must be hundreds of them.

As they pass, I can see their faces, make out their death wounds. Wounds I doled out, every one of them. The cold distant eyes, eyes flat like the ones they left behind in their bodies on Terath, the ones that stared me down so long after the souls left as I dragged them away and hid them in the ground.

They trudge past me one by one, show no sign of knowing that the thing they died for, is but inches from them.

My head grows murky with questions. The shadows crowd around me. Why has none of them crossed over? What are they doing here? The Keeper said souls are drawn to those they knew. Even so, I never expected to face so many of the ones I sent here.

And yet...of course.

Of course, they found me. Always. No matter where I try to hide, they are there. Eventually.

My fingers tremble. So close. So close to me right now. As they pass, some of them brush against my cloak. The box quivers in my pocket as if it knows. I breathe deep and slow. My hand drifts up and presses over it through my cloak.

Just stretch out a hand and grab one of their cloaks,

just wake one up, and the answers I've ached to have for centuries could be mine. So easy.

But something keeps me pinned in place. Something else the Keeper said. His warning. The disruption to the realm. If it's true, every step I take is sending waves through the Underworld already, moving it to fight against me. To wake another soul? It might ruin everything. Already I regret bringing Miriam into all this.

Or, something else in me whispers. *It could give you everything you've been looking for.*

It's barely audible above the rustle of the hoard. A shadow that hovers just out of sight, like the strange rustling thing we saw among the treasures. A voice like the one that wanted me to stay on the shore with not-Jordan and embrace the lies.

A dark tempting cloud hugs close around me. *Just one. Just reach out and pull on his cloak.* My hand starts to drift out. So easy, so close, all the answers I've starved for all these ages.

But then I realize what I'm doing and whip it back, press my palm into the rocky cave wall behind my back.

Rona.

I came for her, and I swore to bring her back. I know what I came for, and this isn't it. A kernel of stiff determination takes shape deep inside me, and it won't let me put that at risk. I've put too much on the line, and so has Miriam, for me to cave to temptation now. Something shifts inside me like a gear, clicks into place. I've gone ages without answers. I can go a little longer. That's not what matters right now. That's not what I want.

Find Rona.

My fingers grip hard onto the wall behind me, dig into the dirt and burrow in, grip around rock to keep them from reaching out. There's bigger things at stake right now.

Just one. It won't take long. The answers to all the questions you've asked for ages are right in front of you.

But answers alone aren't enough anymore.

They owe it to you. You can finally take it. You can make them explain.

No.

I could. But I won't.

Find Rona.

I let it all go and watch the answers to all I've endured pass me by, one slogging soul at a time. They wander on aimlessly and disappear.

If that's what you want.

As the last few trail on, the shadow wraps around me and dissolves. I'm cold with panic, but then something grows inside me. Something so sudden and warm and blindingly bright that I stumble and fall to the ground.

"Are you alright?" Miriam's cold hands are on my shoulders, trying to help me up. But I don't need it. I hardly feel her. I'm more than all right. I'm great.

The light tugs at me to get up, to keep moving. *This way, this way, come with me,* it chants. And somewhere deep inside, I know where it will lead.

"It worked," I say, pushing myself up. "Come on!"

As soon as I am on my feet, I let the light race me down the tunnel.

"Wait!" Miriam cries. "Where are you going?"

I can't leave her for the light again. We need to stick together. I turn back, the light fighting, fighting, and tugging me the other way.

"We're going to the Pits."

Her eyes grow wide and she takes a breath as if to say something. But before she can get the words out, the light surges inside me. I grab her hand and we chase the light through the tunnels.

CHAPTER 21

I TEAR THROUGH the tunnels as cautiously as I can, squeezing Miriam's hand, the light tugging me ever forward. Toward Rona, I'm sure of it. My head throbs in rhythm with my pace, heavy and quick. The walls are a blur at the corners of my eyes.

The tunnels spit us out into a clearing. The ground is rough and cracked under my feet. The light is tugging at me to move forward again before I can even catch my breath, its intensity growing. Rona must be close. But I force my legs still and look around.

"Where are we?" I pant, the light throbbing in my chest.

"I don't know." Miriam glances all around. Her voice is tense, full of tight restraint. Her eyes are bloodshot and strained. The realm is trying to take her again. "Do you think this is the Pits?"

A musty haze floats through the air and round my head. Dank. Heavy. It crowds around me from every side, builds like a film on my skin. The realm hums through it and within me. It's stronger here. Tugging at my mind.

"It must be. She's here, somewhere." The light is impatient. Pulls at me again. "This way." Forward. Deeper into the haze. Miriam nods.

I see the realm working away at her too. Her expression is slack and dazed already. Does she remember herself? Where we are? Her hand relaxes and slips away from mine. She trails behind me. But the light urges me forward.

I move slower now. More carefully. Who knows what might be out there, just out of sight?

The ground becomes more depleted, cracked, hardened. It splits more and more as if preparing to crumble away. Below in the earth's splits, mangled up shadows lend haunting under light.

Souls.

Wasting, wilting souls.

There's so many. The souls stretch beyond what I can see, beyond what I can comprehend. They blend like a festering ocean. Blackened shadow eats away at them and obscures their light. A rotten stench fills the thick air, mingles with the heavy haze. It is like death in hot sun.

What is this place, the Pits?

There's no time to wonder. Thin chilling arms tackle me from behind. As we tumble to the ground, painful chills shoot through me. Miriam's voice hisses in my ear, stiff and forced: "Give it to us. We brought you here, we did what you wanted. Now give it to us."

My shoulder explodes with pain, but I ignore it, whipping around to slam her against the ground before she can grab for my pocket.

We both are still for a pause, panting and weary from the drag of the realm. Miriam blinks, shakes her head. "What's happening?"

I loosen my grip on her shoulders. The light floods them and dissolves the cold. My head throbs with anxiety. Is she herself again? Did slamming her into the ground shake her free? I stare into her eyes and try to find her there.

"Welcome."

A thin voice creaks through the haze, echoing strangely. It bounces, twists, and comes at me from every side, prickles at the back of my neck. I flinch and scramble to my feet to arch for its source, leaving Miriam splayed on the ground.

"We have much to discuss," the voice presses.

It's getting closer. A pulse throbs in my throat. Tight and constricting.

"Come out where I can see you," I call into the abyss.

The haze breaks down my words and swallows them.

But a figure starts to take shape through it. Tall. Spindly. It stretches over the ground's deep cracks with hardly a strain.

The throbbing rises to my ears with a wild *whoosh-whoosh-whoosh*. Miriam pushes herself up and stands next to me. Her face twitches, straining against the realm's pull again already. Dread knots in my stomach—I can't fight her off and this new threat, too, if the realm takes her over again.

"I have come to see the one who has broken through the barrier into my realm."

His realm. A chill of fear rushes over me. Then he must be—

"Abazel." Miriam says it accusingly, the syllables cold and sharp in the air like shards of ice.

King of the Underworld. Highest of the demons.

Kythiel warned me, but words are nothing compared to Abazel's live presence. He creeps steadily forward until he is uncomfortably close, only inches from us. My mind buzzes with blank panic. It never occurred to me I'd come face to face with this monster. And yet—his body is boney and brittle. Up close like this, his eyes are dark and menacing, but his skin is pale and tired.

He skims over Miriam and looks to me. The thin lips part to say, "Why don't we have this conversation alone?"

Miriam folds her arms over her chest. If she feels the fear as I do, she doesn't show it. "Because he doesn't need t—" Abazel stretches out a single spindly finger and touches Miriam's forehead. Miriam goes blank and idle. Empty. Like when I first found her on the boat.

"Miriam?" I grab her arm. "Miriam!"

Blazing flames of dread lick over my body. Under it, a rush of secret relief betrays me. Her feet begin to shift, to drift her away.

I pull her back to me. "Miriam!" Shake her by the shoulders. Try to pull her out of it like I did before.

"It won't work this time," Abazel says.

I whip around to him. My fear of him is consumed by hate.

"What did you do? What's wrong with her?"

But he smiles. A grimacing, teeth-baring smile.

"Nothing is wrong with her. She is as she should be in my realm."

"Miriam!" I yell in her face, shake her as hard as I can. "Miriam! Miriam! Miriam!"

"She'd only have kept getting worse." His words are cold. "Is that what you want for her? For her to keep up this struggle until her mind dissolves?"

Lies. My mind hisses. *Don't trust him, not for a second.*

But I know better. I saw enough to understand where it was heading.

I slowly release my fingers from her shoulders. She blinks at me without seeing, then blankly turns and drifts away. I watch her as long as I can as she disappears into the haze, a darkness welling up from my gut.

"There. Now we can talk," Abazel says.

He takes a deep breath and whistles, a sound quick and clear that cuts through the thick air. A shadow dashes from out of nowhere and materializes on his shoulder, turning into a creature with dark skin that clings to its bones and feral pointed teeth.

Just like the creatures from the realm trap.

Just like the strange shadow trailing us since the treasures.

It's real.

A slow sinking sensation fills me. It was following us. The anger fuels the fire of my hate.

It whispers into Abazel's ear, purring chirps like taunting laughter. A bolt of nerves shoots through me. How much does it know?

The light still wrestles anxiously inside me, strains for me to keep moving forward. *Rona, find Rona.* But I dig in my heels. Wait to see what the demon tells his king.

When its chirping ceases, Abazel scratches its head, then folds his hands together, spindly fingers pointing to his chin. He takes a step closer through the haze.

"You've made quite a stir. I have never felt the realm so uneasy," Abazel says. His voice is thin, quiet. "But do not mistake your foolishness for victory. When the boatman told me of what you came to do, we laughed. Many before have tried to save someone from death. None have succeeded. We did not think you would make it even this far."

The back of my hands prickle. The Keeper betrayed us, just as Miriam said he would. What else has he learned of my plans? I rummage through my mind for everything I told the Keeper. All the demon may have learned from watching me. Not everything. But enough. Enough to ruin it all.

Did he tell Abazel about the box? My breast pocket quivers, four pointed corners pressed against my skin.

Abazel continues. Something dark hovers around him.

"This is the problem with you creatures of Terath. Always meddling, negotiating, and trying to get around the Gods' rules. Unable to accept your place in the Order, yet unwilling to fight to break free of it. You have left us to take up your fight for you, and then turned your backs on us when we lost." His voice is slow, cold, calculated.

It takes me a moment to understand what he means. "The Realm Wars."

Find Rona, find Rona, find Rona. The light beats its

demanding rhythm inside me.

"Yes," he says. "I was the first to break free and see the Gods for the tyrants they are. Did you know that?"

I didn't. The Texts don't tell much about the creatures who rebelled. Just that they fought to break the Order.

Abazel continues. "I showed the others what was possible when you let go of the Gods and dared to think beyond them—free will. We would have been content to go our own way and rule ourselves, but the Gods would not let us. They forced their Order upon us."

Abazel shakes his head. His focus has drifted off to somewhere far away.

"After the First War, in the wake of the destruction they provoked, the Three saw the error in their ways and tried something new. Man."

The word shoots off his tongue as if spitting out spoiled fruit.

"They gave men free will. They hoped if they did not hold them so close, that men would not see in them what we did, I suppose. But, cowards that They are, the Three cut them off from the powers we enjoy."

Something twitches in the shadow that surrounds him. I lean closer to see what it is, squint into the haze.

Wings.

Large, inky-black wings. Just like Kythiel's.

The realization hits me like a punch to the gut. Abazel isn't a demon.

"You're an angel." But he can't be. "Angels can't enter the Underworld."

"The Gods created the rules," he sighs. "And the

Gods made an exception. It takes its toll, withering away in this darkness. And yet so it is. We are but pawns in the Gods' game."

He pauses. Looks down to his frail, thin hands.

Takes its toll — I've only just gotten here and already I'm ridden with pain and cold. I can only imagine how the ages down here have weighed down on him.

"Which brings me back to my point. The Three favored their newest creation, the humans, and it sowed envy among the First Creatures. More and more joined our numbers. Even some men. Again, we fought, and again we were defeated. The Second Realm War. The Three bound us here, to the in-between of the Underworld. But a Third War was foretold, and we knew our time would come. This time we will be ready."

I'm only half listening, my eyes still gazing at his dark wings. But Abazel, his war, his Gods, are not why I am here. The light throbs inside me, bursting wild, bright, and hot. *Find Rona.* It grows impatient, and so do I.

"This has nothing to do with me," I say.

"You entangled yourself in our fate when you crossed over into the Underworld," Abazel says. "We have been preparing for the Third Realm War here in our exile for hundreds of years. And now you have brought us our chance. When you broke through, you weakened the barrier the Three created to hold us here."

My racing thoughts come crashing to a halt. *Don't believe his lies.* I step back, out of his reach. Enough talking. "What do you want from me?"

"Stay," he says.

"What?" It doesn't make sense. My mind rejects it, refuses to understand.

"Stay in the Underworld," Abazel presses. "You will prepare with us. And fight with us, when we're ready. Why accept a world dominated by the commands of Gods and makers who do nothing for you? You can choose; you can make a difference here. Stay. Join us."

The light throbs in my head, pulses at the edges of my vision. I shut my eyes against it and try to process Abazel's preposterous suggestion. Me, fight in the Realm Wars?

The light surges, swarms within my head. I shake it side to side. "Your fight is not my fight."

"And what is your fight? Finding Rona? Is that your great cause?" Abazel snaps.

The words hit me like a bolt of lightning. I told the Keeper many things. Too much. But I didn't say her name. Not even to Miriam.

The demon is chittering into his ear again.

A buzzing terror rises over me like a fever. "How —
"

"You can't hide anything from me, Adem," Abazel cuts in. "The demons can sense your thoughts."

No wonder his lies are so powerful. He knows just what to say, I'm giving him all he needs to do it. My throat tightens. The light pounds inside me. I have to find Rona; I have to leave this place as fast as I can.

The demon chirps into Abazel's ear again. I try to stop my thoughts and lock them away, but they only churn out faster.

Abazel smiles, an awful and strange baring of his teeth. "You have nothing to fear from me. We should be working together. Do you know the power you possess within your particles?"

Why do they all keep insisting there is power in me? The light bursts through me, buzzing between every particle of my being, and I am helpless against it, against Abazel, against the box's pull, against everything. But it is all I've heard since I stepped out of my temple's shelter, and I cannot stand it anymore.

"I am nothing," I growl.

"That's what makes you so curious." Abazel says. "You should be nothing. What magic is mingled with that common dirt? That you hold together at all is a wonder itself. And yet...well. No pain. No death. On Terath you are invincible. So many seek me out for these gifts, thinking it is something I can grant. I cannot. And yet some human was able to grant them to you."

No pain? Not here. It's spreading over me from my shoulder still, regaining its hold on me through the light's disorienting high. No death? I'm closer to it than I've ever been, every breath heaving and hard, the realm's tug stealing my energy.

The light writhes, angry and urgent and turning my head woozy. I've got to get away from Abazel. I have to find Rona. She's somewhere out there, in the sea of souls just beyond him. I look out over the flickering glow with longing.

But he keeps going.

"I know what you want," Abazel presses. The weariness of my long journey bears down on me. The wounds in my back and side fester like licking flames. The light is draining on my energy, pounding through me every second. Its demand rolls through me like thunder. *Find Rona.*

"You want a soul. You want to be *human.*"

The strange smile spreads over his lips again. I can see the forced ways his face creases to make room for it. I can see each tooth, small, jagged, and sharp.

Resentment rises in me like a sandstorm.

"Why do you so badly wish to join the lesser beings of Terath? A soul!" he scoffs. "Look around you, Adem," He points past him into the Pits. "Look what it does to a being to compound soul with the material. Don't you see how feeble they are? Look at how they waste away, too frail even to stand. They are weak, they cannot take on the things that we can."

He pauses. Watches me. Waits for a reaction.

I don't give him one.

"Did my brother Kythiel tell you he can give you this? He was always one to take the easiest path. But he cannot do it." The terrible smile still floats on his face. I hate it. "Why don't you think I offer you one? I would if I could. But I can't. None but the Gods can."

My stomach lurches.

But no. I won't listen. This is just more lies. Like the shore and the not-Jordan. A trick to make me stay.

"Tell me, Adem. What else do you want? Glory? Fight with us and it will be yours. Riches? Peace? I can give you these things. More than you could dream of."

He will say anything to keep me from finding Rona. *Stop listening.* I have to get past him, into the Pits.

"I want Rona."

Abazel blinks. "I could even return you to your little shore in the mountains after the Wars, if that is what you want. It's still there, you know. You could stay there for all of eternity."

The emptiness within me aches to do it.

But no.

"Don't give in to his lies, Adem. Stay. Fight with us."

Me, fight in the Realm Wars? No.

No more blood.

No more deaths.

Only my own. Only when, after all this, Kythiel gives me my soul, and I live out my years in peace and quiet until finally, finally, finally I pass on and return here the right way. The next time I am here will be for my final rest. To cross over. Only when my body finally breaks and I take all of its violence and secrets and burdens with me back into the ground.

But first, I must finish this. First, I must find Rona.

She is here, among the sea of sagging souls at my feet.

Get away from here. Before Abazel can further poison my thoughts. This is what I need to do.

The light burns bright and hot inside me, writhes and tugs with impatience. I give into it.

It pulls me forward, down into the Pits.

I follow. Stride around Abazel, bracing myself for a fight as I pass him. But he just eyes me coolly, his arms crossed over his chest. *Why won't he stop me?* A flash of fear crashes over me, but the light surges against it. I reach the ledge and lower myself into the rancid splits in the ground, into the awful stench of death.

"Rona! Rona!"

Can she hear me?

Would she have it in her to respond if she did?

"Rona!"

I roar her name as loud as I can. It is swallowed in the haze.

But I will find her if I have to check every last soul in the realm. The light will lead me. Won't let me stop until I do.

The chill in the Pits is almost unbearable, even with the light to combat it. They wrestle through me, battling flashes of fire and ice. The air is filled with a dense slippery stench that hangs in the thick haze like seaweed. Its film seeps into my skin, illuminated by the broken light of the flickering souls sprawled around me, scabbed, rotting, and dim.

"You waste your time," Abazel calls down to me. He trails my steps from the ledge. "You will never find her."

Abazel and his demon tower over me from the ledge. He's smiling that monstrous thin smile. This is why he let me pass. He's toying with me. He's this sure I won't succeed. But then why bother showing himself at all?

"I will."

I have to. Without her, there is nothing else. I must bring her back. Must get my soul. Abazel's lies only make me more determined.

"Try if you must. It will not matter," he shrugs.

But he is watching me too carefully — he's worried. I try to block him out. Let the light guide me.

"It is a pity to see you go to such waste. You could

be so much more than the puppet they have made you," he calls down to me. "They feed you commands and you unquestioningly ingest them as if they were your own will."

My mouth goes dry like parchment. A puppet? Not for long. Not with a soul. But first, Rona.

I crouch to one of the souls at my feet. It is curled in on itself like a wounded dog, its light obscured by a number of dark flecks, sores, festering infection. Its head is buried under its arms.

I reach out my hand, my fingers straining to recoil. I force them steady and place them on the soul's arm. My fingers slide against a grungy film covering it as I pull it toward me to uncover its face. Chills burst up my arm.

It gives in without any sign that it feels my hand. Its head rolls toward me. Dried and cracked and blank, puckered in like a skull.

But it's not her.

I step to the next one, untangling its limp form and lifting its head.

Not her.

"Look at all you have suffered protecting their interests. Your maker, and now Kythiel. All those murders you watched yourself perform. The ages you have spent alone and afraid. The injuries and risks you have taken getting here. Even that Epoh woman, she bound you to the child, and you just added it to your burdens without thought."

That Epoh woman. As if Miriam was nothing. As if none of this meant anything.

I don't look up. Try to block him out, focus on

quieting the rage that rumbles through me.

"Do you not feel the weight of it all, Adem? Do you not feel them pressing down on you? All those strings binding you to them, forcing your hand? They are beginning to tangle and knot. They will tie you down completely, if you let them."

It's unstoppable. His words leak into my mind like poison, seep in the cracks.

Because I can feel them.

The strings.

Pulling, always pulling me in all directions. They tug at me all the time, weigh down my every step. There is no choice that is mine. There is only the strings. And now that I feel them, I know they were always there.

One twinges at me now, pulls me back to focus. The light demands that I find Rona.

I step to the next soul.

Not her.

"Where is she?"

I feel the seed he's planted within me growing, twisting around the strings. Questions and doubt choke my brain like weeds.

Not now. I can't do this now. Get Rona. Get out.

Find her.

I will.

Each soul I touch shoots another chill through me. They ball together in my core, a piercing cold I can no longer ignore. My teeth begin to rattle.

The demon chirps into Abazel's ear. Abazel listens, and then nods.

The demon leaps into the air, dissolves into a burst

of shadow, and then twists back together into a new shape. A shape that fills me with rage and longing.

The shape of not-Jordan.

"Please stay," it says. "We will go back to the sea."

It is cruel, how accurate the demon's figment is. The same bright wild hair. The wide eager grin. It tears at my core.

"Don't you like us? Stay and protect us. Please. Don't let the realm's barrier break. Not yet."

I breathe in deep to steady the wild pulsing within me. Step to the ledge.

I grab the child — *not real, not real, not real* — by his shirt and lift him up, squirming against me, so he is level with my face. I look deep into those false gray eyes. Something inside me pleads to put him down, follow him back to the shore and just let all this pain, all these choices and burdens end.

"No."

It shatters into shadow and slips through my fingers. I roar into the fluttering chaos. "Where is Rona?" My voice breaks under the weight of the question.

For a heaving pause, all I can hear in the wake of my howl is the faint moans of the dead and inside my head the charged buzz of adrenaline. The after burn of not-Jordan's image is behind my eyes when I blink. I shake it away. I keep pushing through the souls, checking each one. Each one I touch adds to the cold. As I reach out my hand, I realize I'm shivering.

A new voice calls to me from where they stand.

"And what then, after you find her? Do you really think you're worthy of going back to Terath?"

It sounds familiar, but I can't place it. The stinging taste of regret coats my tongue.

I can't help it. I look again.

A strong young body cloaked in deep red. Blood drips from the open gash across his gut. It's the Hunter, the last one I killed.

Not it's not. Not real.

"You'll just continue the cycle. You'll just keep on killing."

The blood still drips out of him, hot and fresh. It covers his hands like it did as he lay dying on my temple floor, trying to keep his life inside him.

He's not real.

But he's still right.

In Terath, all the rules will be in place again. The Hunters will never stop coming. And I can't stop what I'll do to them.

But if I stay...at least here I am in control.

Still I have to go back.

Because going back is the only way to end all this, too. I'm done with hiding. I'm done with the box determining my actions. Getting my soul will make it all stop. It will break the box's hold.

I kneel to the next soul. Not her.

"And what of the others who have fallen to your bloodlust?"

A new voice. I whip around to see and immediately wish I hadn't.

The Silencer glares back at me, his head disconnected and limp on his neck, twisted with streaks of blue bruises.

"You think you only kill because you have to? It's

time you admitted to yourself what you really are. You love the kill. You will never stop killing. You will never be free of the thirst for blood."

My fingers remember the feel of being around his throat, the anger, the power, the thrill.

"No. I can control it."

"You don't control anything. They control you."

My fingers twitch. They crave to strangle him all over again.

Abazel steps in front of the demon-Silencer. "You've killed too much to stop now. It's what you were made for. I know the darkness that lives in you, the rage. You belong here with us now. Where you can put it to use."

It's not true, I tell myself. It's lies. Tricks to slow me down. I must be getting close, for him to act so desperately.

But a small voice inside me whispers—what if it's true?

At least part of it is.

Because there is something in me that wants it. The kill. The action. It roars within me even now, begs to be let loose, to rip off the Silencer's head, and end his taunting.

The power, the unrestrained struggle, the lights going dim behind his eyes. There's a brilliant flash of it in every kill. And then it is over and it is swallowed in the guilt, the disgust at what I've done. But it's always been there. I've been afraid to look it in the eye. Afraid of the monster I really am underneath. Can I control it? It is worth the risk, more lives ripped away by my hands?

Maybe I should stay here, find a dark corner to wrap myself away in. Bury myself somewhere I can't hurt anyone.

Something inside me fights back.

Maybe it is the right thing to do. I can't tell anymore. But I can't do it.

I have to go back.

Not just for my soul. Not just for my promise to Jordan.

It's where I belong. After so many ages spent across Terath, it is mine. I am made of its very earth, and my body craves to return to it. It is where my home is, where my hope lies, where the answers are that I need.

"Where is Rona?"

"Why? So you can go back to Terath and send more of its souls to join me?" the Silencer sneers.

"Where is Rona?"

"Is there no end to the wake of your destruction?"

"Where is Rona?"

"Give it up, Adem," Abazel steps to the ledge, the Silencer shatters into shadow and collects again at his shoulder. "This entire mess is far beyond hope. Rona. You. All of it."

The word floats in the space between my ears, swells inside me—hope, *hope*, HOPE—until there is nothing else.

The light expands with it; a wild throbbing that takes over, blocks out the world, and fills me with giddy joy.

Beyond hope?

Jordan's bright eyes come to me in my mind. There is always hope. When you take everything else away, hope is what's left. I have to believe this. How else can I go on?

"Come now, Adem." Abazel stretches out a pale hand to me.

I shut my eyes.

I stop trying and just listen.

The light is strong, angry, and burning hot. Railing at me to go forward. For me to give in to it and let it lead.

So I do. I give in.

The light erupts over me, a painful searing force. It takes over, blinds me, and forces me forward.

It races me through the Pits with my eyes still shut, my legs barely keeping up with the pull. Abazel calls out after me. He sounds far away, nothing more than an echo.

The light grows and grows until there is no room for anything else. Until the light is all I am. I can see it behind my eyelids and feel it tingling in my fingertips. And then without warning, it bursts. Spills over me like a fiery explosion as it leaves me. Brings me to my knees with a raspy cry.

When I open my eyes, somehow I know the soul in front of me is her. From my head to my toes, I pulse with searing elation.

I reach my fingers into the mess of hair, stroking my thumb across her once-proud cheek bone.

"Rona."

I try to keep the roughness out of my voice.

She is motionless. Dead to the world.

"So," Abazel hovers from the ledge, panting. "You found her after all."

I turn to him, still cradling Rona's limp soul in my arms. His mouth is pulled in to a terse line.

"It changes nothing, you know. Believe me when I tell you, her condition made her easy to collect. She chose this. She will not waken. It makes no difference what you try, you will not succeed. She is too far lost. Come with me instead."

I turn my back on him. Focus on Rona. He was wrong I would not find her, and he is wrong about this too.

Rona is all that matters now.

"Rona. Rona, listen to me." There is no way to tell if she does or not. "I am Adem. I have come for you. To take you back to Terath."

She remains a limp heap.

"I have come to bring you back."

Nothing.

A pit starts to form in my chest. She's not coming.

"Do you see now, Adem? There is no point to this. You have done what you came for. You have offered her this second life, and she has made her choice. Put an end to this now. Come with me, and we will find something better for you. Something your own."

Abazel's voice carries a sharp edge to it, thin and tense. I push it away and steady myself with slow breaths, trying to slow my shivering shoulders. I just have to keep trying until she hears.

I lean in close to her so Abazel can't hear. The rotten stench of the souls is losing its sharp edge. What to say? What could possibly bring her back? She must come. I did not come this far to turn back empty-handed.

I kneel down, placing my head in the sod inches from hers. Run my fingers over the side of her face, around her slack jaw. "Rona?"

Nothing. The growing pit in my chest swells with fear. She has to, she has to wake up.

"Rona!" It comes out in a fierce growl this time, the force of all the fear inside me behind it. I give her head a sharp shake.

Her sunken lids lift to me. I choke on a gasp and try to keep my hold on the moment.

I speak softer now. "Rona. Come with me. Now." But she pulls back into herself. Curls in and buries her head in her knees.

"No."

I stand.

"No!" I shake her by her thin shoulder. "No. Get up. You have to get up!" Lifeless at my feet. Deathless.

Abazel's mocking laugh hangs in the acrid air. Too soon. My back stings, my muscles ache, my entire body shakes from the cold, but I'm not done yet. Nowhere close. I kneel to her side again, put my palm to her face. With my other I take her hand, remembering Ceil's soothing touch on my own hand. I squeeze it.

"Rona? I'm sorry, Rona. Please, listen to me."

Her lids flutter halfway open.

"Please Rona, you must come. I cannot leave without you. I cannot face Kythiel and tell him I failed."

Her eyes shoot open. "K...K..."

The pain, the chill, the desperate clinging—all of it lifts from me like magic.

"Kythiel? Yes! Kythiel!"

She bolts upright with speed I could not have imagined she possessed. She turns her head side to side, searching with tense energy. Possessed.

"He's not here. We must go. Let's go, Rona." I try to reel myself in, contain myself to match her energy, to not do anything that might scare her back within.

She is on her feet in a second. Wired and alert on weak, wobbly legs. She is too skinny, covered with bruises and sores. Her clothes are tattered and torn. Through one hole I can see the wound she gave herself in the end, a large cut across her middle, a festering gaping raw slice.

I take her hand. "Come, Rona, I will take you back."

"No!"

It is Abazel, his voice twisting through the haze, sharp and wild.

I turn to him. He forces his grimace back into its stoic mask. A tight grin stretches over his lips. His eyes are hot and simmering. Feathers twitch in his dark wings.

"You will never make it back to Terath. It's a miracle you made it this far." He's quiet, but his voice wobbles as if on a tightrope.

My hand is going numb with cold where it is pressed to Rona's. The throbbing pain pulses through my wounds with each shiver, through my chest, my toes, and my fingertips.

"The realm is already angered by your very presence here. And you want to break the Order and bring a soul back to Terath? Break through the barrier again? Can't you feel it? The waves of your disruption are magnifying."

Even as he speaks, a faint rumble shakes the ground under my feet.

Rona sways, too weak to hold herself steady over the rumbling. I grab her arm to keep her from falling.

I need to get her out of here. I turn to run.

I don't make it one step.

A force drags me down from behind, shoves me onto my back, and pins me to the cracked dirt. Abazel pulls my head up by the neck of my cloak, his great wings spreading their full length.

"Where is it? Where is the necklace? I can feel it, I know it's here," he hisses.

All this and he was after the same thing as all the others. It all comes down to the same frenzied attacks.

But why? What could he possibly want with it?

"You cannot have it."

I have to get away; it's my only chance. I'm no match for an angel, even on Terath. And right now the pain is taking over and my breaths are rattling in my chest.

But not without the box. Is this what he wanted all along? Is this why he let me make it so far? I've brought it right to him. I can't imagine what a necklace would do for him, but if he wants it, he surely has something terrible in store. I can't let him have it.

I wrestle myself free and swing a punch to his head, sending bolts of sharp pain through my back and down my arm.

He slams me down into the ground. "It does not belong to you. The humans have no right to have it in their realm. It belongs to Calipher."

Calipher? Who is Calipher?

I kick him away with all the strength I can muster, turn toward Rona.

Fingers wrap around my ankle, I crash into the ground, rocks scraping under me as he drags me back to him. His knuckles slam into my face and my head rings, a strange vibration that starts between my eyes and waves over my skull.

This is Abazel weakened?

He pats me down, hands frantically searching me over. I shake my vision back just in time to catch a double image of his hand ripping the box from my cloak. The demon cackles from the ledge. But his chest is heaving. He's wearing himself down.

A gruesome roar stretches over the Pits, and I realize as I leap to the box that it came from me.

I throw myself at him and we wrestle for it, a blur of shoves and kicks and punches and searing pain, but I push it to the back of my mind. The box is clenched in Abazel's hand. I reach for it, slamming his arm in the ground to shake it from his grip. Again. Again. But still he holds it tight, holds it as if it is his life. I smash and smash and smash his arm into the ground, he squeezes the box, and finally something gives way.

The box cracks and bursts open. Shimmering shards of painted wood fly everywhere, and Abazel's grip loosens for just a flash as the box crumbles, a shimmer of emerald and gold flash inside his hand. I swipe it away fast, before he can react. Broken chunks of wood and cool smooth chain bite into my fist. My other hand brushes against the ground, scoops up as much of the box's pieces as I can as I turn away and run to Rona. I scoop her into my arms without stopping, running without knowing where to go, just anywhere but here.

"Stop them." Abazel's command is quiet and sharp, huffed out between heaves.

The demon-shadow rushes toward me, materializes at my side to claws at my fist. I whip my arm to throw it off. A rise of screeches and cackles edge toward the Pits, an army of demons responding to Abazel's command, a hoard of shadow closing in from all sides.

Faster.

The shadows whoosh at us, materialize at my sides to claw, grab, and bite.

My strength is no match for their speed, rustling through the air and swarming at us from all around. One keeps flying back to my hand, picking at the chain to free the necklace from my fist. I throw it off again.

I don't know how long I can bear the strain, the hurt, the cold. But I keep pumping my legs, my breaths heaving and rasping, to propel us forward. *Just a little longer. And a little more after that. As long as it takes.*

But then, a faint shimmering in the air at the edge of my eye.

I pull back, my heels digging into the hard ground, dredging it up in crumbles as I swerve away, so abruptly the demon shadows rush right past us. Rona gasps.

Is it?

I squint back at it, strain to find it again.

Yes. There.

It's a glimmer.

I reach into my cloak's side pocket and I laugh aloud at my relief as my fingers run over something cool and smooth. The Keeper's glimmer stone, it's still there. But there's no time to waste. I have only seconds before the demons are back on us. I use it to pull out the stone and turn toward our only hope for escape.

The demons are on top of us again in seconds, surrounding us in whooshing shadows, nipping at my skin.

Almost there.

The ground's rumbles are still growing, the earth cracking and splitting below my feet. It rises through me in panicky quakes, every tremor echoing painfully through my gut, my shoulder, my head, as if my body could just crumble apart.

I reach the glimmer just in time. I shift Rona onto my shoulder, brace against the pain and chilling cold, and roll the stone over three times between my palms and whisper, "The river."

Then I leap toward the glimmer and tighten my arms around Rona.

A demon materializes at my wrist, grabs on with its claws and digs its teeth into the side of my hand. It shakes violently until my skin tears, until my smallest finger separates from my hand with a sickening rip and pain so strong it edges into my vision. I feel a cry rise against my throat rough and raw, like choking on gravel. My hand seizes and draws back against the pain.

As the glimmer pulls Rona and me in and the world collapses around us, I glance back just in time to see the demon materialize on the ground, my finger between its teeth and something gold clinking between its claws.

It got the necklace.

A vacuum of panic swells in my chest as the glimmer collapses around us.

CHAPTER 22

THE GLIMMER CRUNCHES me down to nothing and throws me into oblivion. I can't breathe.

I lost the necklace.

All these ages I've guarded it. All the lives I've taken in the name of keeping it safe. And now it's slipped right through my fingers. For so many years this is exactly what I wished for—to find a way to separate from the box, to leave it behind. And now that it's gone, all I feel is panic. An emptiness so powerful it blocks out all the pain, all the cold, all the urgency floods me. A blankness stares right back at me from within with the certainty that I've just let something awful begin.

The glimmer spits us out and we tumble to the ground. It's still rumbling with the realm's anger, crumbling and splitting from the tension. The river rushes in my ears.

Next to me, Rona is gasping for breath.

"Easy. Take it easy."

I tuck the box's leftover pieces into my breast

pocket, placing my one still-whole hand on her back. I take deep breaths with her until they are level again.

Even then, she can't stop shaking. It's more than the trembling ground below her.

"K...K...Kythiel."

"Yes. Kythiel." The rustle of whooshing shadows and demon cackles are rising from the distance. They're coming. "Rona, we have to keep going."

I scoop her into my arms and step to the water's edge. The river tosses wildly. I'm about to dive into it when a creaky voice reaches out and stops me.

"Surely even you know better than *that*, you heap of mud."

I whip around. It's the Keeper.

He's rounding the river's bend, pushing toward us through the choppy waves. I don't know whether to be relieved or afraid.

He shoves the boat toward us with a grunt.

"Are you trying to destroy yourselves? Do you even remember how you got that wound in your shoulder?"

The beast in the water.

A rush of guilt, then gratitude. He's right. We would never have made it out from here. Not if more of those beasts are lurking under the river.

But he betrayed me. Is he just keeping me here until the demons can catch up?

"How did you find us?"

I almost have to shout to be heard above the rumbling.

He gestures out to the realm. "Everything knows where you are. I warned you. I told you, don't disturb the realm. It's raging now."

The demons' calls are getting louder. Closer.

He pauses and looks me over. "By the Gods. You look terrible."

"Why are you here?" I growl.

The ground is shaking with rage. I am shaking with weakness. In my arms, Rona is shaking with fear.

Another hard push with his staff and the Keeper is at the shore, the tip of his boat at my side.

"I—" he fidgets at the staff with his hands. "I came to help you get out."

"To *help*?" I growl, "You have helped enough already."

He drops his head, stares down at his worn, wrinkly hands.

"It's the realm traps. The treasures. It eats at me. There's a reason I stay at my helm. And that box...its power..." His head whips back to me. His eyes pull together and push wrinkles all over his face. "Where is it?"

"It's gone." Salt in the wound. My anger toward him wells up again.

"Oh. Gods." He shifts in his cloak. The water splatters and sputters around us as the realm's trembling grows and grows and grows.

The Keeper glances past me as he pushes the boat to the shore, the lines of his face deep and grim.

"You're out of time."

I follow his glance over my shoulder—a cloud of whooshing shadows is closing in.

"It's them or me." The Keeper stretches out an arm to pull me up.

I'm out of options, and I've got nothing left for him

to take anyway. I take it, the raw stub where my finger used to be throbbing. He pulls us into the boat, and as he pushes us off into the raging waters, I set Rona down on the bench.

The realm's rumbling swells, the river rages. Thick chunks of crumbled rock tumble from above. Demons swarm around us. But the Keeper is stronger than he looks. Somehow, he keeps us moving forward.

The pain and cold run so deep, it's all I am anymore. But I cling to Rona, trying to shield her from the attack.

Ahead, the river's mouth opens into a wide, churning abyss. The staff cuts into the river, the boat twists against its pull. The Keeper's every muscle is strained with the effort to keep it steady as it swerves. His face is dripping with sweat and splashes from the water. His breaths heave. "Go!"

I stand, lifting Rona into my arms. I step to the edge of the boat, but something tugs at my gut and holds me back.

The Keeper came through. In the end. We made a deal. I can't give him what he wanted, but there is something I can give him.

I turn and reach out to the Keeper. "Come with us."

He draws away. The boat dips warily. "What?"

The cackles of the demons echo toward us, closer and closer.

"Come with us. Back to Terath." I can't just leave him here to their mercy.

His eyes bulge wide. "I cannot leave!" He pushes my arm away.

"But—" I don't understand. "I can bring you back.

You can live again."

"You mean I can die!" he hisses. "If I leave this place I forfeit my immortality.

Even if your angel were to give me more years, I'll end up right back here. I will be forced to go out into the Underworld to cross over. I cannot face it. I will not! Leave me be! Get out!"

His whole body trembles. Fear. He is so afraid to die he will not go back and live.

The surprise, the confusion, the helplessness stir through me—and then they're swallowed in urgency. There's no time. Over the Keeper's shoulder, the cloud of demon shadows are closing in, almost close enough to reach out and grab me.

I pull Rona tight to my chest, step to the boat's edge and jump.

The demon shadows rush around me as I soar toward the water. Their teeth take sharp nips at my heels as we plunge into the water.

And then the river swallows us. Chilling. Wild. The rushing current drowns out all else, the familiar heaviness seeps into me as the water soaks between my particles. I shift Rona against my shoulder and pull hard with my other arm, a pain straining through me with each stroke, biting at my hand, my side, twisting through my shoulder. But I got myself here, and I will get us back.

As we rise back toward the surface, sharp pecks of demon teeth nip at me, a cyclone of shrieks following. The river thrashes and bites, tosses and teases. With each stroke, I *pull, pull, pull.* Somehow, I tug us forward against the current. The water begins to tip, and suddenly I am fighting against an upward current, pulling against a tilting wall, and then finally a surge, the strange sensation of falling up. A sudden burst and we are pulled under, an impossible tug and flow in all directions.

And then suddenly, stillness.

CHAPTER 23

THE NUMBING PAIN of my wounds.

The piercing cold.

The aching exhaustion in my muscles.

It all begins to loosen, break down, and float away into the gentle pull of the waves. The poison softly drifts out of my shoulder, the throbbing sting where my finger used to be eases as smooth skin closes over it.

I stop swimming and pop my head up.

The sea stretches as far as I can see in all directions. Nothing but dark, starry vastness expands overhead, reflecting off the water. The waves are the only sound, a soft whisper. The Keeper, the vicious cackling, and the rushing demon shadows are all gone.

We made it.

Rona's arms are wrapped tight around my neck, but they no longer piercing me with the Underworld's terrible cold. She gasps for air through tight dried lips, coughs up water. I'd assumed that when I got her here she'd be better, healed. Like I did. But she's barely more than a corpse, her skin still as weathered and depleted as the tortured soul I found her as in the Underworld.

But she's here. We made it.

I lean back and stare at the stars, let the relief soak through me.

And then Rona releases a raspy scream that stretches over the waves and rattles deep in my stomach.

I jolt up. Her hands clutch at her middle, a ring of red is growing around her in the water. Dread tingles over my skin. I push her onto her back to see — her death wound is open again, raw and deep in her starved stomach. She's bleeding out.

A quiver of panic shoots through me and settles at the back of my neck. Did I bring her back only to relive her death then return to the Underworld all over? Her curdling scream is still ringing through the air. Her eyes look to me in a panicked plea for help.

I press my palm to her mouth to muffle the sound. "Shhhh. Shhhh. It will be okay." It has to be.

For now, all I can do is get her to the shore.

I wrap my arm around her, hold her close, as if I can keep her soul from slipping away again if I just cling to her strong enough.

Which way to go? The same endless waves in every direction. I keep on the way we were moving when we crossed, and hope it won't be too far. I pull harder through the water than I ever have before. Through the night and into dusk. Rona drags along, whimpering and trembling. It is almost dawn when I see the shore. As I pull her onto the shore, dusky pink light streams over the little hut roofs — we're back at Haven.

Something sweet and peaceful surges in my chest, like coming home, a feeling that all will be well. But not yet.

I shove away Rona's tattered shirt to examine the wound. Her wasted middle is a mess of blood. It pools around the wound and puddles in her starved stomach. I push the waves over her to wash it away and examine the wound. She flinches. More blood begins to pool immediately. I grab the edge of my cloak and press a handful of soaked cloth into her.

The cut is deep, jagged. In the short pauses between the swells of blood, I can see the shiny pink of organs underneath where it splits apart. The smell is strong — the steely sharpness of fresh blood mixed with the awful death-stench of the Pits.

The sun is reaching over the shore, stretching our shadows long over the sand. The villagers will begin to rise soon. The children will come out and start their games. *Jordan.* But I can't think about him now. What matters now is Rona, keeping her alive. We have to get somewhere safe, somewhere hidden.

I break from my mopping, slide my arms under her as gently as I can, slowly lift her up. She gasps, eyes opening wide, and then slips away, unconscious. The blood spills out of her onto my chest, drips down my cloak.

We need somewhere we can be safe, somewhere we won't be seen. I scan past the village and up the horizon.

The cave. It's still there, still calling to me just as it did last time. Safe. Secluded. Hidden.

Yes.

I wade through the waves to hide my steps as I carry her down the shore toward it as quickly as I can. Dank salty air and echoes of the waves and the damp dark rock embrace me into the cave's mouth. I lay out my cloak on a large rock inside it then place Rona carefully on top of it. The pooled blood spills over her sides.

How will I hide her body if she dies? What will I tell Kythiel? The thoughts leak into my mind through the cracks no matter how I try to keep them out. It's no wonder this wound killed her once. I hope by the Gods that Kythiel knew what he was doing. That it won't send her right back to the Underworld again.

The day stretches out. Rona goes on, delirious, stiff and still as death, not even knowing where she is. Her skin is pale and puckered, more corpse than living. I go through more pieces of my cloak, press them against her wound until they are stained, dark, and can't hold any more blood.

She moans, weakly turns her head in short periods of half-waking. In her sleep, she passes between deadly stills and fits of horror. I have to stifle her screams with my hand to keep the village from hearing and I know if I hold her too tight, I will press the life right out of her. But how hard is too hard? I keep watch over her, powerless to do anything but soak up the life leaking out of her. Horrified at what I've brought her back to suffer.

Once it is dark, I step out to the sea to rinse the stiff coagulated blood out of my cloak so I can keep holding it against her. And then again before morning. As I dip the strips of cloth in the waves, I glance to the village. Could they help her? What could they possibly do for someone so far gone? What could I even say to explain? My gut says Kythiel wouldn't want the interference. Surely, he knows. He'll be here soon. Any moment. And he could do so much more for her than any human healer.

Every time I press the salty wet cloths against her, she flinches against it. I don't think the bleeding will ever stop. But eventually the handfuls of cloth I press into her don't darken as quickly. The wound seems smaller than it was before. Her restlessness eases and she relaxes into a more restful sleep. Finally, I can stop, and perch near her on a rock by the cave's mouth.

I've never seen a human heal so quickly — or recover at all, from a wound so severe. But healing it is. Already her skin is regaining some of its color, the stench of death beginning to leave her. I've no explanation, except that her death is reversing itself.

The village is still wrapped in dusk, the waves padding at the sand, when Rona draws slow breaths. In the stillness a thousand anxieties begin to emerge that were until now drowned in the urgency of keeping Rona alive.

Kythiel, how much longer?

If she doesn't make it, the back of my mind whispers, will Kythiel hand over my soul? I've done my part. All I could. He didn't warn me she'd die all over again when she got here. My soul, my soul, my soul, my soul — no matter how many times I roll the words over I can't make them stick together.

And then there is the necklace.

It's gone.

I'm left with nothing but splinters of painted wood.

It's just what I've tried and tried for, the one thing I wanted all my centuries of being. But a well of feeling heavy as bricks drags at me. The wrong way, the wrong hands now hold it. I should be grateful I'll never have to hide another Hunter's body and leave it alone. I should forget all about it.

But.

It's my fault.

Whatever Abazel wanted, whatever he plans to do with it, it's only because of me that he can. I brought it right to him.

Morning sounds begin to rise. Birds call across the sky. Crabs scuttle over the beach. Doors open in the village. Children run through its open center as the women pull out the large pots and begin the morning meal. From a safe distance, I scan through them for a head of red wild curls. I listen for that voice, alive and sparking.

But Jordan isn't there.

A slow terror worms its way into me.

A boney hand clutches my cloak and rips me away from my thoughts. Rona—she grabs me with sudden strength, her eyes rolling to lock with mine. Her cracked lips part.

"Water," she whispers.

She speaks. The excitement raises little bumps down my arms. She's getting stronger. Maybe she'll make it after all.

Still, alarm rings through me about Jordan, but there's no choice but to push it aside for now. Focus on

Rona. On what I can fix.

She pulls me toward her, her eyes wide. *"Water,"* she gasps. Then she collapses back into unsettling stillness.

Water—the word hits me like a tidal wave. Of course. Humans must drink—humans must *eat*. No wonder she has not healed. I look over her depleted body, the ribs sticking out through her shirt like they're trying to break free, the shriveled skin stretched tight against her sharp hipbones, the puckering tautness at her jaw. My fault.

Water. Now. Lots of it. I run out of the cave toward the sea, never mind that someone might see us—if Rona doesn't make it, that doesn't matter anymore.

I scoop the waves into my hands, run it back to her. She appears unconscious. I freeze—which does she need more, the water or the rest? The water drips between my hands and splatters against her face. Her eyes snap open and she pulls my hands to her mouth, gulping furiously.

More.

I run back and forth, back and forth, unable to keep up with her thirst.

I hold another handful to her lips. She parts them hungrily to take it, and then turns away. A hoarse gagging cough wracks her. Thin shoulders shake and quiver. I bring her more. She drinks. Beads of sweat grow over her forehead and all over her face. Her eyes grow bloodshot. But still she reaches for the water dripping from my hands, so I keep racing back to bring her more.

She collapses back. I sit. I wait. But edginess

wrestles in me and I can't let go of the feeling that something is wrong. She's getting worse, not better.

All I can do is sit. Wait. Watch her too-fast breaths rush in and out of her chest.

My hands quiver with rage. Where is Kythiel? This is too much, too long.

Suddenly she lurches up and leans forward. It all comes back up in gagging heaves, all the water I brought her. It splatters hard against the rock.

Over and over.

Tears drop from her eyes, her face is coated in a sticky film of cold sweat. The water she coughs back up starts to show worrying threads of red.

Finally it stops.

She begs for more water.

I run to the shore's edge and draw more of it into my hands, my temples throb with helpless alarm. Even when she gets stronger, she gets weaker again, even weaker than before. She is slipping away as quickly as the water cupped in my hands. And all I can do is meet her demands for more water and watch her struggle to keep it down as the sun rises then drops in the sky and leaves the darkness to wrap its emptiness around me. My mind fills with racing fears I cannot stop.

All this to bring her back, and now the only thing I can do to help her is killing her. And Kythiel, where is he, where is he. Foreboding darkness wrestles in my gut. Behind the anxiety for Rona, more fears unravel and tug at me, fill me like a flood. My fingers compulsively trace the rough nub where my small finger used to be. Somewhere beyond in the other realm, Abazel has the necklace. And Jordan, where's

Jordan? What's happened to him?

"What have you done?"

A sharp voice shocks me back to the cave's darkness. The voice is low and pierces through me with a chill. No one's ever snuck up on me before. Not once. I whip around from Rona's side to face it.

Just outside the cave stands a tall figure, a dark red hood encased in the dim moonlight.

A Hunter.

The familiar murky dread seeps through my chest, quivering with fear and an urge for the fight. But that's over now, there's nothing left to fight for. The box is gone. The necklace is gone.

"Again, so soon?" I do my best to keep the trembling out of my voice. Here we go again. He'll demand the box. Except now, there's nothing left to give. Just broken splinters of wood.

I inch closer to him, try to block his view of Rona. The beginnings of a dark beard frame a dark face and dark, weathered eyes.

"Soon?" His eyebrows burrow down over his eyes. "It has been ten years since we could last even trace you."

It's as if the ground crumbles away from below me.

"Ten years?"

I shove past him out of the cave's mouth, facing out toward the village. Look closer. *Ten years?* It's not possible.

"What have you done with it?" the Hunter urges. "Where is the magic you carry?"

How could he possibly know about the box? But I can't explain it all right now. My mind is tangled up in the first thing he said.

I look around me. For real this time. Carefully.

Ten years?

The sea is the same. The shore is the same. But the village.

The village has grown, with more huts in large rings around its center. I've been too caught up in Rona to notice. My mind lingers back over my journey, traces through the time. How long did I wander those dark paths through the Underworld? It's all a blur. For me a decade can pass in a blink after all my time. Days become meaningless with endless time.

"But..."

Before I can pull the words together to ask him anything more, a strained cry echoes out of the cave. Rona.

The Hunter hears it too. He rushes into the cave. "No—" I chase after him, but by the time I'm there, he is already standing over her, his face blank with shock.

I see her now with fresh eyes. The way the Hunter must see her—not by how far she's come, but how far she is from well. Pressure rises from my toes, over my legs, my chest, my neck, and finally my head.

So small, all shriveled and rotted, she lies limp from exhaustion, her chest just barely rising and falling enough to prove she has life. Her face is vacuous, sallow, and shrinking into her skull. The wound across her stomach is even smaller now, but she is covered in rusty, caked red. The stench of death still lingers, trapped in the cave's dank air.

The Hunter's eyes snap to me as I enter. He stands between us, as if he could block me from her. "I will ask again. What have you done?"

A seed of rage hardens in me against the Hunter. He should not be here.

"What have you done?" he demands. My head grows hot. My fingers itch to snap his throat. His words bore into my conscience. The truth is I don't know what I've done.

"I know what you are here for," I growl, shoving him away from Rona, "This does not concern you. Leave now and I will spare your life."

"All innocents concern us," he says. "We knew something was different when you reappeared. What have you been doing? What have you done to her?"

He leans over, stretches his arms out to take her.

"Don't move her!" I growl. "You'll do her more harm."

I'm all too aware of the suffering I have brought on her, the starved half-life she's living. Every flinch of pain, every drop of blood that surged out of her, every cry. But I swore to bring her back to him. I'm too close to lose her now.

"I am taking her with me."

"No. You will die first."

Rona moans, her eyes roll open. When she sees the Hunter standing over her she fights weakly against him. Looks to me. "Help."

The Hunter steps back. Looks to me, stunned.

Rona's head lies limply to the side, her cracked lips too dry, and her tongue dry as it rolls over them. She needs more water.

Enough.

I step over Rona and dig my fingers into the

Hunter's neck, lift him close to my face so he can feel my height, see the glint of my teeth as I form the words.

"You will not take her," I spit the words into his face. He writhes and twists to keep the life inside of him. "You will come with me, and you will stop meddling in what you do not understand."

I give him a hard stare, and then put him back down. I loosen my fingers, but keep my hand around his neck. He coughs and gags.

"I will tell you what you need to know, and then you will leave."

I tighten my grip on the Hunter's neck, sticky and writhing for gasping breaths, and steer him out of the cave to the waves. I stare at the moonlight glistening off the water for a moment, realizing I must let go of him to scoop up the water. Reluctantly I loosen my fingers, reach down, and fill my cupped hands.

"Follow me."

The Hunter keeps his lips pursed tight, his eyes darting wildly, taking in every movement.

Back to the cave. I hold my dripping hands over her for her to drink.

"What are you doing?" he exclaims.

That question again.

The Hunter's hand is stretched out hesitant, confused. I can smell the fear coming off him in sweaty beads.

"She needs water."

"Not salt water! She'll be sick."

His words yank through me as if a hook were plunged into my side.

Sick?

The water drips between my hands and splatters at my toes.

"What do you mean?"

"She needs fresh water. She can't drink from the sea. It won't help her. It will make her worse."

"Fresh water."

"Yes. A river. Or—" His hand idly drifts to his head and pulls at a fistful of hair, pushing his hood gently away. "Where do the rest of them get their water?"

Haven.

I squeeze my eyes shut and reach back deep into my memory. Before the Underworld. In the village. They brought us buckets filled with water. Where did it come from? My jaw clenches with the strain to dig back. The woman brought it to us. From behind the huts.

I open my eyes.

There's a well.

I passed it when I first carried Jordan here. Behind the village.

"You're coming with me."

I lead him out of the cave by his neck. I don't grip as hard this time.

The well. It was just behind the last row of houses. But that was then. Before I left and ten years passed by. Before the village expanded and the rings of huts grew. We'll have to walk right through them to get to it now.

I guide the way around the huts until we're at the farthest point from the shore. I stay to the soft sand and out of the reeds that rustle and snap. Grains of sand rub at my feet and stick between my toes. The moon is just starting to tip down in the sky over us, swollen, just shy of a full circle. There's no movement, no sound but chirping crickets as I lead us between the huts. Urgency and resolve prickle across my skin.

We're exposed here. Nowhere to hide should one of these villagers hear us, or simply come out to take in the breeze.

Ten years.

I have to stop myself from reaching out and running my fingers along the fresh wood of the huts we pass along Haven's outer rings. A full decade. Yet another that's slipped away from me like no more than a deep breath. But for humans it's an age. No wonder I couldn't find Jordan among the children. He'd be a man by now. There's no telling where he's gone in so much time.

A bucket dangles over the well with a reel. Just as before. I lower it down, each creak of the wooden spool quivering through my fingertips. The Hunter stands by, studying the huts. He stands steady, but I can hear the fast unsteady rhythm of his heartbeats. He hasn't asked about the box again. But he will. The dread quivers inside me with his every move.

A splash echoes up from the well, weight tugs at the reel as the bucket fills.

I wind the rope back up, reach my hands into the bucket to carry back what I can. But the Hunter stops me and pulls out his knife.

Choking anxiety clenches at my throat. *Not here, not now.* A struggle here could wake the whole town. It could ruin everything.

But he just whispers, "More than that."

He presses the blade against the rope to free the bucket. Then he returns it to its sheath. My muscles relax, I take a slow breath in, not sure what I was scared of. He can't hurt me, not here in Terath. After all, he's the one on the right side in all this. I'm the monster who keeps killing them. And I don't have to do that anymore.

The way back is slower. I move deliberate and steady, hold in my breath, determined not to lose a drop. The Hunter stays at my side.

When we are back, I go back into the cave, drop to my knees at Rona's side.

"Here. This will be better, I promise."

She pushes her arms under herself, tries to raise her head, but she is too weak. I place my hand behind her neck, using the other to scoop the water to her mouth. The sharp bones of her spine, her shoulder blades, tighten against my hand as she takes it in. I cup my hands in the bucket and bring it to her to drink, again, and then again.

"That's enough." The Hunter is watching from the cave's mouth. "Give her more in a little while."

She lets out a sigh, rolls her head back. I lay her back across the rock. I watch her a while longer, waiting for the awful struggle to start again. It doesn't.

A soft breeze makes its way into the cave and eases the tension across my shoulders. But it's not over yet.

I step around where Rona rests and face the Hunter. "Come."

I lead him out of the cave into the turning dawn.

CHAPTER 24

WHEN THE SEA breeze touches our faces, the Hunter whips around on me.

"Now it's my turn," he demands. His shoulders are tense and bulging. His fingers hover over his blade.

"What do you want?" I ask.

But I know what he wants. What they all wanted. And I don't have it anymore.

"I want to know *how*," he snaps, his hands balling into fists. "How did you do it?"

My mind goes blank. I don't understand.

"I didn't—I—" The words won't come together. "Do what?"

"You know what," his eyes narrow with impatience. "You cloaked the magic's trace from us. For years. Even now we cannot see all that we could before."

A trace?

The pieces come together in a rush. So this is how they have found me time after time. Just like Abazel and the Keeper, the Hunters can sense the box's magic.

Maybe even mine.

Of course, they can. My slow, dense brain—I should have understood this ages ago.

"I did nothing."

"We know you did," he spits back. "The Sworn have traced all sorts of rogue magic, through Terath for ages. Never have we lost one before."

The Sworn?

It's the same thing the last Hunter called them. The questions pile up and wear on me like bricks, weighing me down. Always, always more questions.

"I was not in Terath."

The Hunter's mouth pulls into a tight line. I hear the quiet rumble of grinding teeth. "And what's that supposed to mean?"

I wrestle for an explanation, for pieces I can give him. The Hunter bores into me with a hard stare, and I'm tired of the secrets, the not knowing, and the dragging it all with me like so much dead weight. It wears me down like the all-encompassing fatigue of the Underworld, and it's too much to bear. But how, how to explain any of it?

A thick pause settles between us as I wrestle with the words, trying to find the right ones. Then the Hunter gasps, looks back toward the cave.

"*Again.*" He whips back to me. "You said you couldn't let her die *again*. She was already dead. You brought her back."

"Yes."

Confessing to it loosens the knotting in my gut.

"Impossible," he accuses. He whips back to me, his face pulled into a fierce glower. "Impossible."

"I..." But I don't have any words for him.

"Impossible!" he yells. "You broke into the Underworld? How? Do you understand what you've done?"

He paces the sand, crosses back and forth in front of me, one hand tangling in his hair.

"Oh Gods." He stops pacing, his face going blank. "What will we do?"

"There is nothing that needs to be done." Cold resentment creeps up from my toes and grips tight across my shoulders. "I saved her. And now it is done. Just leave us."

"How could you dare to so blatantly defy the Order?" His voice is empty now, drifting.

"The Order?" My growing resentment explodes into roaring rage. "I have heard enough of the Order. What have the Three ever done for me? What were they doing for Rona? What have they done for anything, all these ages, or during the Realm Wars? If you could have seen—" I grope for a way to explain it. Rona's soul rotting among the Pits. The terrible piercing cold. The desolation. But I can't find the words. "One of Theia's own angels asked me to do this."

The Hunter's eyes are blank and aimless. He shakes his head slowly side to side and back again, over and over. His eyes pull back to focus, and looks up to me, his face still blank.

"The Order isn't just a set of rules. It's what holds everything together. All the realms...Do you understand what you've done? You have started the chain that will lead to the final Realm War. You broke through the barrier. Gods, you broke through it *twice*. Now that the barrier is weakened, it's a matter of time before the Rebels break free. Before it all begins."

He kicks at the sand, sends grains flying.

"No." The cold tightens its hold like a rope at my throat. "*No.* I've done nothing wrong. I'm helping."

But Abazel. What was it he said? A heavy wave sloshes through me. It was too much like what the Hunter says now.

But no. All of that was a lie.

Wasn't it?

"You've gotten it all wrong," the Hunter presses. "Every step of this quest of yours was wrong. Everything is shifting because of what you did. We have been seeing it in the wind, the sky, the ground under our feet. The entire realm. It's all been shifting. And now I know why. Oh Gods. Who knows where it will settle."

But Abazel wasn't the only one who said it. I drop to the sand under the weight of it all. "He tried to warn me."

"Who?"

"Ceil. This is what he was trying to tell me. But I couldn't understand." My thick, slow, worthless brain. "And Ky—"

And Kythiel stopped him.

"Who is Ceil?" the Hunter asks.

It crashes over me like a fierce wave in a storm. He knew.

"A prophet. In Epoh."

Kythiel knew all this would happen, and he wanted Rona so desperately he didn't care. Why else would he stop Ceil from warning me of it?

"And...what about him?" The Hunter calls me back.

The truth rushes around me, a flood of trouble that is already well over my head.

I turn to the Hunter. "What do I need to do? How do we stop it from happening?"

The Hunter lets go a soft laugh. Shakes his head. His eyes are glassy and bitter. "This is not something that can be undone."

My fists cry to be used, to shatter something to pieces the way these truths are shattering me. It's exactly how Abazel said it would be. It was all true. And I didn't listen. I can see it now, so clearly it hurts.

What else was Abazel right about?

For a pause neither of us speaks. Ocean breezes waft at my cloak. Waves pound nearby. The entire world crashes quietly around me. There is nothing to be said.

Then the Hunter breaks it, clears his throat.

"And what happened to the magic you carry?"

The box. Just when I thought I could not feel any deeper shame.

"It's gone. I lost it."

I lost it, I lost it, I lost it, and now Abazel has it. A phantom twinge pinches where the demon ripped my finger away.

The Hunter's expression empties. "What was it? What happened?"

"You don't know?" I frown. All they've sacrificed. All those lives lost. And they didn't know what for?

He waits.

I owe him the truth, after all I've done.

I dig into my pocket and lay out the pieces of the box's shattered remains. All I was able to snatch away with the necklace when Abazel shattered it in our struggle. Though it didn't matter, in the end.

"I didn't know either. I never would have, if I hadn't..." I swallow the rest of my words. I never would have lost it either, if I hadn't gone to the Underworld. "It was a necklace. A gold chain with a large emerald on it. Big." I show him, rounding my fingers so it would fit just inside. "And rough. Not cut or polished."

I tell him all that I can. How I couldn't stop from killing the other Hunters they sent. How I couldn't protect the box in the Underworld, how I wanted to just leave it there. How the Keeper tried to take it, and then Abazel. I show him the smooth nub at the edge of my hand where my finger used to be, the one the demon bit off. I try to explain the hurt, the awful hurt, and the deep, deep cold of the realm. As I speak, the Hunter's brows knit tighter and tighter together. As he listens, the Hunter's eyes drift off, lost to something beyond me. He shakes his head.

I keep talking. The burden of it all lightens with each word. "He said,—Abazel—he said that it didn't belong to me. That it belongs to Calipher."

The Hunter pulls back, sharp and hyper alert. "Calipher? It can't be." He frowns. "He said it *belongs* to Calipher? Or *belonged*?"

I shut my eyes tight, try to dig up Abazel's demand.

The Hunter grabs my cloak and jerks me forward, leans over the box's pieces toward me.

"Is Calipher alive?"

His face is inches from mine, a cluster of stiff creases, his eyes quivering under the pressure. I strain to dig through all the moments. What was it Abazel said?

"I can't remember."

His hands writhe and twist in my cloak, his breath hot on my face. "Try harder."

"I can't remember," I growl.

I resist the urge shove him away. He can't harm me. Not here, not this realm. A last strain of tension, and then he lets go, slides away. Deflates in defeat.

"Who is Calipher?" I ask.

"Nothing but a myth. At least that's what the Sworn believed."

That name again. *The Sworn*.

The Hunter presses his thumb and forefinger over his eyes. "It was never proven he was real. But the story goes; at the Beginning, Calipher was among the angels who grew too attached to a human. When Theia called them back, he tried to follow Her Order. He left his love and returned to the Host. Before he departed, he gave her a necklace that he had charmed with the power of Gloros. So she never had to be alone and would always be loved as he had loved her himself."

Gloros. "The Goddess of Love." It makes sense.

"Yes. And of passion, lust, desire, obsession, mania. Cycles and interconnectedness," he frowns. "After Calipher left, the story is, he could not forget his human partner, and it eventually drove him mad. When he broke free, his human was aged and had long ago moved on. His disappointment fell into a rage, and he killed her and the man that she'd chosen to replace him, leaving only their young daughter alive, who he took and convinced himself was his own.

"Many ages ago there used to be rumors of such a necklace. But those died out long ago. He was a cautionary tale, we thought. There was nothing to even suggest an angel named Calipher had ever truly existed," the Hunter says. "Until now."

"Is that all the necklace did?"

"If the story is true."

"But—" All this new information. It sticks, catches, and tangles in my mind. "A necklace that causes love? What value could that have for Abazel? He doesn't want love. He wants another Realm War."

The Hunter purses his lips. "I don't know. But magic is always dangerous. I've learned this in my time with the Sworn. And if there's any lesson to be learned in Calipher's story, it's that love can be an extremely dangerous, violent thing."

The sun is coming up and sparkling over the sea. The village will begin to stir any minute. I should be hiding in my cave's shadows by now. By Rona's side. But this is the first time I've gotten answers, and there's so much more to know.

"What is the Sworn? Why do you come for me? What do you hunt this box that you did not even know what it held?"

The questions fly out of me like caged birds set free.

The Hunter stretches his hand out to block himself from them.

"Shael's Sworn," he says. "We are His warriors, giving our lives to fight His cause. We hunt down the magical remains from the Realm Wars and destroy them to restore the peace. We are a brotherhood, sworn and bound to this mission, and we will not rest until all is set right again."

This is why they look for me. Why they keep coming back. I remember the Hunters' souls wandering in unrest through the Nethers. This is why. They won't rest until it's done, all the magic in Terath destroyed. They've been there for ages, will probably be there for ages more.

"And the box?" I ask.

"As I said, we trace the magic that does not belong to this realm. We can find it anywhere," he says. "Well, anywhere in the realm. We knew it was powerful magic, and that it held something else even more powerful inside it. We knew it needed to be destroyed. But it seems we failed."

I shift the broken pieces of the box in my fist and lay the fragments out between us. "This is all that's left of what you came for."

The Hunter leans forward over them, his brow knitted. "Is that a rune written around the border? There's not much to go on anymore, but it might tell us—"

I never find out what it might tell us.

As he speaks, the Hunter reaches to pick up one of the splintered shards to look closer, and what happens unfolds before me as if in slow motion. As if in a dream. A nightmare.

As the wooden shard rolls between his fingers, something else takes over and—*no, no, no*—my hands grip onto the sides of his head—*stop, please, stop*—a sharp snap whips the air as my hands twist his neck until his spine breaks. I am left with another corpse, another flat accusing pair of eyes that never saw it coming, another murdered Hunter, who never got the warning he should have.

A cold deeper than the piercing chill of the Underworld overcomes me. My fingers, my hands, my entire body trembles.

Why is the box's magic still controlling me? The necklace is gone. It was supposed to be over.

But the limp body before me says different.

The old walls that boxed me in all the ages of my existence close in around me again. There is no end. No escape. I plummet through the darkness of this realization, a slow crash and burn as the sun creeps over the horizon, a pain so much greater than the bodily wounds I suffered days before. Too deep to bear.

Answers. He had the answers I need. He helped me. And in my carelessness, I killed him. Why didn't it occur to me the charm might still be on the box's pieces?

"Adem!"

Two short syllables. They crash over me like being plunged into a frozen winter lake. I freeze in the shock of the voice behind me.

CHAPTER 25

THE VOICE REACHES out to me again.

"Adem!"

It is a voice I would know anywhere. In any time.

It's different now. Lower, stronger. But also the same. Still rich with the fresh innocence he had as a boy. Even just one word is enough to know him.

Before me, the Hunter's corpse. The box's broken pieces. A death trap.

My chest swells with eagerness, seizes with panic.

I kneel and pick up the pieces at fast as I can.

"Adem? Do you remember me?"

He takes a hesitant step closer.

"Stay back."

I take the last few scraps into my hand, my head still throbbing from the shock, picking the final one out from the Hunter's still hand. I push them together tight in my fist and tuck them back into the pocket, make sure there's not a single splinter stuck to my hand, no chance of anyone else touching any piece of the box.

Then I turn.

Facing me is a lean and muscled young man. Loose waves of fiery red blow around his head in the breeze. The same easy smile graces his lips.

I feel my own face pulling into something similar, despite what I have just done.

"Jordan."

He leaps forward and wraps his arms around me. How can he be so unreserved? Didn't he see what I did to the Hunter? He must have. A thick pulsing floods my ears. I grope for some way to explain.

But he speaks first. "You are just the same," he exclaims into my shoulder, "Just as large as I remember."

My arm wraps around him too, before I can think.

"And you are all grown," I say. My fist is pressed against his back, a fist that just seconds ago snapped the Hunter's neck. I pull it back.

"You should stay away."

Jordan's smile drops away and his lips pull into a thin line, some of the light falls from his face. "You are just the same. In every way."

"I'm dangerous. This man, he didn't deserve this." I need him to understand.

His eyes drop to the Hunter's body, then back. "I remember the burdens you're trapped with," he says. "I remember all of it."

I fumble for words, trying to tell him again to stay away, but he cuts me off.

"What are you doing here?" he asks. His voice is straining toward joy, confusion, anger, a thousand different directions. "Where have you been all these years?"

It's too much to explain all over again. Too much to relive.

My thumb taps compulsively against my leg, idle, restless, and uneasy.

I search for something, anything else to say. "How did you know I was here?"

He stands a little straighter. "I'm the leader of Haven now."

The other children always followed him in Epoh. He stood up for them. It's easy to imagine the others in Haven doing the same.

"I've been gone to speak with another village nearby. But I felt something change. I felt your magic was back." He holds out his hands to me as he did in the wasteland, feeling around me as if for warmth from a fire. "When I came back, they said the bucket for the well was taken. I followed the tracks down here." A gentle smile. "I thought you had no need for water."

"I have a human with me." His eyes drift back to the Hunter's corpse. "Not him. A girl. She is...not well. She needs water. I had no other way to bring it to her. I was going to put it back."

He nods, his eyebrows pulling together. "What's wrong with her?"

I don't know where to begin. "She...needs time. Rest."

I hope it's true. Either way, there's nothing Jordan can do for her.

"But what village have you been to? There is nothing else out there. Just wasteland." I keep talking just to take the focus off me.

"No, but there is!" His eyes charge with energy,

wide like a child's. "There's a lot of us now, all along the water. Getting back to the old ways, back to the Three. Preparing for the Final Realm War."

It's just like Miriam said. He's already leading the way, and he doesn't even know what fate slotted him for. I wish I could tell her, wish she could see him.

A vague hollowness in my chest — I miss her.

"I had to visit another village nearby. Just a few days' walk. I brought them some supplies. And I talked to a prophet there who had a message for all our allied groups."

His eyes flick to the Hunter's corpse again. A frown flickers over his face.

I can't take it anymore, the way he looks at it.

"I didn't want to," the words burst from me like water from a broken dam. "The box. It wasn't supposed to happen anymore. I didn't think — "

Jordan gives me a weak smile. "I remember, my friend." He clears this throat and looks away, out to the horizon.

Heat closes in around my neck. He's so been so accepting, always. But this, the corpse at our feet, I fear this is his limit. But to lose him too, on top of all the rest that is falling apart, I can't bear it.

Just when I think he'll turn away and leave, he clears his throat and speaks. "The prophet in the other village, he said the signs are changing, the realms are shifting. Something is different in the Underworld and the Third War is coming. Soon."

He steps toward me again. His eyes push with gentle force.

"Where were you, Adem? Did it have to do with

this? Anything you might be able to tell us could help."

Where to start. Too much to tell. It rumbles through me in quivering waves, breaks apart, and crumbles at the junctures of my mind like an earthquake.

"My fault," I mumble to the sand. "It's my fault."

His eyebrows pull together. "What is?"

"The war. The Underworld. I'm the reason the Gods' enemies can get out." The Hunter made me understand. And now I have to confess all over again. It doesn't have the same rush of relief this time. This time every word builds inside my core, cold and heavy like iron.

He shakes his head. "That's impossible."

"No," I growl. "It's the truth. I passed through the barrier that keeps them in and I broke it, and they tried, they tried to tell me, I could have stopped it, but I didn't realize, I came back anyway, and now they can get out—"

Jordan reaches out and grips my arm. "No, Adem. Stop—you're not making sense. It's not possible."

"It is."

I take a deep breath. I have to tell him. Everything. Now that I've started the fierce waves are pounding at the gate of my mind, must be released. "There's more."

He stops and looks back at me, the brightness on his face fading, the corners of his mouth drifting down.

"More?"

I pull air into my lungs, trying to figure out where to start.

But before I can a piercing scream bursts from the cave.

CHAPTER 26

THE SCREAM GOES and goes and it doesn't stop. It jams my ears, grates down my spine, and rattles my skull. Jordan's eyes pull open wide and he turns to the cave. They hear it in the village, I'm sure of it, and it's not stopping.

Rona. I've left her too long. Sand kicks up around me as I turn my back to the swelling daylight and run to her. She lays there, still unconscious, screaming. Her body tenses and her back archs up like a bridge, pressing her head hard against the rock beneath her.

"Rona!" I lift her carefully.

It has to stop. Make it stop. Make it stop.

"Rona!"

How long can she go without taking a breath?

"Wake up!" I am shaking her now, but she remains stiff and unconscious. "Stop!"

It's not working. Her scream buzzes in the air around me. I can't think. It has to stop.

Jordan rushes past me. Lifts the bucket and throws the water over her.

Rona's body drops limp across the slate of rock. Sweet silence sets in. The air loosens in relief; my fingers relax from their fists. But the relief doesn't last. Quick tension fills the vacuum as Jordan takes in Rona's depleted form.

"Adem?" He sounds just as he did as a child. "Who is this?"

"I..."

I want to explain. I want to unburden myself of all that's happened.

But Rona is awake.

She pushes herself with her wasted arms, wet, shivering, heaving, sucking in the air, looking all around like a hunted animal. She looks up to me and peers into my eyes through wild hair.

"He's coming. We have to go," she says.

I am so relieved the piercing scream is gone, so shocked to see her fully conscious, I can't think. I blink down at her. She pushes herself onto weak legs, stumbles and falls forward. I catch her and try to guide her back to read on the rock.

"No," she tries to fling my arms off from around her shoulders. "I have to get away from here. We have to go."

I reach out my arms to lend her support, get her off her shaking legs. Jordan stands with his back pressed to the cave wall, confusion in every crease of his face.

I grope for words, any words. "What do you mean? Why?"

"He's coming." Her wound still grows smaller and smaller, but it is flooding red again. She beats weak fists into my chest. "You're wasting time."

"Who's coming?"

She narrows her eyes. "Kythiel."

"Kythiel!" It springs out of me with relief. "Yes. He's coming. He sent me for you. To save you. So you can be together again." *And then I will get my soul, and I will be human, and this will be over, all of it.*

I wait for it to sink in. For her to remember, relax.

She crumples into a desperate pile on the sand and curls into a trembling ball.

I try to make her understand.

"I brought you back. You're alive again. You're safe."

She's rocking now. A terrible trembling force, her eyes hollow and desperate. She pulls her legs up and into herself, wraps her arms tightly around them, as if to keep herself from falling to pieces.

I try again. "Kythiel never stopped trying to bring you back. He found me and sent me to save you. You'll be together again soon."

Her face drains of color. "I thought you were saving me *from* him," she whispers. A tear rolls down her cheek.

"What?"

Nothing is fitting. The pieces splay out without any way to bring them together. She can't mean what I think she means. "Save you from whom? I will protect you. I promised Kythiel. Nothing will harm you. You are safe here, and soon Kythiel will come for you."

"*Kythiel* is after me!" she screams. Her eyes are big and black, fully dilated even in the cave's shadows. Her words tremble in rhythm with her body, a force all its own.

Her words hang in the space between us and suddenly the cave feels much too small and the walls are pushing in on my brain and I can't think, I can't breathe.

"Oh Gods. We're back in Terath?" Her shaking hands clutch fistfuls of tangled hair. "No. I can't be. I'm dead. I'm safe." Her voice rises, hysterical. Echoes off the cave. "This is impossible."

"Hard. Not impossible," I mutter. "You are. You're in Terath. I brought you back."

I have to fight a growing lump in my throat to get the words out. Staring down at my feet, I make sure they're still on the ground, because I can't feel anything anymore. It doesn't make sense.

But no. She's not right. The trauma of coming back was too much for her. This has never been done before. Who knows what damage was done in bringing her back. What awful things happened to her mind in the warp of the Underworld. It isn't, it can't be true.

She starts shaking her head like she can't understand. Or doesn't want to.

Jordan finally moves. He steps over and sits next to her. Wraps an arm around her. No hesitation from the rotting stench, the skeletal frame, the blood.

"It's okay; it's okay," he soothes. "We want to help you. But you have to tell us what happened. Help me understand."

Jordan's palm brushes back and forth across her back and shoulders. His other arm reaches across him and sits reassuringly on her knee. She takes a deep breath. Her shaking eases. Jordan cracks a smile, the same smile he had as a child, the one that makes everyone else smile too. Rona gives him a quick smile through tight, cracked lips. Already her eyes are closed and her breathing is slower and deeper. But her hand clutches onto his, a tight fist on top of her knee. His fingers are going white at the tips, but he just smiles at her. Now that Rona's calmed, the waves rise to my ears again. I stare at Jordan tending to her, so sure, so easy. I'm still trying to unwind what's happening into something I can understand.

"He said — Kythiel — he said he loved you. That you loved him...that..." Should I tell her his whole story? Will that help her remember? I gather it all together to the front of my mind.

"I did," she sighs. "Things changed. He changed."

She takes a deep breath.

"I can imagine what he might have said to you," she says. Every word bites, sparks like it is on fire. "But he didn't tell you everything."

Her voice fills the cave, crashes inside me.

Jordan keeps his voice low. "Help us understand. We want to help. Tell us what happened."

"Okay," she whispers. She pulls herself up with Jordan's hand and sits on the rock's side. She lets go of him to push the wild strands away from her face. I step closer. Her hands grip the sides of the rock on either side of her and she stares down blankly, her eyes fixed on the rocks.

But suddenly my soul feels farther away, almost out of reach. I scratch and claw to keep it close. I'm not sure I want to understand anymore.

"Whatever he said, it wasn't all lies. It just wasn't all the truth."

She closes her eyes.

"This starts at the Beginning."

CHAPTER 27

JORDAN AND I wait for Rona to continue, sitting as still as the rocks around us.

She shuts her eyes tighter and sighs, then opens them.

"At the Beginning it was wonderful, probably just what Kythiel told you. When he was called back to the Host, I would have given anything to keep him with me. I didn't know what it would do to him."

She stares down at the sand, avoids our curious gazes, fidgeting with her fingers.

"After he left, a great emptiness overcame me. The longer I was without him, the worse it became. Finally my father arranged a marriage for me, hoping to make me happy again, or shock me back to myself, or at least to keep me too busy to be so miserable."

She pauses a moment to breathe. She's still so weak, so wasted from the Underworld.

"I don't know if he told you—Theia used to speak to me. The night before the wedding, Kythiel used Her portal to break through to me in my dreams. He begged me to stop the wedding, but I didn't have the will for that fight in me, not then from the depths of my grief. But Kythiel kept coming to me, and I spent most of my time in dream with him."

Rona pauses again, brings her hand to her face to brush away a tear. She bites her lip but it won't stop trembling.

I fight the urge to stand up and pace — Kythiel already told me all this. She said he was on his way. How long will it take him to get here? When he arrives, she will see. Her confusion will fade away.

Jordan reaches out and rubs his hand soothingly across her shoulders again. "It's okay. Go on."

She nods with a heavy breath.

"I didn't realize it then, but as soon as he broke through to me, a wedge began to push its way between Kythiel and Theia. Every time, it grew deeper. Soon Kythiel's presence drowned out Theia's voice in my dreams, and I could not hear Her anymore."

An uncomfortable crawling sensation is spreading over my skin. I don't like this story.

"In time I began to see the love in my husband's care for me, and the pain I was causing him. I tried to start caring for him as a wife should. But I still went to Kythiel in my sleep. It was like being awake all the time. I started to lose myself. I knew what I had to do. I had to choose."

She tightens her arms around her legs again, begins to rock, her shoulders shaking.

"Angels are not like men. Their hearts are constant and do not change. It was impossible for Kythiel to let go. It was not fair of me to ask him to. But it was destroying me."

She shuts her eyes tight, tucks her head into her arms. We have to lean in to hear her story through her muffled voice.

"The night I told Kythiel we had to stop was the most terrifying of my life. The wedge between him and Theia had grown too deep, and his mind was unraveling. When I told him, something in him broke. My body bore the marks of his rage even after I woke. He wasn't my Kythiel anymore."

Jordan looks to me, his eyes heavy with meaning. I blink back. The crawling buzz over my skin burns deeper into me.

Rona keeps going. "Worse, he kept coming. He acted like nothing had changed. When I resisted, the rage took him over. I tried avoiding sleep, but it was impossible. Eventually sleep would overcome me anyway, and when it did, Kythiel was there waiting for me."

She lifts her head and glares at me, panting from the effort of so much talking. Little dots of sweat dapple her face.

"I became obsessed with finding a way to escape him. Finally, I did—I had to go where Kythiel couldn't. I took a knife and sent myself to the only safe place I could think of."

She pulls away from her knees, trails her fingers over the gash in her stomach.

"I sunk into blankness. Numbness. Quiet. And it was more than enough." Her head lifts and she glares at me. "Until you dragged me back here. And now he is in me again. In my dreams. And he is coming. Now."

Her voice is loud, practically a yell, crowding in on me off the cave walls. She lifts her head, her face writhing to hold back tears. She pushes herself onto shaky feet and stumbles to me, gripping my cloak to steady herself.

"I cannot go back to him. It would be worse than death. Kill me. Send me back where I am free of him. Please."

Her words tumble past me, on and on like they are falling into an endless pit. I understand what she says to me and I do not.

She presses her forehead into my chest. "Kill me," she begs.

I can't get it all into my head. Can't bring it together. Can't force it into anything that makes sense. I realize the world is tilting side to side...I am shaking my head.

"Kill me."

No.

Kythiel, a violent madman? All of this effort for nothing?

No.

Pressure tightens through the air all around me and I am up to my head in it.

Barely staying afloat.

On the cusp of drowning.

It can't be. Something inside me twists around my hope for a soul and chokes it.

"Kill me," Rona's voice turns into a raspy scream, and she beats her fragile fists into my chest and shoulders, and my head is still shaking side to side. This cannot be true, this cannot be possible, and then she collapses and I almost don't move my arms in time to catch her as she crumples against me, unconscious.

My soul.

It all depends on delivering Rona to Kythiel.

All I've been through to bring them together. The pain, the struggle. All the pieces crumbling away at the barrier between the realms because of what I did to bring her back to him.

I stare at the heap she has become, leaning against my cloak, still rough and stiff with her blood. It's strangling me.

"No." I say it aloud.

I pull forward every detail I can remember from when he came to me — so far away, ten years away, is that all? — My memory drags forth the soft glow, the grace that glossed every move, the easy peace of his presence.

"It can't be."

I can't force it together with the Kythiel she described. He isn't capable of the things she said. He couldn't be.

"Adem."

There's a hand on my arm and a voice in my ear.

"Adem. Adem."

Jordan.

He pulls me out from the fog of my mind. I look at him. His eyes are sharp. Biting flames. "Come outside with me."

"It's light out. The humans will see us."

"It's okay. They will not bother us." He tries to give me a comforting smile, but it is too tense.

The air is crowding tighter and tighter in the cave,

accenting the hard low walls and distorted echoes and sticky salty wetness. There is no room to think. Outside, yes, outside is better. Rona is still in my arms, collapsed against me. She isn't strong enough for this yet, it was too much. I lay her back on the large flat stone to rest. Turn and leave the cave, eager for the breeze.

As soon as I'm out, the Hunter's blank eyes accost me from the sand.

Golem.

Cold. Flat. Accusing. They stop me in my tracks.

Muffled steps rustle through the sand as Jordan follows and stops behind me. He ignores the body.

"What needs to be done?" he asks.

I stare into the dead face staring at me. The mid-morning sun is swollen and glaring. The back of my palms tingle like a thousand prickling needles.

"Adem. What are we going to do?"

We. As if he has any part in this. I should tell him to leave, that he has no role in this tangled mess. But I don't know what to believe anymore. I don't know what to do, and the "we" drapes over my shoulders like a warm blanket. I should tell him to leave. But instead I take his "we" and I pull it close around myself.

Jordan stares at his feet. Waves of water drag along sand. Neither of us wants to say it aloud, the thing that must come next.

"Kythiel expects to meet me. When he gets here, you stay with Rona. Distract her and keep her calm until I can warn him of her condition."

Jordan steps back, eyes popped wide, sputtering.

"But—you're going to—her *condition*?" He pulls his hands through his hair and down his face. "That's your plan? You can't possibly still intend to hand her over to that thing. After the things she said—"

"She doesn't know what she's saying," I growl. "She's not well. You saw her."

Not well, not well, not well. The Hunter's hard flat eyes staring up at me. Judging.

But no. That's all this is. She's not well.

"You can't be serious," Jordan hisses. "I don't fully understand what's going on with all this, but even I can see what's right here. You can't just hand her over to him."

He stands, stares, waiting, his arms folded. I feel his eyes on my back, and I do not move. Something tells me the emptiness of the Hunter's eyes is easier to bear than whatever lies in Jordan's right now.

"Adem. I know you. You don't want to do this." Jordan reaches a cautious hand out to my shoulder. "You might not realize it now. But you don't. You have a good heart."

He realizes his slip as soon as the words leave his mouth. Bites his lip.

"I have no heart."

But I could, I will, I'm so close I can almost feel what it will be like. To be human.

I just have to I get my soul.

Kythiel will be here soon.

Just give her to him. That's all. She is not well. She does not know what she says.

The sun beats on my shoulders, presses over them through my cloak. The heat is a physical pressure building under my skin, tightening around me like claws.

Jordan steps around to face me. *Don't*. His expression is begging me, *Stop*. But he doesn't know.

"You don't know how it was down there. In the Underworld." So long I was buried down there, but still it feels strange rolling off my tongue.

"It will do anything to trap you there. Fills you with its lies. Whatever it thinks will hold you there. The realm itself can sense you, listens, learns how to prey on you."

The Keeper's raspy words tumble through my mind and out of me. I wonder how much time has passed for him on the other side. What they did to him for helping me escape. Another piece of collateral damage to add to my pile. All of it to get Rona back to Kythiel. And now I may have to turn my back on the deal. Because how can I possibly hand Rona over to something that is more monster than angel? But no, she is confused. She had to be.

"It?" Jordan's brow pulls together. He takes another slow step toward me. "Adem. I don't know what happened to you. It must have been awful, more than I could imagine. But that doesn't mean—"

"I saw *you* down there," I growl. "You were still a child. With your own shore exactly like this one. You begged me to stay there with you." I can hear myself yelling and I can't make it stop, words thundering down like rocks caught in a landslide. "I almost did. For you. But it wasn't you. It wasn't real. It wasn't real, and this story Rona told us isn't either. She is just still confused from the Underworld."

As if I can make it so by repeating it enough times, force it into being with my breath. But I can feel the foundation slipping away from under me like quicksand. Breaking apart to take me in and swallow me.

Jordan is shaking his head. One side to the other, slowly, over and over.

"You can't do this. Even if it really weren't true, she believes it. She's terrified of him. You saw her. You said yourself, she's not well. It's all she can do to stay alive right now. You can't hand her over to something that scares her enough to kill herself."

"I'm telling you. It wasn't him. Not really." But I'm sinking, losing the ground under my feet. "Kythiel's an angel. He can help her. A lot better than we can."

Something twists in my gut. Something dark, angry, and desperate. It clings and won't let go. It nags, screams, and begs me to listen. I shove it away. My soul is at stake. Hundreds of lives, of Hunters and others who will just keep coming and try to take the box's pieces. Even if what she says were true, what's one to the hundreds of lives it will save to hand her over, to end the box's power over me?

"You know you can't do this. You heard her. Kythiel lost himself a long time ago. He's mad. He's dangerous."

I tug it shut like a curtain. Will myself not to hear. *My soul.*

"That was a long time ago. You didn't see him. If he changed once, maybe he changed again."

"Angels don't just *change*, Adem," now Jordan's yelling too, his hair catching in the setting sun as it flies around his face, as if it were catching fire. "They *fall*. You can't fall back up. You fall down and then you're stuck there."

There's no more space in my mind for what he's saying. Too loud. Too many demands, too many voices there already. Each syllable crams against my skull and the pressure builds and builds until there's no space left to think and my vision beings to tilt and the Hunter's stiff eyes stare through me like I'm nothing, less than nothing.

"If you do this," Jordan grinds his teeth, "You're the monster you think you are, after all."

Red rage explodes within me and blocks out all else. My fist flies through the air and connects with Jordan's jaw. The regret floods me bright and burning before he even hits the ground. The one person left still on my side, whoever was really on my side. But the rage is bigger, and my voice runs away without me.

"You didn't see him. Rona didn't see him. I saw him. He's fine. Her story isn't true."

And then I turn my back on him and stomp back into the cave. I can't deal with this now. The sand shuffles as Jordan pushes to his feet behind me. I sit on my rock next to Rona. Her breaths come easy and deep again in her unconscious state. Jordan hovers outside, tense and pacing.

The sun drags lower and lower and darkness pulls in all around. The moon is high in the sky, a full flat circle. I cannot believe it. Will not. It simply cannot be. It sticks in my throat like splinters, as if the words themselves are fighting against me.

But my soul. It hangs in the balance. My life. My

one chance for anything more than the trail of corpses I leave everywhere I go. I don't want to kill anymore. I want to be free.

Kythiel is fine. He is fine, because he has to be. Because I have to get my soul. The rest, it's all lies. She's confused. A victim of the Underworld's tricks. Kythiel is fine.

The sun begins to set into a tense twilight. Still there is no sign of Kythiel. Jordan keeps up his pacing outside the cave. Rona is still unconscious. I shove myself to my feet—I have to do *something.*

I walk outside and cut through Jordan's pacing. I pick up the Hunter's stiff corpse, sling it over my shoulder, and carry it around behind the cave, up the shore to where the sand becomes silt, where the cattails spring up.

"Adem!" Jordan is following. It does not matter.

I find an open patch of ground. This will do. I drop the corpse. Don't look. Don't look at the eyes. I kneel down and push my fingers through the sand, shove it away.

"Adem!" He quickens his pace to a run, tries to catch up.

Everything crumbles as soon as I touch it, breaks away like the ground under my hands. I can at least return over on this one thing. He should have been buried already. Before the humans were out.

"Adem."

He's right behind me now. I push my hands deep into the ground. Losing myself in the digging, I try to block him out before he can start.

"You can't do this Adem. I think you know you

can't."

I keep my head down, my eyes locked on the hole I'm digging. It doesn't matter what Jordan thinks. He wasn't down there in the Underworld. He doesn't understand.

"Leave me alone."

"So you can cover up your sin with the dirt before you go and commit another? This one is different, Adem. This," he points to the corpse, "Is forced on you. I know that. These burdens belong to someone else, whoever bound you to that box. But if you go through with *this*, if you give Rona to that lunatic, that's on you."

My hands stop moving. A burning mix of rage and guilt and stinging bitterness clouds my chest.

Jordan opens his mouth to say more, but then he stops. The air is tightening. Thinning, pulling, and flattening until there's none left to breathe in. I stop digging and stand up. A blinding burst of light flashes over the water.

Kythiel. He's come.

CHAPTER 28

AS SOON AS the air begins to flatten, I break into a run.

"Adem!"

The air snaps and crackles with pressure as it whooshes over my arms, my legs, my face.

"Adem!"

Jordan is chasing after me.

As I approach the shore, a large form strides up from the tumbling waves, its silvery glow mixing with beams cast down from the full moon. He is headed toward the cave.

Kythiel.

He has to bend down low to fit inside, flatten down his inky wings. And then he is swallowed into the rocks.

Rona.

My head pounds with pressure. Rona is in there. Alone. She will panic and ruin it all. But Jordan and I are not far behind. I hear his huffing breaths and thunking steps behind me as we race toward her.

I stop short at the cave's mouth. Jordan crashes into my back, heaving in uneven breaths.

Kythiel is at Rona's side, kneeling next to her unconscious body, splayed across the rock. But the way he looks at her sends chills through me. With one hand he caresses her head, runs fingers through the matted hair. The other holds onto the tight curve of her hip, pulls her close. He isn't seeing the starved, recovering corpse in front of him. He seems to be seeing Rona from the Beginning, the woman he knew. And somehow, in the soft light coming off him, she almost seems whole again. The glow of his skin pools in the cave's crevices and collects in a ring around them like a halo's cast-off light.

Even as we stand in the cave's mouth gaping and huffing, he does not take his eyes off her. I watch his face carefully, studying it for any sign of menace. His strong chin is softened; his perfect lips tremble. He could not possibly be the monster Rona described. If she would only wake up right now, she would see it herself.

I don't belong in this moment. I want to take it back, snatch away the suspicions sneaking into my mind, pull away, and let them be. I begin to step away.

But then he says, "Golem."

"I am here."

But he doesn't look up. As if his eyes are bound to her. He could not be what she said. He is an angel. Sad. Desperate. But not insane.

He pushes a lock of hair from her face. "You have brought her back to me."

His voice is grace and melody, pearly smooth. I

forgot how overwhelming his perfection is.

"Do you have my soul?"

My soul.

It echoes through me in tense quivers. No more box. No more killing. Just freedom. Just quiet. My soul. My very own.

Kythiel's jaw clenches. "Yes. I have it."

His eyes peel over her like a map he is studying to an old beloved place.

His hands run over her hair, over her cheeks and down her thin throat. Rest at her clavicle, still protruding too harshly, skin stretched too tight over her bones. His eyes run over her hungrily.

"She is not well," Kythiel says.

Something in me wants to push him away, shove him off her so hard he will never make his way back. The memory of her piercing scream bursts free in my head, loud, wailing, and unwelcome, as if she had awakened with him over her. My hands ball into fists. Should I tell him what she said, what she thinks? Something angry and desperate rises in me in resistance to the thought, and I swallow them back down.

"No. But she will be. She is still healing."

He keeps going. Over her shoulders, her breasts, her pinched ribs, her too-narrow waist, the jutting bones of her hips. He pushes up her shirt and stares at the wound across her stomach. The skin has knitted together into a dark scab.

"Let her rest," I say. I try hard not to yell over her screaming in my head. Can't tell if it comes out too loud or in a hoarse whisper. "We have business to settle."

He eyes me, a hint of shadow flickers over his face.

"Yes. Of course," his voice is steady and smooth but something about it bites. "*Golem.*"

He takes her in one more time, runs a hand over her hair before standing and striding past me out of the cave. The reeling screech in my head subsides.

I turn to follow him.

"Adem," Jordan snatches my arm as I walk by. Holds it tight in his hot palm and looks up to me like he is still the child I brought to this place. His eyes meet mine, wide, wary, and lost. "Do what's right. Or so help me…"

"This *is* right. This is the deal." I yank my arm away from him and follow Kythiel down the shore.

It is *right.* I tell myself. *It's what was promised. He loves her. He will take care of her.* She will heal and she will see she is not in the Underworld anymore and all is right and she is safe with him. The darkness down there seeped into her mind, twisted her memories. That is all.

And I will get my soul.

Even if it was true, what she said, what's one life to the thousands that would be spared the fate of dying under my hands because of the box?

It's right.

Isn't it?

Soft moonlight reflects off glossy wings, outlining his perfect glowing figure. He stares up at the round beaming moon and they are like a matching set.

I meet him at the water's edge. He watches me the way a child watches an ant, idly curious, uncommitted.

"My soul," I prompt.

"Yes."

I wait for him to continue. He doesn't.

"Where is it?"

"I have it."

His eyes flick impatiently back to the cave. To Rona.

I wait for him to take it out. To put it in me. I wonder how he will do it. If it will hurt. My shoulder prickles and I remember exactly all that word means. Pain.

I wonder what it will be like to be real. To be human. Fragile and sensitive. And free to choose. I'm so hungry for it I could burst.

But he doesn't make any move for it. Stands silent, perfect, and still. Watches me.

"Let me have it." Shadows push at the back of my mind, begin to creep out through the cracks. "We had a deal."

His hands fidget, wringing at his neck, folding over his chest, unfolding again. The feathers of his wings rise and ruffle.

"When she is healed. When I know she will not slip away into death again."

"She is already past the worst. All she needs is time and rest." So far, past the limp corpse I carried to shore just yesterday, unconscious, and bleeding out onto the sand. What would Kythiel have thought if he had seen her then?

"She is not strong enough for the journey we must take. She will stay here until she is. When I take her, you will have your soul."

I follow his gaze back to the cave. Rona. I wonder

where he will take her. And suddenly, I feel hollow. Suddenly I cannot see past seeking her, caring for her, to anything beyond her. All I had before this was the box. There's nothing to return to.

He shifts, stretching and folding his wings. "You've done well, golem. I didn't know if this would work. Sending the lowest of creatures in the Underworld. I didn't dare believe it. When she shut me out, when she sent herself out of Terath and left me alone, I couldn't bear it. I almost went mad with desperation. But all is right now."

When she shut him out? The words jam in my ears. Too much like Rona's story.

No.

I shake out the thoughts stirring inside me. Try not to let myself think it.

Rona might believe what she said, but it wasn't real. It was delusions, nightmares, lies the demons fed her to trap her there.

My soul. It is somewhere on Kythiel right now, just an arm's length away. So close. Painfully close.

But then why did she kill herself?

The echo of her scream is ringing through me again, piercing me.

And Kythiel. He won't look at me. Stares off to the horizon. The shadows are taking over my mind, gnawing at my gut. I try to shove it back, to ignore the rising scream but its building, building, building inside me like a volcano, like I'm about to erupt.

"Kythiel —"

Too loud. A roar. It bursts from me large, wild, and desperate, gusts out over the waves.

His head snaps up. His eyes flick to me like sparking embers, meeting mine.

I look into them. Look for real. Look deep. And the cracks burst open and the shadows rush out and swallow me. Because I see it.

The rootless chaos in his eyes. Dark, churning, restless. Lost.

Just like Rona said.

How did I not see it before? The empty chasm that fueled him. That hidden under the grace, the beauty, and the perfection is a soul that unhinged long ago?

And just like that, my hope extinguishes and I know it's over.

"I can't."

It spills out of me before I can think. Soft, hardly even words. It's as much to tell myself, as it is to tell him.

There will be no other chances. I know there can't be. This one should never have been in the first place. But I can't. Not like this. Not even for a soul. I remember his marble hands running over her face, her hair, her neck, and it makes my stomach churn, how close I let him get to her.

"Hmm?" Kythiel's already drifted off again, staring back toward the cave.

"I can't." My voice is coming back now. Rough but certain. "I can't let you take her."

Why did I trust him so blindly? Protecting her now that the truth has finally sunk in, it's the only thing I can do.

He turns back to me, the content smile fading from his face. Replaced by something removed and hard.

Then he laughs, a peeling like smooth pearly bubbles.

"Of course you will."

I choke down the urge to take it back.

"No."

The laugh drifts off his face and its hard marble skin goes smooth and hard.

"We made a deal. You swore to bring her back to me."

I plant one foot and then the other, firm, shoulder to shoulder with him. My toes dig into the sand. I try not to expose the wild way my mind races in the moonlight.

"You lied," I growl.

The slightest twitch moves through the feathers of his dark wings.

"What did she tell you?"

"Everything."

He stares back at me, unforgiving menace boiling just below the surface. There is no questioning the lost hazard in his eyes, now that I've seen it.

"She is not right. She needs me. I can make her better. But the things she says, they aren't true."

His voice is quiet but his words are hard and cold. It's too late. It doesn't matter what he says now. He takes an aggressive step closer, and I am in his reach. I hold my ground.

"The Underworld. It would cause anyone to get confused. They fed her lies, they..." His fingers curl, tense and searching, open, close, open, close, tug on his hair, curl in fists to his sides. The feathers of his wings flay with aggression. "I need her. She needs me."

"No more stories, Kythiel."

"We had a deal," he hisses, shoving me backwards. My feet stumble and trip to keep me upright under the force from his hands. He follows with easy strides.

"You bring her back to me," he shoves me again, "And I give you a soul," and again. My feet can't keep up and I fall to the ground with a thud, skid across the rough sand.

He stands over me, his dark wings spread wide, blocking out the moon. "And now it is time to live up to your word. Hand her over, golem."

Every inch of me burns with volatile rage.

"You knew. You knew this whole time."

That Rona would not want to come back. Maybe even that crossing through the barrier would bring the next Realm War. He knew, and he didn't care.

And I trusted him, my ignorant slow mind, trusted him blindly, all too eager to get my own reward. It comes over me in a rush, like falling down a bottomless pit. So many warnings, so many times I could have listened and made it right. But I was blinded by my craving to escape myself.

Kythiel is raging, huffing air in and out, his whole body quivering from his chest to the tips of his spread wings. His jaw is clenched, eyes wild. A madman.

All that I've done, all I've broken, all to bring Rona back to this monster. It's time to do something right. To start making things better, not worse. I push myself to my feet, the edge of my hand pulsing where my finger is missing.

"By the Gods, Kythiel, leave her. I'm warning you. Walk away."

The moon is bright above us. The majestic glow of

Kythiel's skin fades against its stretching beams.

He snorts. "By the Gods? The Gods do not care about you, or anything in this forsaken realm. It's just you and me out here." His face curls a feral snarl, baring pearly sharp teeth. A growl rolls out from his clenched jaw, so beautiful it could be a purr. "Do you really think you can keep me from her?"

The giant wings spread to their full span, his smooth muscles flexing and rippling.

No. He is larger, he is smarter, and he likely has ancient magic I can only imagine.

"I have to."

His fist springs toward me.

Hot tension floods me as my jaw unhinges, snapping apart under the pressure. Everything goes dark, and the after burn of his grimacing face imprints in the back of my mind.

I brace myself for the pain.

It doesn't come.

I am on Terath again, and I am strong here. He can't break me like they could in the Underworld.

I let the fury expand, expand, expand until it consumes me. It bursts out of me in a terrible roar that shakes the water and stabs at the sky.

I charge at the angel with all I have.

One way or another, one of us is not leaving this fight.

I'm determined to make sure it's he who falls — not only my own sake, but for Miriam. For Jordan. For Rona. Every Hunter I've buried.

CHAPTER 29

IT WOULD BE a relief, really. After so long. All the problems I've created. For it to all end. Even like this, under Kythiel's raging fists. It was part of what a soul was going to give me, after all. An end.

But I have so much to make up for first. So much else to set right again. As the angel moves toward me, I catch Jordan in the corner of my eye, standing protectively in front of Rona at the cave's mouth. They're out of direct danger. For now. As long as I can keep Kythiel distracted.

The soft glow of his skin, the graceful motion as he shifts, the gentle flutter of his wings. All a perfect disguise for the madness underneath. Only those eyes, those aimless churning eyes give any sign.

"You cannot protect her from me, golem," he throws his words at me like daggers.

Golem.

That's exactly what I am. A brutal, fierce, ruthless beast. The only monster to ever break into the Underworld and crawl back out of it. I take a deep breath and let the simmering adrenaline pulse through my chest, my shoulders, my fingers, my toes.

I haul into his face with my fists. *Slam* he stumbles backward. *Slam* his head whiplashes like a spring. *Slam* I knock him to the ground.

His perfect straight nose shifts out of place, and silvery blood seeps through the splits in his skin where my knuckles landed.

The pressure builds in my hand with each blow, a satisfying tension as the bones split and crack, the cool sticky silver coagulating across them. I pause to let them pull back together.

As soon as I do, two fists to my chest send me flying, and the world blurs as I soar through the air, skid across the sand.

Kythiel is too fast. Too strong. Maybe even more indestructible than I am. Can this battle ever end? All I know is I can't let him reach Rona.

He rushes at me as I stand. I throw punches that toss him clear across the shore. He rips me from the ground and flies me high into the stars until the air is too thin to breathe, then sends me crashing back to the earth. I shove him to the ground and pound more silvery blood out of him. He mutters curses that shoot sparks from his fingers, that bite and sting and burn through my skin. It goes on like this all through the night.

I struggle to keep up with his speed. Engulfed in blur of cool silver and dark feathers. Bursts of force hit me from every side, no more than a blur of throbbing pounds and the grinding of sharp teeth. My broken limbs make delayed attempts to fight back as he comes at me again and again, shattering my body into splintered pieces. I must find a way to stop him before he breaks me too much to fight back. I'd recover, but would it be fast enough to stop him from taking Rona?

Too little. Too late. Too slow.

I channel all the rage, all the pulsing energy in me, and charge. I leap at him, grab hold, and pull him down with me. We knock to the ground in a tangle of arms and legs and feathers, and before I can break free, he has my head clenched in his hand and my mind fills with the *thunk-thunk-thunk* of my skull slamming against rock. A hot wet rush covers me where my head keeps meeting the rough stone. I see red, I see stars, and I can't break free.

But if he's here slamming my head on the rocks, he's not in the cave taking Rona away.

I'm limp, helpless, lost in the dizzying rhythm. For a moment I give in to it. Thin fracture lines spread over my skull with each hit.

Focus.

All I can see is a blur. My fingers reach out, fumble across the sand and find sharp shards of rock. This will do. I wrap my fingers around one tight. This strike has to count.

I swing around toward Kythiel with all my strength, all my force. Dig the rock into him like a blade. Vibrations roll through my fingers as the perfect silver skin rips apart. I tear through it as long, as deep, and as hard as I can.

A garbled cry sounds.

A huff of wind blows off dark writhing wings.

My head is free. I feel it start the work to reshape

and heal, the pressure begin to relieve. But there's no time to wait for it to do its work. I stumble away, ready for whatever he comes at me with next. Moonlight catches in a copious flood of silver draining out from his neck. I've ripped a gash down his neck and across to his shoulder. Kythiel stumbles back, hands outstretched and trembling, his eyes wide in shock. He opens his mouth to speak and more silver spills out over his lips.

I strike again while he's vulnerable, splitting open his abdomen. He gasps, doubles over, pulling his arms around himself. The silver blood oozes out in a sheet, drips down, and puddles on the sand.

A whisper of victory grows in my chest.

But then Kythiel straightens his back. Slowly. Carefully. Quivering.

Soft curls, encased in light, tumble into his face. He shoves them back, staining his hair with his blood. Then he hovers his hand over the gash in his stomach, closes his eyes. He murmurs a short chant. As he finishes, the wound heals itself. His power is greater than mine. Great and flawless and brutal.

When he is done, he lifts his head to me. He's smiling. Suddenly, even with the sharp rock in my hand, I feel helpless and vulnerable. *Why is he smiling?*

He steps to me and raises a fist to the sky. "Goodbye, golem."

He murmurs another chant. The wind rushes around him and he strains with the pulsing power. Then he slams his fist to my head.

I don't even feel the impact.

I am propelled backwards, and land with a crash as

overwhelming darkness edges in on me. I try to push it away and scramble to my feet, but am unable to control my own limbs. Kythiel turns his back on me and strides toward the cave. The last thing I see as the darkness closes in is Rona's terrified face, too thin and scrunched with fear, and Jordan pulling out his blade as he steps in front of her.

Everything fades to shadow. My entire being swells with blank terror.

CHAPTER 30

SAND.

I wake up face-down in it. Grains press into my cheeks, my forehead, and my chin. They are inside my mouth, my eyes.

I lift my head and open my eyes. They are attacked with overwhelming light. I shut them again and pull my arms up to shield them.

"Get up, Adem."

The voice is deep, wide, and everywhere, surrounding me. It echoes inside my head, beyond the shadows. Vibrates against my skin.

I push myself up. Rub my palms over my face to push out the sand.

I am just where Kythiel left me, halfway up the shore between the water and the cave. But everything is bright, so bright, unbearably bright. I squint against it. Everyone is gone—Kythiel, Rona, Jordan, even the village is abandoned.

The light is warm and soft, but a wave of panic overcomes me. My fingers curl into my hands in tight fists.

"Adem."

Where is the voice? A wind swirls around me, kicking up sand into its pull. It catches on an invisible form just feet from me.

It knows my name.

The panic mixes with confusion and rage. Adrenaline still pulses in me hot and thick from the fight.

"What is this? Where did they —"

"Adem. Be still." Through the broken wind and flying sand, an arm reaches out to me. "You are not mine, Adem. I did not create you. You do not answer to me, and I cannot expect you to follow my commands."

I cannot see it, but somehow beauty and peace emanate from it. It is just what I crave, and I soak it up like dirt takes in rain after drought. But what is it? My whole body reverberates with fear. The wind is building, swirling around us. More sand rises into it. Small pebbles begin to lift into its fold.

"All the same, you have broken my Order," the voice continues.

"What are you?" I ask. It is swallowed into the building wind.

"I am the One who forged this realm. The One who planted the Order into everything in it. I am all that is."

Each word quakes through me as if they rolled up from within the depths of Terath, shakes free everything within me, leaves behind only awe.

"You are Theia."

The wind builds. Rocks as large as my fist begin to rise, to join the wind tunnel's mass around me.

And then my mind reemerges from Her overwhelming presence. The desperation, the rage, the burden of all I've done come back to me. Jordan. Miriam. Epoh. The ages before that. The Wars. All the brokenness of the realm melds together in me into a lump of cold leaden anger.

"You abandoned us," I accuse.

I wait for the Goddess to speak. The ground rumbles. She says nothing.

"You have to come back. You have to help your people. Everything is falling apart. I've done things, awful things, things that could destroy the whole realm if you don't—"

"End this, Adem."

End this? That is all the Goddess of the Realm has for me?

If only I could.

I would give anything, everything, to make it end. I tried.

My failure wells in my throat. My words have to fight to get out.

"I can't."

"You must."

"How?"

One word. Almost a cry. One word, but it's everything.

"The very fabric of my realm is your being. You are the dirt. You are the earth. You are Terath."

The voice is too big, everywhere at once. And it is inside me, a comforting whisper. The wind whips at my ears, fills my head with violent noise. I don't understand. My dense, slow mind. The root of all the disaster I've brought forth.

"You have caused great destruction with your foolishness. What has already passed is only the beginning."

I feared it; no, I knew it was so. Kythiel is only the first stone to fall in a landslide, a landslide tumbling my way, threatening everything, and somehow I'm supposed to stop it, catch each stone, and set it all back into place?

I cannot. I open my mouth to tell her so again, but she holds up an invisible hand to me, sand blowing around it in the wind.

"I cannot claim you. You are the only thing in all of Terath I cannot, from the trees' deepest roots to the highest stars of the sky. But the dirt within you is mine. You have broken the Order, and started a chain of events that will cause great destruction across Terath before it is through. And yet, it was my own creature who led you into it. Perhaps we owe something to each other."

The ground's rumbling continues to grow and my knees are shaky and weak on it. My fear grows with it. Around me, rocks anchored in the sand are sweeping into the building wind. Sand blasts my face, bites my skin. It builds a wall around us. Grains stick to the invisible form across from me, reveal a face beyond beauty, beyond grace, solemn and fervent.

She speaks again.

"Adem, set right what you have wronged, and I will uphold my creature's promise to you. I will give you a soul and claim you as my own."

A flicker of hope lights within me. It's not lost yet.

A new chance might yet be mine.

But. "How?"

A plea.

"Do you pledge to take this on in my name?"

"Yes." To gain a soul? To fix all I've broken? Yes, oh yes, oh yes.

"Then fear not. I will be with you. Kythiel has walked too long through this realm. Cast him out. The war is coming. Fight at the side of my chosen warrior and cast out what you have set loose. End the Realm Wars once and for all. Restore my peace to Terath. Do this and I will make you my own."

The charges pile up on me. Heavy. Impossible.

The same word still hammers at my mind. "How?"

"It is already in you."

Her words don't make sense and it's like I'm sinking deeper and deeper, being buried in the whirl of sand and rock churning around us.

"But I am nothing."

"You are more than you know," She says. Her tone is clipped. "Your maker's power is your power. All these years you hid in the dark, it has compounded inside you. It is yours if you will take it. So take it."

Bewilderment whips around me in raw, stinging fragments.

"But—"

"What do you think is causing the earth to rise?"

The question drains me to blankness. Before I can think, an arm of sand and wind reaches out, presses a finger to my forehead and burns into me, a whipping pain that scorches under my skin. My mind goes blank and I am thrown back, back, back—

Back to a boy in wintered woods, back to a place that is strange but familiar.

I walk around to peer into his face. Dark hair. Flushed cheeks. Shoulders just beginning to broaden into manhood. I've seen him before.

It is the boy that Ceil tried to show me.

My mind clouds with questions and guilt. Why did Theia send me back here? It's too late now, I've already done all Ceil was trying to stop.

The boy treads just on the fringe of a village, watching the bustling life pass by with disinterest. Carts' wheels rumble, punctuated by a cheerful rabble of voices. Something in me is drawn, connected to this boy, and his sullen anger writhes within me. I step closer to him. A high laugh floats through the forest branches, the same laugh that echoed so strangely through the trees before, and suddenly the boy ducks behind a tree.

And then they walk by. A loose pack of boys about the same age, led by a girl. They joke and play to entertain her, pick wild flowers from the forest's edge, and present them to her. She rewards them with more of the dancing laughter. The boy's craving for her wells up in me, a hungry mix of curiosity and secret longing. Her look is plain, touched only by a necklace. A simple gold chain with a large uncut emerald dangling from it.

My necklace.

The backs of my hands tingle, my mind buzzes with dread. Ceil. This is what he meant to show me. I'm sure of it. And I didn't know enough to understand. Why show me this now that it's over and lost?

The group passes by and the boy steps back out from behind the tree, stares after them. The girl twirls, looks past the trees, and pierces the dark-haired boy with a weighty glance. When she turns back, the flowers in her hand are black and rotted. She whips around again and stares at him. They freeze in the moment, their eyes lock, until the flock of boys calls her attention back and she finally must turn and walk away with them.

"That was very good."

The voice is like honey, reaches out from deeper in the woods. The boy jumps and whips around, startled to find he is not alone.

It's an angel. She emanates a rosy golden glow, tall and grand, skin smooth and perfect as Kythiel's. Her face is pointed and proud. She smiles at the boy.

"Do you study magic?"

He shakes his head, bewildered.

"Would you like to?"

He bites his lip, glances back at the town.

"They do not see me," *she says.*

She reaches out her arm and spreads her fingers, palm down. "Aaeros." *A rock floats up and nestles into her hand.*

"Now you," *she nudges.*

The boy hesitates. She raises an eyebrow. "Unless you don't think you can?"

He frowns, the flush of his cheeks spreading over his face, and sticks his arm out. He waits.

Nothing happens.

"Like this," *the angel reaches out, rearranges his fingers so they are spread out and strong.*

"You have to say it." *She places her own hand over his.* "We will do it together. Ready?"

He nods.

"Aaeros." *My own lips mouth the word with them.*

A rock shoots into his hand.

"Very good." *The angel smiles at him.*

The boy is dizzy with the power, and I feel it too, his tingling fingers, his spinning head, and the warm rush that floods over him.

"Tell me your name," the angel says.

"Maelcolm."

"Maelcolm." *She smiles down at the boy.* "There is much more I can teach you, if you want it. Do you?" *He nods, his hot cheeks flushed to his ears.*

"Very good," *she smiles.* "I am Syliel."

Syliel says more, but I do not hear it. I am pulled away from the forest, away from the village, away in a sudden rush back to the shore.

The Goddess's hand settles back at her side, but the center of my forehead still burns where she pressed into it. Around us the swirling wind has risen to a raging cyclone, pieces of the cave tear away and are consumed by it, joining the torrent. I stand in its center unanchored, lost and overwhelmed, the wind's power filling me and rushing through me and jumbling all my thoughts, leaving me dazed and powerless.

Theia's voice is around me and in me. "End this, Adem."

I shut my eyes, shut them tight, and try to wipe my mind clean. But my thoughts lift and join the torrent, and I can't catch them, can't focus on them long enough to make them into anything.

All I know is that something terrible is on the verge of Terath, something that I have caused, and I have to stop it.

It has to *STOP.*

It's a shriek, a cry, a plea, a command. Everything stutters to a standstill, and I know before I even open my eyes, the rocks have dropped back to the ground.

Without the wind and flying sand I can't tell if the Goddess still stands in front of me or not. But then two whispered words — *End this* — come over me in a soft breeze and blow everything away to nothing. I claw against it, *no, please, I have more questions, I do not understand, I need more.*

But nothing responds, and I collapse into darkness.

CHAPTER 31

AGAIN I WAKE, rough sand pressing into my face. The waves are loud and angry.

I force myself to my knees, inebriated and wobbly from the vision. I rub the sand away from my eyes and open them.

I'm back on the shore. The real shore. Just as I left it.

Kythiel is making his way up the beach to the cave, Rona trembles, and Jordan stands in front of her wielding a knife that will mean nothing against an angel.

Somehow, I am whole again, all Kythiel's damage washed away. More than whole. Stronger. A hot angry pulse thunders through me, and fury splays off me like sand kicked up in the wind. I unlock the monster within, and I am rage, I am wrath, I am *golem*, a violent heat radiating from my forehead where She touched me and simmering just below my skin.

And I am more. I am Theia's instrument—Theia's weapon—chosen and sent here to stop this, to stop Kythiel.

End this.

I will.

I just wish I knew how to do it.

My forehead burns, burns, burns and I feel it reaching, settling into my mind, growing roots, taking hold over me. And it is good.

I rise to my feet. My head rushes, the ground sways under me.

Rona's eyes flit to me. Jordan grabs her arm, a warning. She pulls her focus back to Kythiel, but it's too late.

The inky wings bristle. He whips around.

He looks like hell.

His lip pulls back, baring pearly teeth. The smooth skin still bears smudges of silver blood, catching and glaring against the rising sun behind me over the sea. The shadows around his brooding lost eyes are dark, menacing, and sinister. The glossy curls are disheveled, fractured light catching in them like a halo battered and broken.

"We're done, golem. Give it up. Or I will send you back to the dirt, where you came from."

"Then come do it. Let's end this."

He charges toward me, and I toward him, and soon I fear he will be breaking me, soon he will be defeating me again. But he's moving away from Rona, and I have to keep it that way, keep him away from her, until I figure out how to make it stop.

The words Theia planted in me are stretching still, needling into me, working their way through my mind's crevices. They struggle to find room, to make sense. The spot on my forehead where She touched me throbs, bursting through me in waves of power.

We rush into each other where the shore meets the rockier ground scattered around the cave. Kythiel swings a fist. Every particle of my body is in overdrive, and I watch it come toward my head in slow motion. I duck, and his body propels forward as his fist swipes through empty air. I throw out my fist, slugging him across the jaw. He brushes away a drop of blood from the corner of his mouth with the back of his hand, smearing a streak across his cheek.

We circle around each other, fists up, eyes wary.

He seems somehow lesser now. After the other angel in Theia's vision. Duller, less radiant in comparison. Did I simply not see it before? Or is his wildness growing?

He takes another swing. It's frantic and uncontrolled. I step back and it misses me again.

Syliel. That was her name. And the boy...something about him. A connection. How did the girl have my necklace? Where were they? When were they? Ages and ages back, I think.

Stars explode in my eyes as Kythiel lands a hit at my temple. I spin off kilter, landing hard on my arms among the rocks.

He's too strong, too fast. And he's got magic at his command. How can Theia expect me to have any chance? A wave of resentment at her surges. Why come to me at all? Why send me back to this?

I push my hands into the sharp rocks to stand back up. What choice is there but to keep fighting?

The rocks.

It ignites inside me like a spark in dry straw. This is

what She was telling me. This is how it ends.

I stand. Turn to Kythiel.

A half-cocked smile is spread over his face.

I hold out my hand, spread my fingers out tight like Syliel did.

"Aaeros."

A rock quivers, slowly rises. The power bursts within me, a strange mounting pressure. I muster all my focus toward Kythiel and push my arm forward. The rock drifts toward him, slowly dropping until it meets the ground near his feet.

A hard, dry laugh drops from his lips. He kicks the rock away. It makes sad skipping taps as it scuttles against other rocks in the sand.

But I felt it. The magic is in me. And now it's stirring. Waking up.

Another fist comes at me, proud and sure of itself.

I brace myself. Let it come. It lands square in the middle of my chest. Spindly fracture lines stretch through my sternum, my ribs. They are already knitting back together before Kythiel's arm is back at his side.

I ignore it, stretch out my arm, and try again.

"Aaeros."

The rocks rise to me quicker this time, a cluster of them. I shove my hand toward Kythiel and they fly at him, bounce off his chest.

Kythiel's face clouds, his full lips pulling into a flat line.

"You dare use my own gift against me? That is angels' magic, golem. Stop meddling with what you cannot understand."

He starts toward me again. But he's angry now, distracted.

I muster my strength, my will, my desperation, everything I have, and roar, "*Aaeros!*"

The earth rumbles. I brace myself, holding my ground. Raising my arm, I order the rocks to follow my command.

And the rocks rise.

First, the smaller ones lift. Then more. The large shards around the cave pull free from the trembling ground and join them. The power shoots through me in quivers. I breathe slow and deep to hold myself steady. The air is sharp and tight with force; it snaps and pulls. I shove my arms toward Kythiel. The rocks charge, mixed with sparks of raw power.

His wild eyes pull wide. He throws out a hand, cries "Repelle!"

Our waves of magic meet and my rocks are lost in light, blinding and hungry and all-consuming, brighter than the sun. The force is too much. The rocks inch toward him quivering and unsteady, until his light and my sparks combust into each other. He is swallowed into the explosion, the light eating into him, and breaking apart at his fingers, his shoulders, making his face like crumbling embers. I stand my ground, sparks and rocks biting at me from every side. I try to keep them steady and charging, the power coursing between my particles like a current.

I stand my ground until my knees give out and I collapse.

This time when I fall into the darkness, there is nothing beyond it.

CHAPTER 32

SOMETHING NUDGES ME. I have the vague urge to fight, to defend myself. Someone needs my help.

"Adem?"

I roll over onto my back and open my eyes. Two faces stare down at me. Bright light reaches around them and blots out their faces. From an explosion?

No. It's just the sun, rising behind them and reflecting off the sea.

But there *was* an explosion.

Wasn't there?

"Adem?"

A deep voice, young and warm and full of life — Jordan. He sounds tense.

My body is a thousand tiny fractures knitting back together. I stay still and let them heal. While I wait I strain to remember, dig through my memory, but my mind is blank.

"What happened?" I ask.

Jordan and the other figure exchange a look. The second figure pushes back long tangled locks with a too-skinny arm.

Rona.

And suddenly it all starts rushing back to me.

Kythiel. Theia. The rocks.

I bolt to my feet and swing around, my head buzzing. Past Jordan and Rona, a crowd hovers together, their expressions bewildered.

"Where is he?" I whip around in a circle, brace for the next attack. "Where's Kythiel?"

"He's—" Jordan's eyes flicker away and back. "It's over."

I follow his glance and find the rubble.

Shattered rock everywhere, large shards and broken crumbles. I step past them and walk through it. My hands into fists, trying to hold the moment together.

"It was incredible. What you did," Rona says. She's just behind me. "I've never seen anything like it."

"It obliterated him." Jordan steps to my side. "Where did it come from? All that power?"

My eyes drift back to the hovering crowd. All of them just stare back at me.

"What are they doing here?"

They shouldn't be here.

"They came from the village. To see what has happening. The fighting could have been heard from miles around, if anyone was out there." Jordan says.

I stare out at them all. They stare back. Wide-eyed and blinking and unsure. There is too much to process, my mind is too confused. I push them out of my mind and try to focus on what happened.

The broken rocks are thickest at the middle. Under them, Kythiel's bright white robe lays crumpled and limp, glistening ash strewn through them like crushed diamonds.

"Is that...is he dead?"

"Yes. And no. I don't think so," Rona stutters. "Angels don't die, really. In the Host, they're all soul. He doesn't need his body to survive. It was just for Terath. But he's gone. He's broken. I don't think he can come back, not for a long while."

Her voice falters, a drop trickles down her face. They were happy once, I remember. I wonder if part of her still loves him, despite it all.

I don't dare ask. Instead, I kick at the rubble.

Clink.

Something hard is wrapped within the remnants of Kythiel's robes. The shards of rock bounce back off it. I crouch down and dig into the folds. My fingers find smooth glass. I pull it out, shaking it free of the ash.

A jar. It emanates a soothing light. Fills me with quivering excitement.

My soul.

The jar catches the sunlight and multiplies its rays.

It's mine. It's here. It's real. Resting right in my hand. I don't need to wait for Theia. Finally, I can be free.

But how do I put it in me?

"Oh—" Rona gasps. "Oh Gods."

Jordan steps closer. He looks at the jar from over Rona's shoulder. His face drains of color.

"Is that..." He cuts off, for once struggling for the words.

Their expressions flatten with confusion and disgust. My mind muddies. Something is wrong.

I look again at the jar clutched in my hands, and something jagged knifes at my gut.

Streaks of dark liquid red stretch over its inside walls. They were hidden under the sun's glare off the jar. The light writhes and twists. For a flash as it struggles, I see a face pressed against the glass. A shudder overcomes me and the jar falls from my hand. It cracks into pieces on the rocks. The soul leaks through, expands to full size on the sand.

A twist to my gut—if this soul is mine, why does it look like someone else? This one is thin, short, and frail. And it's somehow different from the souls in the Underworld, somehow less. Writhing, gasping, seizing.

Helpless.

And I am helpless watching it. My arms hang in limp horror and I am frozen by the grotesque struggle.

"What's wrong with it?" I cry.

"I...I don't know." Rona kneels beside it. "I think...he cut it out of someone. Someone living."

"How do we send it on?" Jordan's voice is tight, and loud, despite the quiet.

Rona shakes her head, eyes wide and dilated. "I don't know how it's here. It should have gone right to the Underworld. He trapped it in Terath somehow."

The soul writhes, gasps, and flails like a fish dredged up to the shore. Its eyes bulge and blink without seeing.

A tingling panic rises up from my toes up my legs my chest sets my head ablaze. I need to do something. But there is nothing we can do. We stand frozen, helpless horror etched into our faces, watching the soul's struggle. Finally, slowly, it fades to nothing.

"Is he..." But he was already dead. "Did he pass on?"

Rona shakes her head again. "I don't think so. I don't think it could. I think it might have just...*ended*. I'm not sure it exists anywhere anymore. Gods," she wraps her arms around herself. Still staring where the soul flailed. "I knew Kythiel was beyond help. But this. Who cuts away a man's soul? What would make him want to do that?"

Her eyes are full with tears.

It bites at my skin and singes through my mind. Burning shame. All-consuming.

"It's my fault."

Add it to the great pile of the awful things I've caused.

"I told him I'd bring you back for a soul. He said he couldn't, but I said it was the only way. I didn't know. I never would have..."

But there's no point. What difference is it what I would have done? I would not have done many things, if I had known. There is only what is. My head sinks. I stare at the broken, bloodstained glass. It wouldn't have worked. Even if I had returned Rona to him. This soul would never have been my own.

"No. You didn't know. You couldn't. It's my fault," Rona says. "It's because of me that he's become this."

"No. It's not your fault. Neither of you." Jordan's face hardens with anger. "Kythiel made his own choices. But that's not what's important now. What matters now is what comes next."

He face hardens with determination. He kneels, lifts up the largest piece of the jar, picks up the smaller pieces out of the sand, and places them into it.

The vision comes rushing back to me, Theia's final whisper, *End this*. It's massive, more than I can carry. But I also can't let it go.

"I've got to fix it. I swore to Theia I would."

They turn to me and stare.

"To Theia?" Jordan frowns. "I thought you didn't follow the Gods."

I need to tell them. But where to start. How to explain.

"The rocks. You asked how I did it. How I stopped Kythiel," I take a deep breath. "Theia came to me."

And then it all comes pouring out.

About the box, the Hunters, how Kythiel came to me, how he begged, how we came to our deal. I tell them about the Underworld, about the Keeper and the beasts and the traps, the little boy who was so much like Jordan, and yet not. I tell about Abazel. How my mistakes made it so they can break free and start the Third Realm War. The Hunter who saved Rona only to die under my hand. And I tell them what happened when Kythiel knocked me out. The Goddess, the vision She gave me. How I swore to Her I'd fix it. All of it.

They stare at me. Eyes wide. Mouths open. Brows pulled tight.

Rona reaches out and touches my forehead where it burns. "Is that how you got this mark? You didn't have it before the fight."

I reach up and touch it too, brushing against her fingers. It's hot against my fingers. "Yes."

"And there's one more thing." I turn to Jordan, my throat tight. "I saw your sister there."

Jordan steps forward.

"Miriam? You saw her? Is she okay?"

"Yes." The memory of watching her drift away into the abyss rises in my mind. "She is at peace." Surely, she has made it back to the Crossing by now.

I glance toward Rona. I don't know if I should give him what I know in front of her. But I have to tell him. "She told me what all the training was for."

I don't know quite where to begin, how to say it. I explain to him all she said about his mother, the voices she heard, how Miriam herself had only just started to believe.

"But believe *what*?" he asks.

"That you were chosen by the Gods. That you'd lead the Three's army in the final Realm War."

Rona gasps. Jordan's lips pull together tight. His eyes drop to the sand and the moment is filled with a great quiet. He was so talkative as a boy. But there is a stillness in him that is strong. I wonder what lies beneath the stoic expression? But he doesn't tell me. Instead, he turns to face the villagers. I forgot they were there.

They huddle together, whispering to each other, but when Jordan turns to address them, they hush each other and quiet to listen to him.

"I know you came to the shore in fear last night, but you have witnessed the turning of a tide. You bore witness to the first battle of the Final Realm War," he says. He gestures toward me. "Theia's own agent defeated a First Creature who turned his back on the Gods."

My stomach tosses. *Theia's agent?* Hardly. I'm just

trying to set right what I've broken.

"Soon this will get bigger. Soon it will be all of us fighting." A murmur grows among the crowd. "But we are ready for it. This is what we have been waiting for. Preparing for. Training for, for generations. Soon it will be our time to take a stand. We will fight with our Gods at our side, and just as we saw on this night, we will find victory."

The murmurs break into cheers.

Jordan calls over it to hush them. "My friends, our moment is near. But not now. Not today. Go back to your homes. Rest. Enjoy each other. Tomorrow we keep preparing for what is coming."

Jordan raises one hand, fingers spreading, and says a short prayer and blessing. The villagers bow their heads and close their eyes. Rona joins them. But I just watch him, Jordan, the strong man he became while I slipped away to the Underworld. He's already just where he ought to be to lead Theia's people in this war. Did he sense it in himself somehow? Or did Miriam and his mother train him so well that it happened on its own?

The blessing ends. The people begin to disperse and walk back to the village. Jordan watches them a moment before turning back to us.

"You'll stay in my village until Rona is well," he says. "And then we will figure out what needs to be done."

"No." It launches out of me with blunt force—I can't go back there, live on the fringe of their preparations, on edge and waiting to hurt someone again. Too many have been hurt by my blunders already. No more. "You take Rona. But I must go."

Go where? Do what? I don't know yet. Whatever is next is dark and blurry. But it's bound to mean more danger, more fighting, more death. There's been too much of these already.

"'Take Rona?' I've come back from the dead, I'm not a child whose fate is to be decided for her," Rona retorts. "I'm coming too."

Rona's declaration floats, just hangs in the air. Her face is hard and determined, but her legs still shake with fatigue. There's no way

"You're weak—"

"I'm *not*." She stumbles in her passion and has to grab Jordan's shoulder for support. "Well, I am now. But I'm healing. I will be strong."

She tilts her chin proudly, the strong cheekbones showing themselves in her determination.

"It's too dangerous," I growl. "I can't be responsible for—"

"*Responsible?*" she scoffs. "You brought me here. I didn't ask for this. But now I'm here, and I'm a fighter. What are you afraid of? That I'll die? That I'll go back where I belong?"

That I'll do her more harm. Cause her more pain.

"If the war is really coming, you'll need me. I was there for the first one. I'm good in a fight. And Kythiel might try to come back. I'm the only one who can warn you if he does. He'll come to me again, I know he will."

"But that's all the more reason..." But I'm stumbling over my words, not quick enough to keep up with her.

"I'm coming too." Jordan's bright eyes are ablaze with determined flecks of orange, catching the sun's rays.

"No." The ground is slipping out from under me. This is the opposite of what I swore to myself. To put an end to the wake of destruction. To keep them safe. Both of them.

"Adem, listen," Jordan steps toward me. "Haven has resources—allies, armies, prophets. This is what we've been preparing for. You just told me, my whole life was preparation for this. You know." he puts a hand on my shoulder, his eyes bore into me. "You *know*. I'm already part of this. You don't have to protect me anymore."

But he doesn't have to be in this part. Neither of them do. His fingers are tense against my shoulder.

"You've done too much alone already, Adem. Look where it's gotten you," he says. "You have to let us help. You need us."

His words stick inside me like rocks sinking into mud.

How much of this could have been stopped if it hadn't be left up to me? Would the necklace still be safe? Would I have known about breaking the barrier in time? Would I have known what Kythiel was before any of this started?

Theia Herself tasked this to me. But I'm weak. Dense and ignorant. How much worse can this still get? The fall down seems bottomless. The stakes are too high, the fate of the entire realm. Too much to bet on just me.

I hang my head and nod into my chest. Jordan squeezes my shoulder and releases, turns away to give Rona support and lead her into the village.

I don't follow. There's one last wrong I must right first.

CHAPTER 33

THE WAVES SIGH.

My legs stretch, ambling up the shore, through the cattails where the rough sand gives way to rich silt. To the Hunter.

He still lies there, stiff, broken, and dead.

The eyes, stare blank and glassy at the horizon, catch light off the mid-morning sun.

I reach out and push down his cold eyelids with my fingers, sadness brooding thick in the air around me. This Hunter was not just another assailant coming at me from the darkness. He was a friend. For that short time. An ally. And in a blink, gone.

More blood on my hands. More lives lost. More weight to add to the burden I carry always.

And it is far from over.

The box is nothing but shreds of wood, and even still, it rules me. Can I ever break free of it?

For now, all I can do is this. It's a drop in the bucket. More penance than progress. But I need to do it.

I drag the Hunter's body up the shore and among

the cattails. I kneel in the dirt, and I dig. The silt is soft, damp, and cool in my hands, rough against the fresh skin grown over the nub of my last finger. It pulls away easily, willingly, to accept the Hunter into it. The cool rich soil in my hands feels good, right. Warm sun reaches out to me in thick rays. A soft, salty breeze brushes over my face. I soak it up, taking in as much of it as I can. I don't know what's next, but I know I won't be here long. It's a welcome break from my weariness, eases the heft of the great burden upon me.

Even if just for the moment.

But the pressure is mounting between the realms. I can already feel it. All I've done, the damage I've caused, the aftermath still to come, it weighs heavy on Terath. The debt I owe to set it right again weighs heavy on me. It is a load that is building, building, building on my back, my shoulders, and through every muscle in my body.

But it doesn't cripple me like before.

When the hole is big enough, I brush off the dirt from my palms and lift the Hunter into it. The body settles into the ground, looks to be at rest. A wave of relief comes over me. I lean in and fill the dirt back over him.

The spot on my forehead where Theia touched me still tingles, a gentle buzzing burn. A reminder of all that's passed, memories clear and painful and vivid. A reminder of what I've promised, of what Theia has promised to me. My soul. Not something torn from another, but something that is truly mine. Of the vision, the knowledge She planted in me. *What does it mean?* It was more than how to float the rocks. I have a connection to that dark-haired boy in the forest's shadow. I know it, I feel it, restless and calling to me, just out of reach.

I pat down the soil, smooth it out flat and even.

A voice stretches toward me from the village. Jordan. He stands between the village huts and waves me in.

Almost ready.

I pick out some nearby pebbles and place them over the Hunter's resting place. I press my thumb into the ground over them to form Theia's symbol. The seed.

But it doesn't leave me satisfied. It's not enough, this small mark in the sand.

No more hiding in the shadows. No more rootless impermanence. It needs something more, something that won't roll away with the next breeze.

Near my foot, a sapling is just starting to take root and sprout its first leaf. I push away the dirt and gently lift it up, reopen the ground where I pressed Theia's symbol into the earth and settle the sapling into its place.

I stand and look at my work. Better.

Footsteps brush the sand behind me.

"Come," Jordan says. He places a warm hand on my shoulder. "Rona is settled and resting. Let me show you your hut. The others will not disturb you. I'll talk to them."

Now that the Hunter is buried, I don't know what to do next. I nod, and let him lead me.

A new day is here. Already the village is coming to life, pulling out their pots, and gathering in its heart. A surge of warmth comes over me.

I know it's far from over. And I don't know what it all means yet. But for once, there is something beyond the burden. Action. Answers. Life.

For once, I'm not alone.

THE END

Thank you for reading! Find book two in the Chronicles of the Third Realm War coming soon.

Please sign up for the City Owl Press newsletter for chances to win special subscriber-only contests and giveaways as well as receiving information on upcoming releases and special excerpts.

www.ejwenstrom.com

@EJWenstrom

All reviews are welcome and appreciated. Please consider leaving one on your favorite social media and book buying sites.

For books in the world of romance and speculative fiction that embody Innovation, Creativity, and Affordability, check out City Owl Press at www.cityowlpress.com.

Turn the page for a sneak peek at the next book in the
Chronicles of the Third Realm War,

BY: E. J. WENSTROM

Coming Soon from City Owl Press

Haven.

Sanctuary. Safety. Refuge.

As a village, it's not living up to its name at all. Things have been tense—at least, ever since I arrived here, they have.

But then, bringing me back is what started this whole mess. That's what shattered the barrier between the realms and released the rebel First Creatures determined to take down the Gods.

And the Gods are furious about it.

The rebels have tried this twice before—the Realm Wars. Last time they almost succeeded. Now they've had ages trapped in the Underworld to let their rage simmer. They haven't broken free yet, but it's only a matter of time. I would know. It's where I've wasted away for the last thousand years.

The Third War isn't a surprise, exactly. It was foretold. The people of Haven have been preparing to fight on behalf of their Gods for generations. But not even the greatest prophets have been able to divine how it turns out. And no one expected it so soon.

So there's reason enough for Haven's people to be tense. I sure have been.

If anyone had bothered to ask me, I could have told them this would happen. I would have told them to leave me in the Underworld and let me rot. I sent myself there for a reason. And it worked. I was at peace, or close enough to it. At least Kythiel couldn't reach me there.

But ever since I came here—no, was *dragged here* by that golem—my life has been a barrage of sensory overload. As if my body is catching up on the hundreds of years that have passed since I was last alive, all at once.

My body aches with exhaustion. It wrapped back around me when I re-entered this realm with a vengeance, as if to pin me down and hold me here, a garment too tight and stiff.

Then there's the irritating buzz of people constantly hovering around me, sun up to sun down, insisting I rest, and eat, and rest more and eat more, to nourish away the depletion of my body.

They're angry. Some of them still don't trust us, Adem and me, no matter how Jordan assures them. It's okay, I get it. As far as they know, when we arrived is when everything started to go wrong. It's the rumors of upheaval and coups that make me uncomfortable.

Despite it all, Jordan comes to my hut every day with the golem — Adem, they call him. They hover and pace away hours around my bed, and we try to force together the clues we have to stop another Realm War.

It's been weeks of this. We still have nothing. Just a description of a necklace, a name, and some rumors from the beginning of the rift between the Gods and their First Creatures. But we keep at it anyway, driven by our collective sense of guilt.

Then the sun goes down, everyone files out of my hut, and finally I can breathe. But sleep? That's a completely different story. My sleep has been agitated and broken ever since I came back to this realm. Restless dreams of hostile darkness wake me abruptly over and over in a cold sweat.

Which is why I'm up now. Once I shake my mind free of the haunting dreams, I don't mind too much.

Now, before the sun is up, it's quiet. No one else is awake yet to tell me what to do, or remind me how fragile I am. I can stretch my legs and take in some fresh air.

My bare feet squish through the mud. It's cool and soothing, like the sweet morning breeze that rustles through my hair. It's dark still, the only hint of morning a tinge of pink on the horizon behind the village huts.

I didn't exactly rest in the Underworld, either. Which means it's been hundreds of years since I've had a good sleep. My body feels it, too, achey and wobbly and strung out. But anything is better than the terrors that rush into my mind when I close my eyes. The whoosh of demon shadows, whispers of age-old visions from the Gods, Kythiel's crazed eyes. It's all trapped inside me, just waiting to pounce at me should my mind begin to quiet.

As I reach the shore, sand sticks between my toes with the mud. I pull off my dress and toss it onto the sand without stopping. The body I expose is one I hardly recognize as my own, weak and still too skinny despite all the eating they force on me. I'm stronger every day, though. Just a couple weeks ago I couldn't have made the walk all the way down to the sea on my own.

I keep walking right into the ocean and let the pull of the waves lead me in. Its chill reminds me what it was to be alive — really alive, not this sheltered half-life they'd boxed me into since I came back. When I'm deep enough, I drop to my knees and let the water rush over my head.

And as the chill seeps deeper and turns my fingers and toes numb, it reminds me of what it was to be dead. Death, that safe, easy numbness. I sunk into it so easily. The Underworld was grim, but its emptiness was a relief after what I'd been through with Kythiel. Part of me aches to go back—to shed this miserable starved body and let the numbness take over again. I could do it. It wouldn't be hard. Just like before, a quick slash across my middle, and it would all drain away in minutes.

I lay back and close my eyes, let the water's current toss me.

Maybe I should stick around for a while, though. After all, Kythiel's gone, too far destroyed to reach me on Terath now. In a way it's my fault he was left out there to prey on Adem in the first place. Instead of finishing him, I just fled to where he could not reach me.

No, I won't flee this time. I'll do all I can to set right what I helped break. Adem and Jordan are not going to be able to right this on their own, and they shouldn't have to.

When I open my eyes, there is a lean, tall figure standing over me. Loose curls of red hair blow around his head and catch in the sun rising just behind him. His face is hidden in shadow, but I can tell he his smiling by the pull of his cheeks.

That godsdamn smile. He's always smiling.

"Jordan." It comes out with a heavy sigh. I bring myself to my feet, my dripping hair clinging to my bare shoulders and chest.

"Um," Jordan pulls his eyes away, his face flushing

red as his hair. "You weren't in your hut."

His bashful reaction to my body boils under my skin. I stand still and tall, rejecting the impulse to cover myself.

"No, I'm not." I'm not going to give explanations for myself—they can all insist that I rest all they want, but if I want to be out, I'll go out.

"Well...I just wanted to let you know," he forces his gaze up again and makes eye contact. "Adem and I are leaving in a little bit to visit another village."

What? Both of them? I can feel the frown creases forming across my forehead. "What for?"

He pauses. "Why don't you come back up to the shore? We'll all talk about this together."

I glance back toward the village and see Adem lurking on the sand. Resentment twists through me. "Fine."

Jordan turns and wades his way back, his pant legs dripping. I look out to the endless waves, take in one last moment of the sea's tranquility, and then follow him.

Adem gives me a furtive glance as we approach, then stares back down to the sand. His shoulders are hunched in tight, as if to shut us out. The guilt has surrounded him like a storm cloud ever since the fight with Kythiel. It makes me want to shake him with all my strength until it disperses.

Jordan hands me my dress. I pull it on, sand dusting over my head and sticking to my shoulders as the cool fabric falls around me. Both of the men relax and turn their eyes back my way once my skin is covered.

"So what is all this?" I prompt.

There's a beat as they make eye contact, and then Jordan clears his throat. "Adem and I are going to another village not far from here. We'll only be gone a few days. We just thought you'd want to know."

His tone is forcefully casual. I narrow my eyes, studying his face. His lips are pursed together tight, his mouth a thin line. He meets my gaze and holds it, waiting for me to respond.

"What for?" I ask.

It must be awfully important, whatever it is, for Jordan to be willing to leave his village while it's so unstable. Or doesn't he know how his people are splitting apart? It didn't occur to me before, but he's so optimistic, he might not be able to see the anger bubbling among them.

Jordan fidgets his hands. He wants to lie, I can see it. But if there's one thing about Jordan, it's that he has this thing about integrity. He can't help himself.

"It's nothing, we're just talking to someone."

I huff out the air from my lungs in frustration and turn to Adem, my hands crossed over my chest.

"Adem?"

Adem isn't like Jordan. But he means well. And his guilt for bringing me back and all that followed weight on him. He will always give me what I want.

He stares blankly at me a moment. It's so strange, he looks so human. But always that blank stare gives him away as a lesser creature. But for what is essentially just a pile of mud, I guess he does alright. I wonder if he's thinking, weighing out what he owes Jordan versus what he owes me. But I'll always win in that measure. He brought me back unwillingly from the dead, damnit, and I've been in unrest ever since.

He shoots Jordan an apologetic glance before he speaks. "It's a prophet."

I knew it had to do with the Wars. I whip back to Jordan. "I can't believe it. We agreed."

All this time plotting together, puzzling, trying to figure it all out. *Together,* we all agreed we were in this together. And they were just going to leave me behind.

It's not just about feeling included. They're going to need me. I was there when it all happened. I saw everything fall apart the first time. Besides, they're the ones who dragged me into this Gods-forsaken mess.

And just look at these two. Leave the fate of the realms to these two fools? Not a chance.

"No!" Jordan is so insistent his voice is a high-pitched squeal. "You're still healing. If we're going to do this together, we need you strong. This is just a conversation with someone. We don't even know if he can help yet. And it's a full day's walk each way. You're not strong enough."

"I'm plenty strong," I snap. These two are so determined for me to be fragile. "And I won't get any better wilting away in that hut. I need to do something. I'm coming."

"No," Jordan says again. "Besides, there's no time. We're leaving as soon as the sun comes up. I just have to leave some parting instructions with Lena first."

Already the village is stirring, the morning cooks preparing everyone's breakfast around the fire.

"I'll be ready."

Jordan frowns, but neither of them argues. I'm in. I

bite the corner of my lip to hold back my excitement and turn away to walk quickly back to my hut and pack my sack.

If I'm honest, I still feel fragile, just like Jordan said. Brittle, like I could snap right in two. But my soul craves to be out, to do something. Can I really walk a full day in the sun? My body cringes at the thought.

But I'm losing my mind stagnating away here. I have spent enough time cooped up and doing what others tell me to. For better or worse I'm alive again, and this time I'm setting my own terms.

I hope I've got it in me. Guess we're about to find out.

ACKNOWLEDGEMENTS

No matter how many mornings I dredge myself out of bed and open my computer, there are certain people without whom not a single word would matter.

First and always, many thanks to Christopher. Thank you for believing in my writing from the very beginning, even sometimes when I did not. And for giving me the space, time, confidence, and sometimes the finances to make this book the best it could be. Most of all, thanks for being so totally cool about it that time I set the alarm for 5 a.m., crawled over you, and started typing away a good two hours before you had any interest in waking up, for five years straight, even when we were in a teeny studio apartment and there was no escaping my noise.

And, of course, to my parents. Thank you for filling my brain with everything from ballet to piano to softball, and for making imagination mandatory. To Mom for the summer short story contests. To Dad for reading to us every night. To you both for accepting "making stuff up" as a legitimate career choice.

To Rebecca and Sam, who always make me feel like a rock star, even if it's just because I was born first. Reba, for the Black Fridays and the early morning '80s rock jams in the car, and always being available as a sounding board for literally anything. And Spiderbutt, for the Bob Evans breakfasts and the movies no one else appreciated but us, and a life full of Potato-Head face moments.

Also, to those who have lent time and thought to help me improve my writing. To The Writers Center, an absolutely invaluable resource. To my D.C. writing group—Adam, Gary, Jennifer, Michael—for all the monthly meetings, shared laughs and support over drinks, and thoughtful critique. And to the beta readers who so kindly showed interest in my work before there was any reason to and gave me such wonderful feedback.

Many thanks also to Heather, Tina, and the whole City Owl team, who have given me an amazing opportunity. Your expertise, guidance, and passion have made *Mud* a better book, and me a better, savvier author. You have made this journey to publishing my first novel less daunting and way more fun.

And, to the person who started all this and does not even know it, a certain former editor at Grand Rapids Magazine who took me in as an intern, even though I was clearly clueless, and drew out something in me I did not know was there: that I could write, and that I loved it. It opened an entire career path for me, and gave me a coveted creative outlet I could not navigate this world without.

ABOUT THE AUTHOR

E. J. WENSTROM is a fantasy and science fiction author. A D.C. girl at heart, she currently lives in Florida with her husband and their miniature pinscher. Her first novel, **MUD**, is being published by City Owl Press. When she's not writing fiction, E. J. drinks coffee, goes running, and has long conversations with her dog. Ray Bradbury is her hero. Keep tabs on E.J.s writing and other antics at

www. ejwenstrom.com

ABOUT THE PUBLISHER

CITY OWL
PRESS

CITY OWL PRESS is a cutting edge indie publishing company, bringing the world of romance and speculative fiction to discerning readers.

www.cityowlpress.com

CPSIA information can be obtained
at www.ICGtesting.com
Printed in the USA
LVOW08s1632220317
528098LV00001B/178/P